ENTANGLEMENT
Andrew J Thomas

First published in Great Britain in 2019 by Ursus Publishing.
www.ursuspublishing.com

Copyright © 2018 by Andrew J Thomas.

The moral right of the author is hereby asserted in accordance with
the Copyright, Designs and Patents Act 1988.

A CIP catalogue record for this book is available from the British
Library.

ISBN 978-1-9160440-0-5 (Hardback)
ISBN 978-1-9160440-1-2 (Paperback)
ISBN 978-1-9160440-2-9 (ebook)
ISBN 978-1-9160440-4-3 (Audiobook)

Praise for *Entanglement*

"A great read"
Alex, London

"I couldn't wait to find out what happened"
Jess, Newbury

"An excellent story; I became very wrapped up with the characters
and found the ending surprisingly emotional; in a good way."
Peter, London

"Treat yourself to a tranquil, offbeat and thoroughly absorbing
adventure across parallel worlds with a fascinating set of characters"
Terry, Somerset

"Entanglement is an enjoyable read about friendship, possibilities and
a mystery to solve. Oh, and did I mention the cakes?"
Diane, California

"Entanglement has compelling characters, a mystery to solve and a
great sense of humor. I enjoyed every minute."
Glenn, North Carolina

"An intriguing and downright funny book with a warm and engaging
cast of characters. You'll join them as they attempt to uncover what
has happened to their friends, some moles and a random brick. Loved
the cake recipes too! Highly recommended."
Dave, West Sussex

Thanks

Dave Loewy, Diane Rupert and Terry Thomas for being my sounding boards, reading and commenting on the novel's various versions, and offering loads of valuable insights and encouragement along the way.

Jess Allen, Chris Ridgewell, Lawrence Porter, Peter Slade, Iain Farquharson, Jacqui Chappell, Vicky Stewart and Anna Loewy for their questions, challenges, and input on topics from the musical tastes of millennials to character traits, quantum physics and Scottish place names.

Police Scotland and the RAF for clarifying terminology, and official roles.

Credits

Cover & interior icons	Dave Provolo
Editors	Kay Leitch, Alex Hammond
Map	Andrew J Thomas
Author photograph	Dave Loewy

Author's notes

Science

All scientific theories referred to in this novel are genuine aspects of current thinking in quantum physics. All scientists referred to, but who do not have speaking roles in the story, are real people in the public domain and are referenced solely to provide a factual context for this work of fiction.

Footnotes

This novel contains a number of footnotes, which started out as funny, albeit informative, asides. Then when American friends read the novel, I realised how many words and phrases I use are UK-specific, which is why some of the footnotes now relate to UK/US language differences.

Contact the author

Web	www.andrewjthomas.net
Instagram	@andrewj.thomas
Facebook	@andrewthomasnovelist
Twitter	@andrewthomas109

For my Mum & Dad, who taught me the value of love, laughter and a little bit of madness. In life and in writing, they'll always be my inspiration. Cherry & Terry Thomas, you're the best.

Entanglement

ɛnˈtaŋg(ə)lm(ə)nt/

1   a.   Relationship, Romance, Deeply involved, Entwined together.

      b.   A mysterious affinity or complex situation.

2   a.   According to modern physics, Entanglement is central to the many-worlds theory of parallel universes.

      b.   Entangled particles can stay connected over small and cosmic distances alike, so if particles can do it, why not people?

ENT

ANG

LEM

ENT

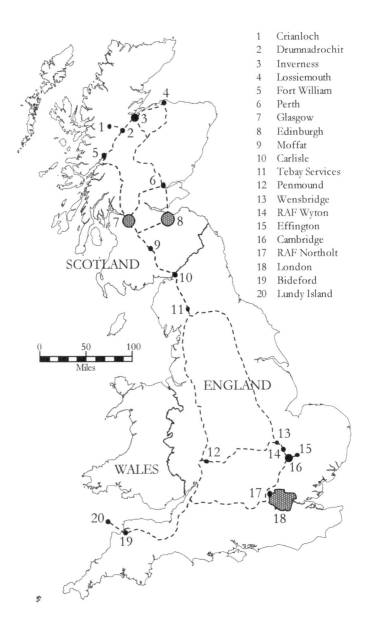

1   Crianloch
2   Drumnadrochit
3   Inverness
4   Lossiemouth
5   Fort William
6   Perth
7   Glasgow
8   Edinburgh
9   Moffat
10 Carlisle
11 Tebay Services
12 Penmound
13 Wensbridge
14 RAF Wyton
15 Effington
16 Cambridge
17 RAF Northolt
18 London
19 Bideford
20 Lundy Island

SCOTLAND

ENGLAND

WALES

0   50   100
       Miles

It all started well enough   1
   Somewhen else …   8

Everything goes wrong   10

Weird coincidences   36

Meaningful meetings   59

Finding out, Covering up   86
   It minus 11 years   107

Travelling north   112

First answers?   143

The thing about coincidences   165

Days 7, Answers 1½   188
   Soon?   206

Truth emerges   211

Green and Blue   238

Parallel running   257

All's well that ends well   284

What came after   296

Some words of thanks   299

It all started well enough

Fate was bored. Nothing funny had happened in days, and it needed a laugh. When the UK's most secret research station vanished though, it smiled. When odd things started happening to some moles and a brick, it chuckled. When it realised what was coming next, its laugh was heard across every world. It was going to be a *very* good week.

But what *was* coming next? Well, imagine you wake up in a parallel world where everything looks familiar, but no-one knows who you are. Worse still, you've no idea how you got there. Then you shift to another world, and another, and another, year after year, until eventually you find yourself in one where it's you who doesn't know anybody. No friends, no family, no-one. Could you cope? That was what a woman called TC was about to find out.

Then there were the cakes.

I'll get to all that though, as our story begins two years before. In GCHQ[1] no less, that ultra-secret government building which sits in plain sight, disguised as a giant, silver doughnut.

In a basement room sat the Director General of MI5, the UK Secretary of State for Defence, and five eminent scientists. They were there to discuss the security implications of some recent findings at CERN[2]. It was an unusual mix of people, all of whom had different agendas. Even so, they still reached a conclusion, and three months later, the DG also got the support of the head of the Royal Air Force. Three months after that, the DG and the Defence Secretary met again, only this time in 10 Downing Street. The Prime Minister was testing both their knowledge and their patience.

"And you're sure he's the right person for the job?" demanded the PM in a thin, nasal whine.

"Well, both groups like him," snapped the Defence Secretary.

"Both groups?"

"The scientists and the RA ..."

"Remind me what role the RAF plays?"

The Defence Secretary ground his teeth. He hated being interrupted, and he'd already taken the PM through this twice. He was about to respond when the DG interrupted in his calm,

---

[1] Thought by many to refer to the building alone, GCHQ is actually the name of one of the UK's three Intelligence and Security Agencies, alongside MI5 and MI6. It just doesn't have spy films made about it.

[2] Birthplace of the World Wide Web, CERN (from *Conseil Européen pour la Recherche Nucléaire*), is the Geneva-based organization that operates the Large Hadron Collider. Housed in a tunnel, 100 metres underground and 17 miles in circumference, that's the same size as one encircling the City of London, Hampstead, Vauxhall and Kensington. Or the whole of Manhattan from Battery Park to 69th Street.

soothing voice.

"Group Captain Marston has a double first from Oxford in Meteorology and Computer Science, Prime Minister, which ..."

"So, what's our cover story?"

"A weather research facility, Prime Minister, to study high altitude weather conditions. And as the RAF will have aircraft on site, having one of their people in charge is standard operational practice. He's an excellent officer too. Trustworthy, well-liked, more than capable of doing the job ..."

"... and the fact that he looks like a movie star doesn't hurt. Is that it?"

"It can't do any harm, Prime Minister," replied the DG with a nod. "After all, the names of my predecessors have been common knowledge since '92. And Crianloch[3] would be open to even more scrutiny if its real purpose ever got out."

"So, he's the acceptable face of ... What do we call it anyway?"

"My office refers to it as *Spooky Affairs*, Prime Minister," replied the DG with a wry smile.

"Well we need a better name than that."

"I gather *Operation Carter* is the preferred name in the Civil Service."

"Why Carter?"

"Some science fiction reference I think."

"Hmf," snorted the Defence Secretary.

"So, we're agreed. Marston will head up what from the public perspective, is an ordinary weather station. But when we're talking about other matters, Operation Carter it is."

[3] Pronounced *Creeyun-lock* with the emphasis on the *creeyun*.

David Marston had joined the Royal Air Force after university, going straight to Cranwell officer training college, where he came first in his class. Then, when the top brass at RAF Wyton approached him, David leapt at the chance. He knew it by reputation as home of the *Joint Force Intelligence Group* and the *National Centre for Geospatial Intelligence*[4], so it was an easy decision. Careers move on though, and now he had his first base-command post. OK so it was at Crianloch rather than Lossiemouth, as he'd told his family, but he could get around that.

At 32, he wasn't the youngest person ever to hold the rank of Group Captain. But at 6'2" with blond hair, and eyes that matched the blue-grey of his uniform, he made a striking figure. What his challenges might be at Crianloch, he didn't know, and not because he hadn't been briefed, because he had, extensively. The thing was, the notion that the station itself might vanish had never been considered, and no-one had imagined a scenario that might change the entire world. Unfortunately, they should have, and sensing somehow that things were about to change, the planet waited. Not consciously like you do for a bus, but waited, nonetheless.

It was therefore ironic that when **it** happened, only a handful of people noticed, and none of them had a clue what it was, let alone what caused it. For one thing, they only saw their own parts of the puzzle. And although some parts were bigger than others, they were each so bizarre that only one person wondered if they might be connected. The trouble was, he wasn't the sort many people listen to.

For now then, the world slept. Group Captain David Marston

---

[4] If you check the RAF website, you'll see this is all true, as Wyton doesn't hide much.

did too, slumped over his desk as he often did. His fiancée, on the other hand, was sleeping soundly in the hotel room she'd called home for the last few months. And her soon-to-be-new-best-friend slept surrounded by cats at home. The only person not sleeping was David's cousin Nigel, but that was normal for him, so the world kept spinning. Kept waiting.

So, picture the scene ... An unforgiving highland landscape made of granite and carved by glaciers in a time when woolly mammoths walked the Earth. A grassy glen now, with a small, playful stream gurgling through its centre, laughing and dancing as it splashed over the rocks. High above, barren peaks grumbled amongst themselves as they gazed down in disapproval of anything so frivolous. And well they might, for the stream seemed almost to sigh with pleasure as it finally disappeared into the lush, green bogs.

Appearances can be deceptive though, and like *The Great Grimpen Mire* in *The Hound of the Baskervilles*, they were also the spots where many a small creature had lost its way ... permanently. As far as wildness goes, Dartmoor had nothing on Glen Crian though, and if Conan Doyle had ever visited, he might well have set his story there instead.

With eighteen-hour nights in winter and six months of rain a year, it was never going to be a major tourist destination. That said when you add in its mild, year-round temperatures[5], and the fact that it's hidden from the nearest village by a series of hillocks, you have one thing ... The perfect site for the UK's most

---

[5] Admittedly, *mild* may be a bit of an overstatement, but with actual temperatures in the area ranging between 9 and 14°C (48 to 57°F) in September, it's not that bad.

secret research station.

It didn't take long to put the press stories in place either, all leading with a central message about the station's low environmental impact. It would have a single, short runway, with everything else underground, and be so remote that the security guards would have more sheep to worry about than people. In fact, it's only claim to fame would be the hundreds of boffins[6] working there, and what could possibly go wrong with that?

Over the next twenty months, Glen Crian was transformed from a tranquil highland valley into the site of a high-tech research facility. It lived up to its low-impact promise too, and if you flew over it, all you saw was the green tarmac of the runway, a couple of single-storey buildings and a fence. Not a high fence either and no razor wire in sight.

Mind you, as the Ministry of Defence now owned the entire glen, it's not like people could walk in without being noticed, as the valley floor was dotted with hundreds of hidden sensors. Consequently, anyone who came visiting set off an alarm in the underground control room, and if they kept walking, they were picked up on camera. It was deliberately low key ... up to the point that they were greeted by heavily armed members of the RAF. Purely as a courtesy, you understand.

As for air traffic control, gone was the usual, tall concrete tower. In its place, the job was done by dozens of networked cameras positioned around the valley sides, all with inbuilt infrared to handle night flights.

What wasn't made public, was the massive mining operation

---

[6] This slang dates from the 1940s and describes a brilliant scientist who's also rather eccentric or peculiar. Hair that looks like it's been plugged into a light socket is an optional extra.

needed to construct the station's three underground levels. Nearest the surface were vast hangers such as on aircraft-carriers, and on the level below that, twenty-five parallel corridors, each running the full length of the station. Each half-a-mile long, with dozens of offices, laboratories and living quarters leading off on either side. Below that again sat a server-farm the size of a football pitch, and numerous other basement rooms even I can't tell you about.

As for people, naturally the station had its complement of RAF personnel and meteorologists, but that was only the beginning. Its real purpose lay with the dozens of computer scientists, astronomers and astrophysicists, all crunching petabytes[7] of data from around the world.

Then on Friday, September 10th, everything went wrong.

---

[7] On the off chance that you're even faintly interested, one petabyte of data is equal to one thousand million million (10^{15}) bytes. To put it another way, 1PB would store 223,000 DVDs or almost three and a half years of 24/7 full HD recording of your cat.

Somewhen else ...

 Data aside: reality is a funny old thing. I mean, it's always the same distance between London and New York, but it still feels nearer if you're going on holiday rather than on business. "Ah, but that's just different perspectives," you might say, and you'd be right. What happens though if you come across something so weird, your mind refuses to accept it, even if it's right in front of you? If it's a gigantic, salivating monster ripping the roof off your house, you probably run like hell. On the other hand, what if the person you've been secretly in love with for years suddenly notices you? In that case, I guess you either run towards them or faint with shock.

But what if the *something* is small? What if it's insignificant? What if it can't possibly matter, but it still bugs the hell out of you all the same? In that case, I reckon you worry. Not perhaps in a front-of-the-mind kind of way, but more like a coffee percolator. The bubbles are barely noticeable to begin with, but as they start to heat up, they get bigger and bigger.

So what was TC's reality like?

Well, no-one noticed her much as a child. Her parents loved her, and she had her fair share of friends, but she was nothing out of the ordinary. She didn't excel at sport, she was an average pupil, and although she took piano lessons, the music she played was at best, accurate. She had two pet rabbits called Bill and Ben, half a dog named Amber, and anyone she allowed into her room found the floor covered with clothes.

The walls were very much her too, which at six years old meant posters of unicorns. At ten that changed to ponies, and from twelve onwards it became a succession of boy bands … with a few photos of kittens thrown in for good measure. She was loved, she was liked, and her best friend thought she was ace, but extraordinary? Not really.

At eighteen, all that changed.

.

Everything goes wrong

Friday, September 10th

Group Captain David Marston took it in his stride when the air traffic control cameras failed. Likewise, when the goods-lift broke down, leaving the weekly delivery of groceries stranded on the runway. It was only when the coffee machine in the Senior Officers' Mess stopped working that his day really started going downhill.

"At least that's three now, sir," his steward said cheerily.

Marston glanced up.

"They say problems come in threes don't they, sir."

"Well, let's hope so this time." Ever a man of few words, Marston's accent was clipped and nondescript, yet easy to listen to. He smiled and stood up from his desk. Issues with air traffic control and the station's food supply were bad news. Ever one for prioritisation, he, therefore, headed straight for the civilian mess to see if their coffee machine was working.

He liked the openness of the place and the way it served as the station's social hub. Plus, it had a commercial grade coffee machine like the Senior Officers' Mess, and today that was important. As colleagues had quickly discovered, Marston was a coffee aficionado[8], and while some people have favourite cars, holidays or pizzas, he had a favourite coffee machine, and the *Gaggia D90 Evolution* was it. Thankfully, the one in the civilian mess was working. So, after chatting with a few of the scientists while he got his morning pick-me-up, he strode off to look into the station's other problems.

Later that morning, with the air traffic control cameras and the goods-lift working again, he headed not back to the civilian mess, but to the smaller one intended for him and his senior staff. It was private, and over time, had become a dedicated, meeting room for them. It was also where, as they sat down this particular day, all the lights went out.

"Oh, what now?"

"What the heck?"

"Oh no, not another ..."

Confused, complaining voices rippled around the room as laptop screens provided the only glow of normality in the darkness. Seconds later, the emergency generators kicked in, and the lights flickered back on. Marston's operations manager was already punching keys on the conference phone in the centre of the table.

"Systems Control," came the instant reply.

"Jim, it's Doug Smoke; what just happened?"

"Everything tripped, sir. We don't know why yet. I'll get back

---

[8] That, plus listening to AC/DC, Disturbed, some blasts from the past like Led Zeppelin and his one guilty pleasure, The Proclaimers.

to you."

The line went dead.

"He's brisk," commented Marston with a smile.

"He's a good man, sir. He'll find out what's going on."

He didn't though. At least not before the shutters over the helicopter bays had refused to open, and the air conditioning decided it was a good day to imitate an arctic winter. Consequently, when the top team met again, they were wearing padded jackets, furry hats and gloves. They made a comical sight with their breath steaming out into the cold air. None of that mattered though, because that was when **it** happened.

The time was 13:32, and as the station was plunged into darkness for the second time in as many hours, everyone's first thought was that it was just a power cut. This time though the generators didn't kick in. There was also the odd, green light. An impossibly bright pulse that had filled every corner of the station for a fraction of a second, then nothing.

Anyone on the peaks surrounding Glen Crian would have seen it too because it enveloped the runway and surface buildings as well. In fact, for barely the blink of an eye, it blanketed the whole valley floor. But as there were no hikers about, and the hills shielded the place from the outside world, no one saw anything.

Even so, the milkman and the newspaper boy still thought it strange when the station wasn't there the following morning. They'd always felt there was something funny about the place though, so they figured it must just have been more secret than they'd realised.

Why didn't either of them rush to tell the police?

As for the newspaper boy, he was saving up for a new

mountain bike, and the way he saw it, if there was no station, then he was out of work. OK so he'd have to hide the extra newspapers for a few days, but that was fine. He already occasionally dumped some in skips around the village when he couldn't be bothered to finish his round.

And the milkman? Well, he went the other way altogether and started by telling the couple who run the Post Office and village store. From there he told his mates in *The Shepherd's Arms*, and with that done, he was happy to let the rumour mill do the rest. Like the paperboy though, he didn't go straight to the police. The whole thing was just too strange.

Not strange in the way clipped poodles look mind you. Or the way celebrities on botox do, let alone the notion of pineapple on pizza. No, this was the sort of strange that makes governments tremble, and fills headlines the world over.

As for the pulse of green light, the last thing Marston saw as it flooded the Senior Officers' Mess was Doug Smoke reaching for the conference phone again. As the station's operations manager, problems were literally his problem. This time though he had no ready answer for Marston, for along with everything else, the phone was dead.

"It must be some kind of EMP[9], sir," he said in the darkness.

"They're real?" asked Marston, "I thought they were only in movies."

"Oh, they're real alright, sir. Off the top of my head, it's the only thing I can think of that could make everything go down

---

[9] Electromagnetic Pulses are momentary discharges of electromagnetic energy that can knock out electrical items, or even entire power grids. The effects aren't permanent, but for a while, you have an instant return to the Middle Ages.

like this."

Suddenly Smoke had a thought, and pulling his phone from his pocket, he pressed the power button. It still worked.

"Well, at least it's not affected batteries. With your permission, sir, I'll go down to Systems Control. Find out what's going on."

"Fine," replied Marston, "you do that. There are emergency torches at every corridor intersection? Yes?"

Illuminated by the glow from his phone, Doug Smoke nodded.

"Good. The rest of us will go around the offices and reassure the scientists. Meet back here in an hour?"

Smoke nodded again and left the room. As he walked to Systems Control, he was struck by how odd everywhere seemed in the dark. It was a route he knew well, but apparently not today. Distances felt different, and corners weren't quite where he remembered them.

From time to time, he encountered people coming out of their offices to see whether it was only *their* power that was down. Apart from the few who'd remembered the emergency torches, they were all using their phones, and it gave a spooky feel to the place. Navigating the stairs down a level was interesting too, and by the time Doug reached Systems Control, he was happy to be in familiar territory.

The room was in the basement where all the station's main systems were housed. Consequently, as well as the mains power and the generators, it also had battery-powered lights. This *triple redundancy* was something Doug Smoke had insisted on with the planners, and right now he was glad he had. If the lights were working, chances were the battery-backup had kicked in for the server-farm and the station's experimental systems too.

The faces that greeted him as he entered Systems Control were clustered around a table in the centre of the room. Laid out in front of them was a pile of station blueprints.

"What have we got?" he asked.

"The primary circuits tripped again, sir, only this time, for some reason the generators didn't kick in. Luckily the battery-backup is working fine, but all the comms are down."

"What, voice *and* data?"

"Everything, sir. Landlines, satellite and mobile. The lot."

"Well that's not good. What do we do next?"

"We've already reset the breakers on the generators, sir, and are ready to start them back up."

"But no idea yet what caused it?"

"No, sir."

"Any risks in restarting?"

"None that I can think of."

Doug Smoke had worked with Jim Waynes long enough to recognize the worry in his deputy's voice, but that had to stay between the two of them for now. At any rate, Waynes had trained his team well, and without further ado, they all took up their positions. He nodded to each of them, then counted down from five. At zero, they each threw one of the generator switches and brought the station back to life.

First, their own room was flooded with light, then the critical and experimental systems came back on. Laboratories were next, followed by meeting rooms, corridors and finally sleeping quarters. The station was alive again. Most importantly, the coffee machine in the civilian mess started gurgling back into life.

Doug and Jim exchanged a sidelong glance, which the latter knew to mean that his boss was pleased, but still wanted answers.

"It may not be tonight, sir," he said.

"First thing tomorrow?"

Waynes nodded, and Smoke left to re-join Marston and the others.

~~~

That same morning, around the time the air traffic control cameras failed, Nigel Bellroy woke with a start when a bird flew into his bedroom window.

"Oh you poor thing," he muttered, looking at the splash of bloody feathers and the pattern of hairline cracks on the glass. "Why d'you do that?"

His voice held a soft hint of the urban south-west of England, although years of working for American companies had knocked off its edges. Low in tone, it rose in pitch when he became animated about something, rather like an excited puppy. He wasn't that now though, so glancing at the alarm clock, he threw on his dressing-gown, and headed downstairs. Tea beckoned.

The warmth of the house beyond his bedroom hit him as soon as he stepped onto the landing. He couldn't stand sleeping in warm rooms, so the rest of the house often seemed luxurious in comparison. Except for the stone tiles of the kitchen floor, which were always a bit of a shock.

Filling the kettle for his tea, he wondered why some people put the milk in before the boiling water, but he did the opposite. He knew it was something to do with either flavour or exploding crockery[10] and had even done his own experiment once to prove which it was. Unfortunately, it had ended rather abruptly when he dropped the kettle on his foot, and he'd lost interest after that.

---

[10] In fact, it's either, or even both. On one hand, some say putting the milk in first improves the taste. On the other, it also dates from when only the rich could afford crockery that would withstand hot liquids. The rest of us needed a way to cool the tea down so our cheap cups wouldn't crack.

It didn't matter to Nigel now though, as he generally used a travel-mug these days, even at home. Why? Because one of his core skills was not finishing mugs of tea, and it only took a few days for his desk to fill up with half-empty ones. Everything has its downside though, and walking to the front door this morning, he cursed as he scalded his tongue on the mug. "Note to self," he muttered. "Leave it to cool down for a while before drinking."

A little under six feet tall, with eyes the colour of coffee beans and hair to match, he stepped outside to see if the bird had survived. If the kitchen floor had been cold, it had nothing on the garden path. He shivered and glanced around as the last vestiges of sleep evaporated. It was shaping up to be an average kind of day. The sky wasn't quite enthusiastic enough to be blue, there was a breeze in the treetops, and a hint of rain hung in the air. Autumn had begun in earnest.

There was no sign of the bird though, so he went back indoors.

He had a productive morning after that, researching questions for a quiz he was writing for the town's *Winter Fair*. At around half-past one, he was sitting at his desk when he heard a bang. Flicking his eyes to the window, he saw not another bird, as he'd feared, but well, nothing. He trotted down to the front door and peered out. Lying on the path to his left was a brick.

"What the hell?"

Without thinking, he glanced up at the wall of his cottage, although as he did, he cursed himself. The house had been built centuries before, so bricks of any sort weren't a feature of it, let alone modern ones. Except that is for the one lying at his feet, which seemed to stare back at him as if to say ... "Yes? And what of it? I've got every right to be here."

He shook his head and picked it up.

"Weird," he muttered, turning it over in his hands.

As he did, he noticed something else. The brick wasn't always there. Oh, it was there all right ... except it wasn't. Or to be more exact, he could always feel it, but he couldn't always see it. Even that doesn't describe it though because it's not like it kept going transparent or something; it simply wasn't there. It was like a thought that leaps out of your mind as you're about to speak it out loud. It's still around somewhere and more often than not you remember it a second later, but where's it been in the meantime? That was the brick.

Nigel stared at it, trying to work out whether it was there or not. It certainly had no right being both. Then an idea struck him ... The town library.

By this time, *Fate* was having a ball, and not content with only two oddities to keep it amused, it turned its gaze eastwards to the small, Cambridgeshire village of Effington. There, a colony of moles was doing what moles do - scurrying around their tunnels, digging new ones and catching earthworms. All of a sudden, a tiny flicker of green light pulsed in the air, and everything changed. Well maybe not everything, as there aren't many elements to a mole's life, but the tunnels were now different. They were still there, and so were the moles, but the soil felt different. Sandier.

Luckily, moles are so used to being underground that they didn't panic or start gasping for air. They just grumbled to themselves in a moley kind of way and carried on digging. Moles you see are remarkable creatures, plus there are two for every three people in the UK, so they're not exactly rare. It's therefore unlikely this particular colony[11] would have been missed if it hadn't been for one thing. It was the subject of a research study by Professor Elizabeth Benning of Cambridge University; Liz to her friends.

The fact that the moles had vanished was only half of the story too, because unknown to anyone yet, they'd actually relocated to a small island off the North Devon coast.

Not far from the moles' former home, Liz Benning left *The Spotted Pig* at about 2 o'clock in the afternoon as usual. Effington's only hotel had been her home for the last few months, and after a short drive, she pulled over and parked. She was a hundred yards or so from the field where she was conducting her research, and she always parked a little distance away so as not to disturb the moles.

She stopped for a moment to tie back her dark, curly hair and adjust her glasses. Then she set up her camping table, and as she'd done twice a day for the last six months, she turned on the laser grid. Next, she checked the ground vibration sensors, and last of all, she sent up the afternoon drone. The grid seemed fine, the sensors beeped when she stamped the earth next to each of them, and the drone took to the sky without a hitch. In other words, everything behaved precisely as it always had.

The drone was airborne for almost twenty minutes, and once she landed it safely, she opened her laptop. She grimaced as it pinged into life, and with that cue, I should explain her

---

[11] As well as being able to see in the dark and survive on freakishly low levels of oxygen, moles can shift over 500 times their own weight in earth and tunnel 650 feet every day. They could have built the Large Hadron Collider in no time at all!

relationship with technology. By *landed safely*, for example, I mean the drone didn't break when she let it drop like a stone for the last six feet. And by *relationship*, I mean the sort you have with a sister you can't stand, but who you still have to see at family parties. To put it kindly, Liz had something of an on-off relationship with technology. In reality, she was yet to have an *on-day*, but the technology lived in hope.

Connecting the drone's USB cable to her laptop, she transferred the aerial footage. Next, she uploaded the sensor data, and with that all done, she opened *SurveyMaster*. This was the programme she used to predict ground movements, and which the IT team had preloaded with a detailed map of the site. It also showed the sensor locations and the criss-cross pattern of the laser grid, so all she had to do next was wait. She sipped her coffee as *SurveyMaster* merged the data and compared it to the last upload. Then it did the clever bit. It extrapolated where the next molehills were likely to appear and marked those positions on the map as well.

The trouble was, today it didn't.

"Damn," said Liz under her breath, frowning and chewing her lower lip. She could barely tolerate technology when it did what it was supposed to, but when it acted up, she wanted to give it a good slap. That not being an option, she contented herself with kicking the nearest sensor.

Over the next few minutes, she proceeded to double-check everything, grumbling and swearing at technology in general as she did. It was a world-class example of multi-tasking, and when she finished, she looked at the laptop again. She let out a disgruntled snort. The drone footage wasn't corrupted, the laser grid data was clean, and the ground sensors all appeared to be working fine.

"Bugger."

So, everything was fine, except, of course, it wasn't. Liz poured herself a fresh coffee, polished her glasses, then turned her laptop off and on again. Its friendly greeting tone annoyed her even more this time, and when *SurveyMaster* restarted, she re-ran the data. It was still the same, and she was baffled.

Like most scientists, she liked precision, and being confused wasn't a state she enjoyed. Suddenly she had an idea. She ran *SurveyMaster* yet again, only this time with the time-window reset to include her arrival on site. It took a few seconds to return a result, but it seemed longer, and when she saw the data, she stared at the screen in surprise.

"But ...?"

She was about to embark on a fresh rant that would have guaranteed her entry into the *New-Luddite Society* when another thought hit her. She closed her mouth, stood up, and walked back to the car. First and foremost, she was a scientist, and no matter how crazy the thought, she had to test it out.

On a typical day, she sent the drone up twice, once in the morning and once in the afternoon. As a precaution though, she always recharged four sets of batteries overnight, just in case. It was wise, given her issues with technology, and this was the day it paid off.

Back at the table, she swapped over the batteries, and moving to the nearest of the four ground sensors, she sent the drone up into the sky again. As always, she flew it in a diagonal pattern across the field.

She usually stood still for this to avoid contaminating the vibration results. Today though, she strolled around the outer edge of the field, and whenever she reached a sensor, she tapped it with her foot. By *her* standards, she even did it quite gently.

Once Liz crashed the drone again, she connected it back up to her laptop and relaunched *SurveyMaster*. Her finger hovered for an instant over the trackpad, moved the cursor to the on-screen *Merge* button and clicked. The white, clock-like icon pulsed to show it was thinking about it. After what seemed like an age, the screen cleared.

"Bugger," she repeated, glaring at the screen. "Bloody sensors must be out of whack."

By now, Liz had had more than enough of technology for the day, and going around each sensor in turn, she turned them all off. They'd arrived in their own aluminium flight case, inside which were four, precise, foam cut-outs to keep them safe in transit. This is Liz we're talking about though and jamming square pegs into round holes is her speciality. Consequently, a few minutes later, with the sensors wedged into the case in ways that would have made the IT guys weep, she turned to her blog.

At this point, she could have typed something innocuous like *Sensors appear faulty. Will seek help*. Unfortunately, *Fate* hadn't had a laugh for a while though, and that would have been far too sensible. Instead, Liz opted for the phrase that was going to grab Nigel's attention.

All my bloody moles have vanished. What's that about and where do moles go on holiday anyway?

Liz had calmed down somewhat by the time she got back to *The Spotted Pig*, and re-reading her blog post, she replaced it with the version Nigel would read to Jenny the following day. It was already too late though, for even as she typed, the more eclectic news services were already picking up the story. She didn't know that of course, and after grudgingly starting a software reset on the sensors, she changed into her running gear and headed back out.

It was a lovely day for it. The morning mist had burnt off long before, the sky was a deep, cloudless blue, and there was a cooling afternoon breeze blowing across the fields. No tech to cope with either; not even a fitness band or an iPod.

Running was her thing, her way of relaxing and clearing her brain. She enjoyed the simple freedom of it, unhampered by anything or anyone. She loved the way time flew by, and how it only took minutes for the stresses of the day to evaporate. Living in Cambridge, she was used to the constant noise of car horns and angry cyclists as she ran. Swap that for the quiet lane leading out of Effington, and her sense of tranquillity bordered on bliss.

A little under 30 minutes and three miles later, a mentally refreshed Liz walked back into her hotel room and threw a cursory glance at the laptop. It had finished the reset. She'd known it should have, but she breathed a sigh of relief all the same. Undressing, she stepped into the shower and soaking up its steamy water, she considered what to do next.

After another half an hour, now dressed in a black tracksuit and Ed Sheeran t-shirt, she headed back to site. She'd do one more flight, one more run of the data, and whatever the result, she'd call it a day.

Back at the field, she replaced the sensors, switched them all back on, and sent up the drone for its fourth and final time that day. Twenty minutes later, with all the data uploaded into *SurveyMaster* again, she hit the *Merge* button once more. Everything appeared to have worked, except when the results flashed up on-screen, they hadn't changed.

"Damn," she snapped, slamming her laptop shut.

After packing everything away, she returned to *The Spotted Pig* again, threw herself into a chair and began mulling over the afternoon's events. After a while, she picked up her phone and dialled a number. It barely rang.

"Hel ..."

"Steve, it's Professor Benning."

"Oh, hello Prof', what can I do for you?"

"I've got a problem with the vibration sensors. Can you come out tomorrow and recalibrate them?"

"Sure. What's the problem?"

"Damn things are working when I tap them, but they're not picking up anything from the moles."

There was a pause from Steve's end of the line.

"OK Prof'. 10ish alright for you?"

"Great, thanks, Steve."

Steve Guthrie put the phone down and cursed. He was the senior technician at Cambridge University where Liz had done her doctorate, and where she now taught. He, therefore, knew her all too well, and when she said she'd tapped the sensors, his heart had sunk. Her relationship with technology was legendary, and the IT guys didn't call her *Bend it Benning* for nothing. His lovely new sensors too.

Almost 100 miles to the west of Steve, deep in the Worcestershire countryside, lies the sleepy, market town of Penmound. That isn't true mind you because the place itself neither lies nor sleeps, although many of its inhabitants do one of these, and all but one does the other.

David Marston's cousin Nigel is the person who doesn't sleep of course, and having recently had his life disrupted by bats nesting in his roof, finding the brick was the icing on the cake. He didn't like cake though, or at least, not yet. It would have suited him too, or at least the crumbs would have. What with his perpetual jeans, check shirt, trainers and fleece (or jumper when he wanted to be smart), he had *casual* down to a fine art.

That didn't mean he was scruffy though, and he was always presentable after a haircut. In fact, if it coincided with him having shaved or ironed a shirt, he was almost good-looking. Not quite, but almost. These days though, since giving up his office job to be a writer, what little talent he'd ever had for smartness had waned somewhat. Being a semi-professional pub regular in a small town probably didn't help either.

His home reflected him perfectly too, littered as it was with piles of books which looked like they might have been there since it was built. Take his study. It wasn't a big room, but with his desk in front of the window, a sofa bed against the opposite wall, and bookshelves all around, it was very much him. Untidy, but friendly and welcoming, as long as you were happy to pick your way through the jumble of papers, magazines and stray bits of technology which littered the floor.

The living room was similar, with its oak beams, fireplace and yet more shelves. The difference was that here Nigel's books vied for space with his collection of antique cameras and an assortment of DVDs. His music had shifted across to iTunes years before, but he still liked the tangible quality of movies on disc. He was a contradiction like that. As proof, his iPad and AirPods currently shared the dining table with several spiral notepads, a jumble of pens, and piles of junk mail. At the bottom of one pile, were the flattened remains of a cheese biscuit. The surprising thing perhaps, was that he knew where everything was. Maybe not the cheese biscuit, but otherwise he was fine. Or he had been until one-thirty-two when the brick had arrived.

"Alwrite[12] Mavis?" he grinned to the librarian whose name was Deirdre.

He's never once got it right, she thought to herself.

"I wonder if you can help me with somethin'[13]," he began. "I need to do some research on bricks and ..."

"Sticks?"

"No, bricks. As in houses."

He held up the item in question.

"Oh, bricks. They'll be under *Construction and Project Planning*. Fourth aisle to the left, past the yucca plant and keep going."

"Past the yucca plant ..."

"... and keep going. If you get as far as *Modern Philosophy* or *Scandinavian Cookery* you've gone too far."

When he first thought of the library, Nigel had no idea how much information he'd find, so a dedicated section was more than he'd hoped for. Passing the yucca plant, he scanned the shelves.

It wasn't a big section, and it hadn't been tidied in a while as nothing was in alphabetical order. *Construction: A career in the making*, therefore, nestled happily between *If you build it, they will come*, and *Tea breaks I have known*. Not only that, but for some reason, there was also a copy of *The Three Little Pigs* nestling in the middle of the bottom shelf. Then he saw it ... *From mud to marvellous: The bricks that built Britain*, written by the appropriately

---

[12] A multi-purpose greeting used by residents of Bristol, covering "Hello" and "Are you alright?", sometimes extended to "*Alwrite my luvver?*" meaning simply "Hello mate."

[13] Another Bristolian quirk is that g's are often lost from the end of words such as *nothin'*, and those ending in 'a' are pronounced as 'awl', such as *Ikeawl* (a Swedish furniture store).

named Mason Bond.

Hardly believing his luck, he took the book from the shelf and glanced around for somewhere to sit. The modern library was spacious with loads of natural light, and quiet areas mixed in with the bookshelves. Every few yards, a potted plant blocked the way ... or added to the ambience, depending on your point of view. After several minutes, he found a small armchair by a window and settled down to read. Inside the front cover was a quote from someone Nigel had never heard of, which read: *Even bricks aspire to greatness*. He grunted, frowned and turned to the contents page:

> *1. Bricks throughout history*
>
> *2. Manufacturing through the ages*
>
> *3. How mortars have changed*
>
> *4. Bricks in art and sculpture*
>
> *5. Construction today*
>
> *6. The era of specialism*

"That doesn'elp," he muttered to himself, flicking through the book. Then as his finger passed over the centre pages, he felt a change in the paper. He opened the book, and there in the middle were twelve pages of illustrations. First came drawings of medieval brick making, followed by two pages on the workings of a modern kiln, and finally, page after page showing bricks through the ages.

He'd found it; brick porn.

Nigel thumbed through the photographs until he came to the last one. It showed something red, rectangular, with ten holes pierced through between each of its largest faces. The caption beneath read:

*Modern Engineering Brick. Used from the early 21ˢᵗ century
where strength and low porosity are needed*

He picked up his own example and compared it to the photograph. It was identical. *So, not an ordinary house brick then*, he mused, *but how did that help?* After all, apart from anything else, there was never going to have been a chapter on bricks in myths and folklore, let alone anything about them appearing out of thin air. But what now? He couldn't very well leave it in the library, although he still glanced around on the off-chance. *Maybe I could put it here with the construction books*, he pondered, *like a sort of themed bookend.*

As if reading the heresy in his mind, Deirdre chose that moment to walk past, pushing a trolley of returned books.

"Did you find what you were looking for?" she asked brightly.

"Oh yes, thanks, Doris."

"Splendid. I wasn't too hopeful when you asked."

"Same here, this one does the trick though," he replied, holding up *From mud to marvellous.*

"Excellent. Well, good luck with it."

She started to walk off, but he called her back.

"By the way, I found this too."

She tilted her head to one side as he held up the copy of *The Three Little Pigs.*

"Yes?"

"Shouldn't it be in *Nursery Rhymes* or somewhere?"

"Oh no," she replied, "that's *Construction best practices.*"

With that she walked off, leaving Nigel to wonder if there'd been any hint of a smile in her voice. Chuckling to himself, he put *From mud to marvellous* back on the shelf, tucked the brick under his arm and headed towards the exit. After a brief stop to move *The Three Little Pigs* to the children's section, he stepped back outside.

As he walked home, he nodded to a few people he knew, stopped for a chat with a friend from his writing group, then made a short detour to Penmound's MiniMart. He'd spotted the day before that it was giving away free Easter eggs with every packet of Christmas cards, and he wanted to check it out. It could have been the other way around, but in any event, they were either spectacularly ahead or behind on things.

To his disappointment, the *Sell-by* dates on the eggs were too blurred to be conclusive, so he decided against the purchase. Instead, he bought a cook-from-frozen lasagne, a cheap bottle of Merlot, and a copy of Penmound's local paper, *The Argus*. It wasn't something he bought very often, but he wondered if it might have anything about bricks in it. Plus, it came with a free lottery scratch card.

Nigel paid, tucked the paper under one arm, and gazed doubtfully at the wafer-thin plastic bag holding his dinner. He wasn't convinced it was strong enough. The brick was still in his left hand too, so he had to open the shop door with his shoulder. It was a bad idea, and when he stumbled out into the market square, it was never going to end well.

A sudden gust of wind hit him, and in a flurry of arms, the newspaper flew up and wrapped itself around his face. As it did, he also managed to simultaneously drop the bag, and launch the brick into the air. The bag crashed to the ground, instantly creating Merlot Lasagne … with added glass and plastic.

As it did, a group of women came around the corner into the square, laughing and shrieking as only friends can. They were out for a 21st birthday party and dressed as they were in high heels, satin sashes and pink glitter, they stood out rather. It was Nigel who was making a spectacle of himself though, and as he turned to look at them, the wind dropped. With that, *The Argus* fell free, and he came face to face with the brick.

He took a shocked step backwards, and as he did, the brick fell to the ground. The noise it made on the pavement was precisely the same as it had that afternoon. He gazed down. It still appeared to be like any other brick. The only thing was, not content with being able to be both there and not; apparently, now it could fly as well. But bricks are like that … Build a house out of a bunch of them, and they're perfectly happy. Leave one to go wandering about on its own, and you never knew what might happen.

"Blast," he exclaimed, looking down at the remains of the lasagne and the 36 pages of local news which were now soaking up his wine.

"Are you alright?" asked one of the women as they clustered around him.

"Poor man's in shock," said another.

"But did you see …?"

"Well, I thought …"

"You've had too much to drink."

"Or not enough."

That set them off into a fit of giggles, and it fell to the birthday girl to approach Nigel again.

"Are you sure you're all right?"

He nodded, still too stunned by what had happened to speak.

"Well if you're sure …"

With one last look, the women walked away, their laughter bouncing off a couple of restaurants and disappearing around the corner as they went. Nigel, meanwhile, was left to mop up the mess using only the impossibly thin carrier bag, the newspaper and a small packet of tissues he found in his pocket. It wasn't easy, but he did his best, and after dropping the remains in a nearby bin, he went back to the MiniMart. The shopkeeper didn't say a word when he bought the same things all over again.

Back home some fifteen minutes later, Nigel poured himself a glass of wine and sat down to examine the brick. It still looked ordinary enough, except as he slowly turned it over between his hands, it suddenly wasn't there again. The next second it was back of course, and that went on for several minutes in what started to feel like a surreal game of hide-and-seek. Apart from that, the brick seemed happy enough though, and deciding against a staring contest, Nigel put it over to one side. As his lasagne cooked, he settled down to read *The Argus*.

"Come on, TC," shouted Sue as they ran for the school bus.

Panting, they quickened their pace, and a minute or so later the two of them flopped into their seats at the back. Sue with her short, blonde bob and the other girl with her long wavy hair, they were best friends who looked nothing like each other except for the large, inquisitive eyes they each had. It was their typical morning routine with one calling for the other, followed by a mad dash down the street. No point in waiting around on the corner. Then there was the usual pushing and shoving to find two seats together.

The bus was louder than normal today too because it was the last day of term, and everyone was excited. As Sue's mother had said to her over breakfast, "The sooner you get there, dear, the sooner you'll be home."

End of term, her friend thought to herself. *Summer holidays*. She smiled, and as she did, another thought danced around the edges of her mind. Then she had it.

"What did you call me before?" she asked.

"Sorry?"

"When we were running for the bus, you called me Teesy or something. What was that about?"

Sue was flustered for a second.

"TC," she said at last, "not Teesy."

"TC? Why TC?"

Another expression flashed across Sue's face; only this time it held more than a hint of embarrassment.

"Well …" she began and stopped. "OK, but you've got to promise me you won't get upset."

"Of course I won't, don't be daft."

"Promise?"

"Oh, come on, what are you? Six?"

"OK. TC stands for … Well, it stands for *Two Cakes*."

"Two cakes?"

"It was Carol who came up with it. She was making up nicknames for everyone, so she didn't mean anything by it. It's just that …"

At this, she ran out of steam again, not sure how her friend was taking the news. "It's just that … Well, have you noticed how much cake you eat?"

"Cake!"

"Wherever we go … you always have a slice of cake, often two. So … well … Two Cakes."

"What's Carol's own nickname?"

"*Trampoline Queen*."

"Bit nicer than mine."

"I don't know; one of the girls has already shortened it to *Tramp Queen*."

They both smiled.

"And yours?"

"*SnS*, after …"

"You and Simon, yes, I get it. And I'm Two Cakes."

It sounded weird as she said it, but it was true, she did like cake. She liked it a lot. Fruitcake at Christmas, lemon drizzle cake anytime, and her favourite, raspberry and white chocolate muffins.

"Thing is," continued Sue, "you never put on any weight either. If I wasn't your best friend, I'd hate you."

That started them both laughing, and they'd barely stopped by the time they arrived at school. It was a lovely way to end the journey.

Not only the bus ride either, because this was the last time they'd go to school together, as later that summer, one would start work locally, and the other would go away to college.

Once TC left home, her life changed. For a start, she'd got so used to her nickname by then, that she introduced herself to everyone as TC. Then on day six, she met *him*. He wasn't, perhaps everyone's idea of attractive, but he was hers, and the feeling was mutual. If love at first sight exists, they were it. Never apart, finishing each other's sentences, and whoever met them was swept along by the dream; they were perfect together. Then he died.

It was one of those stupid road accidents that should never happen, and no one saw her for months afterwards. It was like she'd died too. That was what it felt like to her anyway. A hole had been ripped open in her soul, and her heart had been wrenched out. Even so, like a crack in a frozen lake, the wound closed in time, although as it did, it sealed in a cold emptiness that would stay there for years to come. An aching, hollow centre that even loved ones never saw.

So TC hid away. Hid from friends, family, her college tutors, everyone. People understood, of course, and for the first few weeks, they kept in touch. They called, texted, messaged, emailed, visited, and in the case of her grandparents, they wrote.

By the end of the first month, the only person she'd seen was her father, and the only people she'd replied to were her grandparents. She'd also posted on *Instagram* asking friends to give her time, but had never read any of the comments.

I'll be back, TC had written, underneath a still from *his* favourite movie.

That wasn't to be though, and when her parents visited her a few weeks later, they found her room empty. Posters immediately went up around campus, articles appeared in the local paper, and after a few days, her face was all over the national media. It was to no avail though, as TC had vanished.

The thing was, she hadn't really. She'd merely gone somewhere else.

Weird coincidences

Saturday, September 11ᵗʰ

It was 8 a.m. and in a large, circular room, lit only by banks of monitors and the small red switch of a coffee machine, sat six communications analysts. The room itself, in a secret building somewhere, had a frosted glass door, with access by retinal scan only. As for the four women and two men of the morning shift, their job was to monitor alerts from UK military and government facilities around the world. The only problem was, one of the analysts had been a little late to his monitor today. Only 45 seconds it's true, as it had been his turn to make tea and coffee for everyone. But in that time an alert had flashed up, showing that Crianloch Station had been out of contact since the previous afternoon. Some such alerts stayed on-screen until dismissed, but this one was only from a weather research station, so it stayed there for 30 seconds, then sank into the background unseen.

The morning after the brick's appearance, Nigel rolled over and stared blearily at his clock. It was precisely 8:16 in the morning. He had no idea of that as he'd always hated digital clocks; they were so damn precise. Consequently, as the hands of his old alarm came into focus, the time appeared to be about ten past seven. Hopelessly wrong, but his head was at a funny angle, and he had a hangover.

After a few minutes, he gave up trying to work out the time and glanced instead at his bedside table. On it was his phone, his house keys, and a copy of *The Hitchhiker's Guide to the Galaxy*. He'd finally given in and bought a few weeks before, after months of nagging from his writing tutor, who thought it might suit his sense of humour.

As he struggled towards wakefulness, Nigel's only annoyance was the nagging feeling he'd woken up with. It was a bit like getting to the pub and wondering whether he'd left the oven on. Or like getting there and realizing he'd left his wallet at home. It even felt a little like the sensation he got when he forgot what he was saying halfway through a sentence. Sort of lost or like something was missing, but with the vague notion he'd never known what it had been in the first place. Funny as well, how two of these involved going to the pub. That wasn't the whole of it either as there was something else on his mind, and it was poking at him. Rather like a white-hot needle pretending to be something cuddly and fluffy.

Tea, he thought to himself, swinging his legs out of bed. It was always his first priority in the mornings, although today it had almost been knocked off the top slot by the brick. As he walked into the living room, he glanced over at the shelf where he'd left it the night before. The brick winked out of existence for half a second, just to prove it could.

The local paper hadn't been any help with that either, and once he'd made his tea, he plodded back upstairs to his study. The last time he'd been online, he was googling questions for a *True or False* round in the quiz he was writing. And as results for bricks popped up now, he realised he had enough information for another round right there. His favourite facts were the 8 million bricks needed to construct the Great Wall of China, the mobile kilns used by the Romans to build cities across Europe, and best of all, that April 14th is *National Brick Day*[14].

Given Nigel's butterfly brain, that got him googling other national days, and what with his current bedside reading, it didn't take him long to get to *Towel Day*[15]. With his mind now in full random-search mode, he typed *National Days in September* and hit *Return*. The list was mind-boggling ... *National Chicken Boy Day*, *National Ampersand Day*, *National Mud Pack Day*, *National Ants on a Log Day*; the list got stranger as it went on. He moved onto October, and in amongst an equally bizarre array of celebrations, one immediately jumped out at him.

Mole Day: Celebrated on October 23rd from 6:02 a.m. to 6:02 p.m.[16]

Why this set off something in his brain, he didn't know, but

---

[14] First seen on social media in 2016, *National Brick Day* is a US invention and genuinely is on April 14th. Amazingly, all the other strange dates mentioned are real too.

[15] *Towel Day* was started in 2001 to celebrate the life and works of Douglas Adams, author of the five-part *Hitchhiker's Guide to the Galaxy trilogy* and the *Dirk Gently* books. It's observed on May 25th, which is the anniversary of Adams' death, although the date works for another reason too ... If you add up the hexadecimal numbers 25 and 5 (25 May), then convert the result to decimal, the answer is 42, which is, of course, the answer to the ultimate question of life, the universe and everything.

[16] Ironically, this has nothing to do with our cute, furry friends, as it commemorates *Avogadro's Number* (6.02×10^{23}), which is a standard measuring unit in chemistry. Why it doesn't run from 6:02 to 10:23 though, is beyond me.

moles were in his mind now, and it was a short hop (or tunnel) to start googling other facts about them. *After all*, he figured, *there might be a quiz round in that as well.*

As Nigel started his search, Steve Guthrie was pulling into the car park at *The Spotted Pig*. He found Liz having a late breakfast in the bar.

"Coffee, Steve?" she asked brightly. A night's rest had done much to wash away the previous day's events.

"I've given up caffeine thanks. Do they have any green tea?"

"I should think so. Hold on."

Liz got up from the table, walked over to the bar and went through a doorway at the end. On it was a sign that read: *Kitchen staff only. No boyfriends or other pets allowed.* From the kitchen came the sound of a kettle boiling, followed by a jar being opened and closed. At last, the noises stopped, and Liz reappeared with a tray. On it were a teapot, a tea strainer and a cup.

"Why no coffee?" she asked, putting the things down on the table.

"Oh, you wouldn't believe what it does to your insides. I'm sleeping so much better since I've given it up too. I'm not as restless, and I feel, I don't know, more real."

And for how long? wondered Liz, for Steve was known around the university for his health fads. If she remembered rightly, the last one had involved avocados and had ended rather abruptly ... Something about one of the stones, a knife, and the palm of his left hand.

Steve lifted the lid of the teapot and stirred the contents. He'd only recently switched drinks and was still adjusting to the yellowy-green liquid in front of him, let alone the tea strainer. He was more used to tea bags than leaf tea. He poured a cup, took a sip, and a surprised smile spread across his face.

"Hey, this is nice."

"I thought it might be. Dot's a bit of a tea snob."

He gave her a quizzical look.

"The hotel's owner. She went into the village earlier on."

"You've made yourself pretty well at home then."

"Yes, we get on well. It's my second year, and I eat most of my meals here, so I'm a good customer. Plus, there aren't many other guests at the moment either."

"I see what you mean."

Liz turned her attention back to her breakfast and buttered a now cold slice of toast.

"Any chance of some more?" asked Steve.

She looked at him.

"Toast, I mean. I didn't get any breakfast."

"Oh sure, I left the bread out on the side in the kitchen."

"You want some fresh?"

"Thanks, that would be great."

Steve went through the door at the end of the bar and found himself in a medium-sized kitchen. Gleaming steel units lined the walls, which wasn't at all what he'd expected. He hadn't thought what that was, but it would almost certainly have been something a lot shabbier and grimier. This was like a laboratory.

The toaster (polished stainless steel to match) sat off to his left. Alongside it was an open loaf of bread, so he popped in four slices and scanned the room for any sign of marmalade. He had no trouble finding the fridge, but it took two guesses to locate a plate. As he closed the cupboard, the outside door to the kitchen opened. He turned around.

Standing in the doorway was a short, slim woman with close-cut black hair and grey eyes. She was wearing jeans, an old baseball cap and a baggy fleece, but she was still the most startling woman Steve had ever seen. Not a classic beauty perhaps, but she radiated confidence in a way that almost made him sway on his feet. Dot? The name had conjured up an image of a smiling but bent over old lady with a string shopping bag.

"Oh, hi, you must be Steve. Do me a couple of slices, would you?"

Her voice was light but husky, and with that greeting, she swept from the room, leaving Steve feeling slightly dazed. The toaster popped, and without thinking, he emptied it. Then, putting in two more slices, he carried the first four out to the bar.

Dot and Liz were in the middle of an animated discussion, so Steve put the plate of toast on the table and was about to fetch the last two slices when ...

"Steve, meet Dot," said Liz.

"We sort of met," smiled Dot, holding out a hand.

Steve shook it and smiled back. "This is your place?"

"Not what you expected, I imagine."

"Certainly not the kitchen. It's like something out of a cookery show."

"Thanks; I'm working on getting Cambridgeshire's next Michelin star."

"Impressive."

"What, me or the restaurant?" asked Dot with a mischievous smile.

Steve shifted uncomfortably. "Well, I ..."

"Don't worry, I'm just messing with you," she laughed. "Dot doesn't exactly conjure up the image of a modern businesswoman does it?"

"Well, no," acknowledged Steve.

"Short for Dorothy. My mother had a thing about *The Wizard of Oz*."

"Could have been worse."

"Tell me about it. Imagine if she'd been a *Lord of the Rings* fan."

As it happened, Steve's mind had already gone there, and he could picture Dot exactly like that. Galloping across a windswept plain, wearing armour as shiny as her kitchen, at the head of an army of hobbits. Wisely he kept his mouth shut.

"We should get going," said Liz, draining her coffee cup.

"My car?"

"Better take both. You can get off once you're done, and I'll stick around afterwards to take some new readings."

"OK, I'll follow you."

It was a beautiful morning, with a weak autumn sun glinting off the spider webs in the long, dewy grass, and when they got to the field, Steve took a laptop bag from his car, along with a small, metal case. Steve opened his laptop, turned it on and unclipped the latches on the small, metal case. Inside were various cables, a handheld calibration device, and a box of tiny screwdrivers.

He took out the calibrator, turned it on and clicked the *Connect?* icon on his laptop screen. The calibrator's display blinked as lines of code flashed past. After five seconds or so, the light on the top turned from red to green, and the single word *Ready* appeared on its small screen.

"Right, let's see what's going on."

Steve bent down by the first of the vibration sensors, and after straightening it from Liz's kicking, he scanned its barcode. After repeating this for all four, he sat down at the table Liz had set up.

"So, what's the trouble?"

"Give me a chance Prof'. All I've done is to register the sensors to the programme. I need to run diagnostics yet."

Liz made a noise … "How long?" Her mood had shifted back to the day before.

"Hour or so."

"I'll get out of your hair, then. I've got my notes to type up."

"OK. I'll come and find you when I'm done."

Liz grunted and left.

Freed from observation, Steve relaxed and gazed around the field. He didn't know anything about moles, but he knew a good site for his sensors when he saw one. This one's flat terrain, lack of trees and distance from the road made it ideal.

On his laptop, a button reading *Calibrate* was flashing. He ticked the box for *Sensor 1* and hit enter. Five minutes later he did the same for *Sensor 2*, then again for *3* and finally for *4*. Once they were all done the screen changed, and a new button appeared reading *Link now?* He clicked it. After another ten minutes, he was presented with the option to exit calibration. He clicked *OK* and launched *SurveyMaster*.

Once Steve had reloaded the data from the day before, he clicked yet again and waited. It had all gone okay so far, except when the results popped up, they showed exactly what Liz had seen.

"Improbable," he mumbled to himself.

He breathed in, frowned and let out a long sigh. An idea had struck him, and he leant forward to examine the laptop screen. Rather than choosing *Movement* from the left-hand menu as Liz had, he selected *Topography*. A black and white image appeared. Not all at once, but it built down the screen as line after line of horizontal detail came into view. If you've ever seen an old movie with a slow-loading webpage or watched a cop show where they use ground-radar to search for bodies, you'll be able to picture what it was like. In this case, rather than the image of a murder victim appearing, nothing came up at all. Greyness yes, but uniform greyness and that couldn't be right.

Steve opened the box of screwdrivers and took out the smallest. There was a tiny screw on the side of each sensor, and he adjusted the first one. He did the same on the other three, took a new set of data readings, and re-ran the programme. The result was precisely the same. He sat still for several minutes, cradling his chin in one hand. Then, puffing out his cheeks, he exhaled, stood up and packed away his equipment.

Back at *The Spotted Pig*, Liz Benning was sitting under a large umbrella, bashing away on her laptop. As Steve approached her, it occurred to him why she needed her keyboard replacing more than most.

"You all done?" she asked, looking up.

Steve nodded.

"Everything OK now?"

Steve sat down and looked at her.

"What?" she asked testily, sensing something wasn't right. "Oh, don't tell me you've got to get them replaced?"

"I could, but I've run the calibration twice, and I'm getting the same answers each time."

"Which are?"

"That the sensors are working fine ..."

"So ..."

"Hold on. The sensors are working fine, *but* they're not picking anything up."

"Wait a minute ..."

"I know. It's the same as yesterday, but this is different ... or actually, maybe it's not. The thing is, they're not picking up anything because there doesn't seem to be anything to pick up."

Liz went to speak, but Steve was ahead of her. He opened his laptop and turned it round to face her.

"What am I looking at?"

"This is from *SurveyMaster*'s *Topo* option. It's an underground image of the soil profile between sensors 1 and 2. Here's the same between 2 and 3, 3 and 4 and between 4 and 1."

He flicked between the four images as Liz stared at the screen.

"They're all the same."

"Precisely."

"Look, I know I'm not techy but what am I looking at?"

"They're ground-radar images that have been created by signals between the sensors. They're fairly crude as it's not what the system's really intended for, but they should still be showing differences in the soil."

"Differences meaning ...?"

"Disturbances. Some evidence the soil's been churned up."

"Like mole tunnels."

"Exactly."

"So, you're telling me the tunnels aren't there anymore?"

Steve hesitated.

"What I'm saying is ... if I'd seen these pictures out of context, I'd have said there'd never been any tunnels there."

Liz went to speak, but the words wouldn't come. It was simply too fantastic. *It must be the tech*, she thought to herself.

"So, what next?" she asked at last.

"I need to run some more tests. Get a broader perspective on this."

Liz glared at him. It wasn't his fault, but they were *his* sensors, so it sort of was.

Steve Guthrie was thinking exactly the opposite and had already put the fault down to Liz's handling of the equipment, so rather than heading home from Effington, he went straight to the university. He wanted to get in touch with *Seismic Dynamics* in the States. They were the North Carolina company he'd worked with to customize the sensors, and although he'd never have admitted as much to Liz, he wanted their opinion. As a result, an email and an overnight *FedEx* were soon winging their way over to Raleigh's *Research Triangle Park*, where SD was based.

Unsurprisingly, there were no moles in Crianloch Station either, and much to Marston's annoyance neither were there any answers. Protocol demanded that in circumstances like this, the station go on lockdown for 96 hours, which meant they had until Wednesday morning to sort things out. With any luck that would be enough time, but therein lay another challenge, because although the RAF personnel were accustomed to spending periods out of contact with loved ones, that wasn't the case with the civilians. To make matters even worse, both Gaggias had now stopped working, and Marston was having to drink instant.

"It just isn't the same," he grumbled as he made his way to the civilian mess.

"Well?" he demanded, as he walked in.

"I'm afraid not, sir. Instant?"

Marston grimaced and nodded. What with everything else going on, he could have done with a decent cup about now. Even something from *Starbucks* would have done.

Worse still, going dark on all comms had only ever been intended as a response to cyber-attacks, and the protocols described it as:

> *To neither make nor receive any form of communication, whether by voice, data or in person for up to 4 (four) days or until advised to the contrary by Emergency Command, whichever is the sooner.*

In other words, the assumption was that a base on lockdown would be contacted by the outside world sometime during the four days. Or if the worst came to the worst, they'd get back in touch themselves at the end of the period. The problem at Crianloch was that unless the engineers could find an answer soon, this wasn't going to happen. It wasn't all bad though, because even if they couldn't fix the comms by the deadline, they'd still be able to restart the air traffic control cameras and best of all perhaps, go outside.

Elsewhere, one person already enjoying the fresh air, was Nigel's best friend, Jennifer Stevens, or Jenny, as she liked to be called … so he always called her Jen. As it happens, she didn't like that, but she called him Nige, which he loathed, so it all balanced out. Unlike him, she always slept like a log, and she shared her meticulously tidy home with two tabby cats called Tommy and Tuppence. Jenny had named them after her favourite fictional detectives, so no Jodi Picoult or Jane Austen for her. Instead, her Kindle was full of Lee Child, John le Carré, Tom Clancy and any number of other authors who made her think. Naturally Agatha Christie was in there too, and in Jenny's case, it wasn't only Christie's stories she liked, it was also the portrayal of a bygone age, and the stylishness of her characters.

Partly as a result, Jenny always liked to look smart herself. Almost 30, and 5' 5" tall, she was two years younger and five inches shorter than Nigel. With shoulder-length auburn hair and bottle-green eyes, she was attractive too, and her voice added to the overall effect. Soft, lyrical, with a hint of Scotland about it, it was like a breeze in the treetops. She could even turn heads in the hideous purple tunic she had to wear at work, as when Jenny wasn't annoying Nigel, she could be found at the DIY superstore in nearby Redditch. It had started out as a job purely to pay the bills. Then today, somewhat to her surprise, she'd been put in charge of the paint department.

"Not only the wall paints either," her manager had said, in a voice that bordered on reverence. "Garden paints, varnishes and ... well, anything you can put on with a brush."

Blusher too? Jenny wondered, absent-mindedly pushing her hair from her eyes, as she often did.

Her boss was a DIY-lifer and had spent years working his way up from the stock room. Then Jenny had joined, and in no time at all, she'd walked straight into his dream job. Suffice it to say he was jealous as hell. He didn't totally believe her LinkedIn profile either.

"It's not only about paint of course," he droned. "We sell the promise of a life renewed. A fresh start if you will. A way for people to express their inner selves."

"Don't you mean shelves?" corrected Jenny, who was only half listening.

"Oh, very good." he laughed.

The sound of this snapped her out of her trance, and without even knowing the joke, she joined in. Her shift was finishing at half-past three, so at a quarter to four, with a spring in her step, and autumn in the air, she headed for her camper van. She got into the ageing VW, gave a silent prayer that it would start and turned the key. The engine spluttered into life, and she smiled again.

As she drove through a countryside that was starting to turn brown, her thoughts went back to previous Autumns. She sighed, and for a moment, it seemed like she might cry. Then as the track changed on her playlist, her trademark smile returned. As the landscape flashed past, she found herself singing along. It was a collection she'd created a few weeks before, and as Adele segued into a childhood favourite by Norah Jones, Jenny's smile broadened. She remembered hearing somewhere once that sad is happy for deep people, and that was her.

When she reached Penmound, she got out of the camper van and looked around. A few of the trees were still green, whereas some had already turned gold, and the odd one shone a bright, improbable red. As she savoured the fresh, Autumn air, the sun was already heading for the horizon, and with a few eager leaves still dancing around her ankles, she turned and went indoors.

After feeding Tommy and Tuppence, she settled down to watch a DVD of *Sherlock* that one of the women in work had lent her. Being a fan of the books, Jenny had avoided it up until now but was soon so engrossed she was well into a third episode before she noticed the time. Hurriedly microwaving a fish pie before putting the remains down for the cats, she grabbed her mobile and ran out of the house. It was only a short distance to *The White Hart*, and as Jenny walked in, she scanned the faces of the regulars for Nigel. There was no sign of him, so she rang his number.

"Hello, *Claridge's Tea Room*," he answered, in his best, snobby accent.

"Where are you?"

"On the corner of Brook Street and Davies Street madam. Just a three-minute stroll from Bond Street tube station, although I'm sure a discernin' customer like you would rather reach us by taxi."

"Very funny Nige," replied Jenny, "I mean, why aren't you in the pub?"

Good question, thought Nigel.

"Well?" she demanded.

"Oh, now!" he blurted out, the fog in his brain clearing as he noticed for the first time that it was already evening.

"Get on down here; it's your round."

Jenny hung up, chuckled to herself, and after buying a drink, sat down at their usual table in the corner. Teasing Nigel was her favourite thing, but people-watching came a close second, and the Long Bar of *The White Hart* public house was an excellent spot for it. Sometimes she just watched, and sometimes she listened in on snippets of conversation. Sometimes, like today, she made up stories about the people around her.

Take the young farmer at the bar. Who was the woman with him? She looked strangely familiar, and going by the absence of a ring, Jenny figured she was probably either his girlfriend or his sister, but which? A girlfriend decided Jenny. But why were they here, and why was she with him? As soon as she asked herself that, a story fell into place.

By a strange quirk of history, the north-east pasture of his family's farm concealed a long-hidden military bunker, unknown to anyone except the secret organization Natalia belonged to. It was no ordinary bunker either, for deep inside it, on a rusty old table, lay a small, mildewed, *My Little Pony* satchel. It was in an anteroom marked *No entrance. This means you. Yes, it really does,* and in the bag was a copy of the UK's nuclear launch codes from 1982. That, and some very out of date bourbon biscuits.

As you'll have guessed though, the woman wasn't really a mistress of international espionage. Her name was actually Christine, and she worked at the Jaguar dealership in nearby Solihull. Mind you, it wouldn't have bothered Jenny if she'd known any of this, as the fun lay in the imagining. So, with a slight shrug of her shoulders, she went back to studying the others in the pub.

The place itself was old with an open fireplace at either end, black oak beams and a handful of pictures on the yellowed walls in between. Jenny turned her attention to two old men arguing about something in the corner. *More espionage?* she wondered. Or had one just found out about the other's affair with his sister forty years before? She chuckled to herself again and looked instead at the group of middle-aged women over by the door. Something about cat shows, perhaps? Which bulbs to plant the following spring? Or maybe a trip to see the *Chippendales*?

As a story about them started to form in Jenny's mind, Nigel was rushing around his house like a mad thing. "Wallet, keys, phone," he muttered as he went from room to room. When he was satisfied he'd got everything, he hurried out of the house, slamming the front door behind him. He'd not gone far though before he realised he'd forgotten a coat, so dashing back in, he grabbed one and set off again, putting it on as he went.

"So, you forgot you were meeting me?" teased Jenny.

Nigel studied his beer for inspiration, but none came. He watched the froth spreading across its surface, and that didn't work either. He took a sip, but still the dark brown liquid refused to help.

"Fancy a game of dominoes?" he asked at last.

"You what?" came Jenny's stunned reply.

"Dominoes. You won last time we played. You said you enjoyed it."

"And that's the best you can do?"

When Jenny asked this, she'd known Nigel for two years, four months, seven days, five hours, twenty-six minutes and forty-two seconds. She, therefore, shouldn't have been surprised by his tendency to go off at sudden tangents, and in many ways, she wasn't. It was still infuriating though.

She waited with that frustrated sort of patience you have when you've just missed a bus, and the next one won't be along for ages.

"It was the moles," he said at last. "I got distracted."

She stared at him. "The moles. What moles?"

"Oh ... well ... err ... sorry ... yeah ... I should explain."

"I'll gie ye a skelpit lug," she exclaimed.

Jenny's Scottish roots rarely found their way into her daily speech, and she'd almost entirely lost her accent, although she did keep some favourite phrases for moments like this. Nigel knew this one too, and as he didn't want a slap on the ear, he pulled a rueful smile and surveyed their drinks. Both his and Jenny's glasses were already half empty. He'd only been in the pub a few minutes, so it was obviously one of those evenings when the beer goes down like water.

"I'll get them in," he said.

"But it's my round."

"It's alright, I'll get two. This might take a while."

She looked at him, her earlier annoyance now replaced with a sense of intrigue. She found herself nodding.

"Alright, I'll pop to the loo while you're doing that. Get me some salt and vinegar crisps[17], would you?"

Several minutes later, they were back in their chairs by the log fire. They had beer, the next pints were warming up nicely on the table[18], and next to them was a small pile of crisp packets. No ice cubes, chilled lagers or healthy snacks for them.

Nigel generally took a while to arrange his thoughts, and the break had given him time to do just that. As Jenny sipped her beer, he, therefore, launched straight into his story and was quickly doing his puppy impression.

"So, I was doin' some research for the quiz, an' I found some amazin' things," he began excitedly. "Did you know, for example, that half the population of Iceland believe in elves[19]?"

Jenny shook her head patiently.

"Or if you sneeze at 60 miles an hour, your eyes stay shut for fifty feet! That's as long as a lorry!"

Again, Jenny shook her head. She knew that in his rush to tell a story, Nigel often took a while to get to the point, and it was best not to interrupt the flow. She though tended to go mainly on instinct, and although her stories were rarely as engaging as Nigel's, they did have two benefits. They took half as long to tell,

---

[17] I should explain for any American readers that crisps are what you call potato chips. Potato chips for us Brits are what you call French fries. French fries were not invented in France but in Belgium. Clear now?

[18] Unless you're related to one of Goldilocks' bears, you may have never wondered whether your beer is too hot, too cold or just right. In case you start wondering now, a general rule is that the colder the beer, the weaker and less tasty it is. Mmmm warm beer!

[19] According to a 2017 census, 54% of Icelanders believe in elves, which they say are 3' tall, with big ears, old-fashioned clothes, but not pointy hats. They're taken very seriously there too, as roads have been diverted around boulders they're believed to live in, and a former member of parliament even swears a family of them once saved his life. And you wondered about your politicians!

and if they led to anything needing to be done, she was the one to do it. In short, whereas Nigel might tell fantastic stories, Jenny lived them.

"Anyway, you remember our walk the other week, an' you wanted to know why some of the molehills were grassed-over?"

Jenny nodded.

"Well I thought it'd make a good quiz question, so I googled it an' turns out they're just last years."

He paused, waiting for a pat of approval like any good dog.

"And that's why you forgot you were meeting me?" asked Jenny, at last, brushing a hair aside, so she could glare at him better.

"Oh no, I thought you might be interested is all."

She shook her head in exasperation. "So, going back to our main topic ..."

"Oh, right ... Well, I was havin' a nose around an' I came across a piece about a whole colony of moles that's vanished."

"Vanished? But ..."

"Exactly. Weird, huh?"

"Yes, but ...?" tried Jenny again.

"Just what I wondered. Apparently, some scientist has been studying 'em for the last six months. Even got a government grant for it. Anyway, she was usin' all sorts of gizmos to track them, an' she'd got to the point she could predict where the next molehills would appear. Then this happened."

"But how ...?" said Jenny.

"I know, it's incredible, isn't it?" continued Nigel, oblivious to her growing irritation. "You wouldn't think you could get paid to predict molehills, would you?"

"Will you stop interrupting me?" cut in an exasperated Jenny at last. "What I want to know is *how* did it vanish?"

"Oh ... no idea."

"I mean, that's the extraordinary part."

Nigel pulled a thinking face and drained his pint. Then he took out his phone and started tapping away on the screen. Jenny was used to him googling things at the drop of a hat, so she too drained her pint and was partway into the next one when Nigel spoke again.

"She's got a blog, this Professor Benning, Professor Elizabeth Benning," he said, for once in his life pronouncing the g on the end of the word. "Says here she's been takin' readin's for months, an' everythin' was fine 'til yesterday afternoon.

"When they disappeared?"

"When the readin's stopped."

"Meaning ...?"

"Quite," replied Nigel, his earlier enthusiasm now rekindled. "She did a bunch of double checkin' apparently, but nothin'."

Nigel kept reading to himself, his excitement rising again. He backtracked and started reading out loud.

Have an expert coming tomorrow to re-calibrate the sensors. Spec says they can detect ground movement down to four feet, which should be enough, but today they're not recording anything.

Jenny looked at Nigel. "Well it's odd, I'll give you that," she said reluctantly. "Anyway, change of subject. I have some news of my own."

As she'd expected, Nigel was delighted to hear about her promotion, and some while later, after one more celebratory drink than was perhaps wise, they got up to leave. As so often before, it was only when they did, that they realised they were the last people left in the pub. In the nicest possible way, the barmaid was glad to see them go.

 Now here's a question ... Have you ever given much thought to the idea of parallel universes? Or the many-worlds theory of quantum physics? TC certainly hadn't, and if you're like her, I don't suppose you've ever lain awake at night wondering how any rational theory can assert the objective reality of the universal wave function while denying the actuality of wave function collapse.

Lost you? Don't worry, it's a lot simpler than it sounds. In a nutshell, what it means is that everything that *can* happen *does* happen. It's just that some of it happens somewhere else. When you say *yes* to something, for example, life carries on as usual But what about the possibility of you saying *no*? For that, a parallel world springs into existence, and the future there plays out from your *no*. Result? Millions of parallel worlds where every possible eventuality unfolds somewhere.

There are different theories of parallel universe[20] too, but this is by far the coolest. Why? Because according to this theory, there's a world where you passed your driving test the first time, and where *The Godfather Part III* was as good as the first two. Best of all, there's one where the genetic code for grass that never needs cutting isn't being suppressed by a global conspiracy of lawnmower companies.

"So, parallel worlds, eh? Are we talking pink sky, and turquoise grass?" I hear you ask. Well no, and how can I put this kindly but don't

---

[20] The types of parallel universe currently recognised by Quantum physicists are: Level 1: Space is so big that it stands to reason there's an exact duplicate of our world somewhere. Level 2: Separate universes exist as bubbles of space-time, where even the laws of physics might be different. Level 3: What we're talking about here and without doubt, the best kind. Level 4: Everything else that physicists haven't found a name for yet.

be so ****** daft. Molecules in the air still scatter blue light more than red, and chlorophyll still absorbs green, so no changes there. As a result, if you did wake up in another world, you might not realize straight away.

OK, so it would be obvious if your bearded husband was unexpectedly clean-shaven. Equally so if you woke up to find that instead of two Burmese kittens, you now had an iguana, a Great Dane, and an ant farm. Whatever you found, the key things to remember at a time like that are:

a) You've not gone insane,

b) You're likely stuck there for a while, so best make the most of it, *and*

c) Flying cars are bound to happen at some point, so it's up to you to either enjoy them or invent them.

In any case, if you did find yourself in another world, the one thing I can guarantee is that it would seriously freak you out. Not its strangeness either, but the sheer normality of it. You'd recognize people, but you wouldn't know if they were the same as the ones you knew. Some might dress alike, have the same sense of humour, or like similar movies. Others, might have different jobs, be with other partners or have different personalities altogether. Worst of all, some might never have met you before. All that aside, if you do find yourself in a parallel world, you won't go far wrong if you remember the three *constant facts* about them, the first being that our world is just one of many, and variants of you exist all over the place. The second, as TC had discovered, is that sometimes things go wrong. And the third? Well, however you believe the cosmos started, the third constant is that all the parallel worlds like to stay in balance. "Very sweet," I hear you say, and it is, mostly. The problem comes when this clashes with the fact that sometimes, things do indeed go wrong.

OK, so things going wrong isn't exactly rocket science. In fact, it's actually the basis of most of what happens in the universe. One of the things it means though is that sometimes, someone from one world ends up in another. This only happens very rarely because physics hates being messed about with like that, but there it is, the universe is a funny old place.

Take Vincent Van Gogh for example. If his girlfriend hadn't left him, he might not have cut his ear off and been motivated to create such tortured but brilliant works of art. Instead, maybe he'd have died a penniless but happy farmer surrounded by his seven children, thirteen pigs, and a donkey called Persephone. What though if his girlfriend had planned to leave him, but at the last minute was replaced by a more devoted version of herself from another world? Result? No angst, no artwork, lots of sex, some pigs, and an oddly named donkey.

Bit of a leap of logic you might say but turns out it happens. The good thing is, it's dead easy to tell when it has. Or at least, it's dead easy once someone has pointed it out to you in an "Oh of course. You've shaved your head; I knew there was something different about you," kind of way.

For TC though, such revelations were yet to come.

Meaningful meetings

Sunday, September 12ᵗʰ

In the secret, circular communications room, shift change was at 8 a.m. as always. As the morning crew came on duty, the appointed drinks-maker, therefore, headed straight to the coffee machine. It was surrounded by mugs saying things like *Come to the dark side, we have π*, and *Geeks make fantastic lovers.* There was even one with a maths problem on the side which someone had solved with a *Sharpie*. As for the team members, one of the women had recently contracted a bad case of conjunctivitis, and as retinal scanners don't generally like people with eye problems, it took her three attempts to get in. Now sod's law being what it is, the man she was taking over from that morning had had to leave promptly, with the result that their monitor stayed unobserved for almost two minutes. It was fortunate then, that with this being Crianloch's second alert, the red flag stayed on-screen until the woman dismissed it. All the same, by the time she saw it, she was keen to get on, so she cleared the flag without reading it and settled down to her day.

When Jenny woke up, she found to her surprise that the first sentence to go through her mind was ... *Whatever happened to the moles?* She wasn't someone to dwell on things as a rule, and she wondered why today was different. Especially given how few of Nigel's stories tended to sink in. For some reason, this was an exception, and now she knew about the moles, she needed to know the answer. Consequently, the first thought that went through Nigel's head a few minutes later was: *Who the hell's textin' me at this time of day?*

He gazed around his bedroom, then closed his eyes and snuggled back down under the duvet. He knew it was Sunday because he could hear church bells in the distance, but apart from that, the world didn't need to come into focus just yet. How many had they drunk the night before? Four? Five? Then Jenny had told him about her promotion, and Nigel knew from experience he always lost count after five, so anything was possible.

Hoping for no more suicidal birds, he swung his legs out of bed and went over to the window. He peered out between the curtains and smiled as he saw it was another nice day. A bit bright perhaps, but cool, sunny and with a slight breeze. It only needed a hint of rain, and it would have been his ideal sort of weather.

Walking out of his bedroom, Nigel stepped over a pile of washing without thinking and made his way downstairs. As always, he needed tea. On his way to the kitchen, he caught sight of the message light blinking on his answering machine. No one ever phoned his landline. He only had it for broadband and was surprised anyone had the number.

"Damn telemarketers," he muttered to himself.

A cup of tea and some muesli later, Nigel was starting to feel more human and was about to go and get dressed when the message light caught his eye again. Then he did one of those things that change a person's life.

For some people, it's meeting the man of their dreams, while for others it's getting a wake-up call about their health. For others still, it's swimming with dolphins, seeing the Pope, or maybe just discovering frozen pizza for the first time. For many of us, it's the little things we don't even notice as they happen. It was like that for Nigel, as all he did was press *Play* by mistake instead of *Delete*.

Half a second later he was listening to the ageing but still firm voice of his grandmother. She sounded worried.

"Nigel, it's Gran. Call me back, would you, dear? I'm worried about David."

That was it, just thirteen words. Not significant in themselves, but that's the thing about words; you can never be sure. It was like when Nigel was eight years old, and he'd stood on tiptoe to get onto a fairground ride he wasn't tall enough for.

You must be THIS tall to take this ride, the sign had said, with a thick red line under the words.

Rubbish, I'm big enough, he'd thought to himself.

Five minutes later though, he was wearing most of his chocolate milkshake and being escorted out of the funfair by an impossibly tall security guard. He'd been a kid though, so the only lesson he'd learnt that day, was that chocolate milkshake is far better drunk than worn.

Now was different, so after throwing on some clothes, and waving a brush somewhere near his hair, he headed back downstairs. He pressed *Recent calls* and hit *Redial* for his grandmother's number.

"Nigel."

"Hello Gran, I got your message."

"Of course you did dear. You wouldn't be ringing me otherwise, would you?"

In a flash, he was eight again, maybe six, being told off for stealing apples or something. As then, her usually softly-spoken voice had somehow transformed into something a lot sharper. He could almost picture himself as a child, awkwardly shuffling his feet under her gaze.

"Sorry, Gran."

"Well, thank you for phoning dear. I thought you'd have time now you don't work."

"I do work Gran. I gave up my office job is all. I write."

"Hmm. Writing, no work, it's all the same. Like those people who say they work from home. What's all that about?"

Evidently, she was having one of her challenging days, so Nigel sat down to listen patiently. The complaints slackened off after a few minutes, and she turned to the subject at hand.

"You listened to my message?"

"You said you're worried about my perfect cousin."

"Well, I am, and you shouldn't call him that."

He was definitely eight ... "What's got you so worried, Gran?"

"Not now dear, I'm about to go to pilates. Come over for coffee and bring that lovely girlfriend of yours with you."

He was about to tell her for the hundredth time that Jenny wasn't his girlfriend when the line went dead. This was clearly information his grandmother was never going to absorb. Feeling a distinct sense of resignation, he picked up his mobile to call Jenny. She loved his grandmother as much as him, and she was always up for a road trip, so even at such short notice, he knew

Jenny's answer before dialling.

It was almost a two-hour drive to the small Cambridgeshire village of Wensbridge and coffee time meant eleven-thirty. Consequently, as Nigel was finishing his second tea of the morning, there was a tap on the window, and he glanced up to see Jenny smiling at him through the glass. He couldn't remember when he'd given her a door key, but he had, so she let herself in.

"Morning," she trilled.

"You look nice," he smiled.

"Well, you don't. Go and change into something smarter. You know Gran will nag you if you turn up like that."

The irony of this remark wasn't lost on Nigel, and he was about to ask what was wrong with how he looked when he realised the futility of it. Jenny was right, and he knew it. Frustrating how often that was the case, but there you go.

Like the time she'd advised him against trying that rope swing. It had seemed sound, and it had felt perfectly secure. It just wasn't, and the fish in the nearby stream had been none too impressed when he'd landed in their midst a few minutes later. Nigel, on the other hand, had been just as unimpressed by having to stand around drying, before Jenny would let him back into her camper van.

Shuddering at the memory of finding tadpoles in his socks, he stalked upstairs.

As he did, Jenny looked around the room. She presumed there was some logic to it all, but after two and a half years, she still couldn't work it out. The thing was, she liked almost everything in the room individually. It was just the haphazard way it was arranged that always threw her.

She shrugged, and a few minutes later, Nigel reappeared wearing clean jeans, shoes instead of trainers and a crisp new shirt. He'd even brushed his hair!

"You scrub up all right, you know," said Jenny, brushing her hand across his shoulder with a smile. "Did you iron that?"

"It's the last one from the batch I did last month."

She rolled her eyes. It was true. Nigel had so many shirts he only needed to iron every few weeks, and what with t-shirts as well, he did it even less in the summer.

An hour and three-quarters later, Jenny's car pulled up in front of a small, whitewashed bungalow with a neatly laid out front garden. As always, the front door was unlocked, and pushing it open, Nigel called out. His grandmother immediately appeared from the dining room, pushed past him and pulled Jenny into a warm embrace.

"Hello, Jennifer. It's lovely to see you, dear." she beamed.

"You too Gran, you're looking well."

"Oh, mustn't grumble. I see you've brought *him* with you," she replied.

Nigel smiled. He'd always been close to his grandmother, but they went through the same routine every time. It was one of those family things that never change, much like his grandmother herself. Known as *Gran* to everyone, she was in her eighties now and walked with a stick. But in the same way that 40 seems old when you're a child, she never seemed to change.

"Good to see you too Nigel," she said, now hugging him as well.

"An' you, Gran."

"You even look respectable for a change, and right on time

for coffee too."

She winked at Jenny as she spoke, then showed them both into the long, open living room with its wall of windows looking out onto the back garden. On a low table sat a biscuit tin, which Nigel hoped would have more than digestives in this time. The rest of the room was furnished as you'd expect for a woman of Gran's age. Dark wooden cabinets holding china ornaments, flowered upholstery and faded photographs going back over the generations.

Nigel knew her chair too. It was the one surrounded by crossword books, dictionaries and thesauruses. He and Jenny sat on the sofa and waited. Not for long though as Gran soon reappeared carrying a tray holding a cafetière, a sugar bowl, milk jug and three bone-china cups with saucers.

She liked her little rituals, and after a few minutes of chitchat, Nigel caught her eye.

"Yes alright," she said as if reading his mind. "I'm probably being silly, but I'm worried."

"How about you tell us all about it, Gran."

"He's usually so good, you see. Well, you know what he's like. Calls me every fortnight without fail. Sometimes more."

Nigel pondered this for a moment before speaking. "When did you last talk with him?"

"Two and a half weeks ago."

"He's usually that reliable?" asked Jenny, brushing aside a hair.

"Oh yes," said Nigel. "He's known for it in the family."

"Which is why I called you dear. I thought you could do something. Now you're not working I mean."

Nigel resisted the temptation to debate that again. Instead, he looked at Jenny for inspiration.

"You've tried calling him I suppose," she asked.

"Of course dear, several times."

The elderly woman sounded quietly defiant, although Nigel was also aware of how her voice had trailed off at the end of the sentence. She was more worried than he'd realised.

"We could always pay him a visit," offered Jenny after a moment's silence.

Nigel shot her a quick, troubled glance, but his grandmother's face had already brightened. "Oh, that's kind of you, dear; I hoped you'd offer. It's so far you see, or I'd go myself. Would you like an early lunch before you set off? I've made sandwiches."

It was as if she'd planned the whole conversation, which of course she had.

"You had to offer didn't you," grumbled Nigel as he and Jenny got back into the camper van.

"Well she's worried," said Jenny indignantly.

"I know, but we've already driven this far an' ..."

"Oh, stop complaining," interrupted Jenny. "Where does David live?"

"Cambridge."

"Well, that can't be far."

"I suppose not." Nigel wasn't convinced. He liked David well enough, but they'd never been especially close. He took out his phone, found his cousin's address and tapped the link to open *Apple Maps*.

"What is it? Three-quarters of an hour? An hour at the most?"

"47 minutes."

"Well, we might as well go now. Better than making a trip

over another day."

Assuming they had to go at all, Nigel couldn't argue with that logic, and it was barely two o'clock, so there was plenty of time … He pulled what he hoped was a peeved but compliant face. Jenny smiled, started the engine, and they set off.

They were both quiet at first, as Jenny was near the end of an audiobook of *Magpie Murders* by Anthony Horowitz and Nigel didn't want to interrupt. He was also mulling over what his grandmother had said. He knew some people might think it odd that she was worried about her grandson after barely three weeks. On the other hand, he also knew how infuriatingly reliable David was.

"Maybe he's got flu," he blurted out.

"What?"

"Sorry. I was wonderin' why David hasn't called."

"He really is that reliable? I know you said, but …"

"Oh, he really is."

"How old is he?"

Nigel pondered this for a moment.

"Thirty-one? Thirty-two?"

"And he still rings Gran every other week?"

"Sometimes more. Makes the rest of us look bad."

Jenny chuckled. "He's in the army, didn't you say?"

"RAF. Quite a high-flier by all accounts."

"Oh, very good." laughed Jenny.

"Eh?"

"Air force … High flier."

Nigel smirked at his accidental joke, and after a few minutes he spoke again … "By the way, there was somethin' else I meant to tell you the other night."

"Oh, yes?"

'Well, you'll never guess what I found." The puppy was back.

"Oh, not that pork pie you lost. You're disgusting sometimes Nige."

"No, not that. Think outside."

"I don't know ... An Amazon parcel left in the dustbin like that other time?"

"A brick."

"You found a brick."

"I know. Weird, huh?"

"I hate to break this to you, Nige, but my house is made of thousands of them."

"Mine's not."

Nigel's words fell into a silence that hadn't been there before. It was true, his house had been built in the 1600s when bricks were only for the rich, and everyone else had to make do with sticks and mud[21].

"Not only that, but it kept vanishin'."

"What do you mean, vanishing?"

With this, Nigel started into a description of the brick, how it kept fading in and out, his trip to the library, and last of all, the incident in the market square.

"And the women saw it too?"

Nigel nodded.

"But that's ridiculous. It couldn't have been hovering in mid-air."

"And on the same day the moles ..."

"Oh, come on Nige. You're saying the two things are ..."

"Connected? Well, stranger things have happened."

---

[21] A wooden frame, typically oak, with the panels in between filled with *Wattle and Daub*, i.e. interwoven sticks padded out with mud and animal poo. Luckily for Nigel, the smell had long since faded away.

Jenny made a disbelieving noise, threw him a glance that clearly questioned his sanity, and turned her attention back to the road. There was a sign up ahead reading *Cambridge, A1307*.

"This exit?" she asked.

"Uh-huh," nodded Nigel, looking down at his phone. "Follow the signs to the city centre, and at the first big roundabout, take a sharp left."

Jenny did as he said and was soon being directed to take the fourth right, then to stop at a three-storey block of flats on their left. She drove into the small car park and turned off the engine. It was a charming, tree-lined street with semi-detached 1930s houses on either side. The only modern building was Greystoke Court.

Walking up to the door, Nigel selected the buzzer for number 3c and pressed. There was no reply, so he pushed it again, this time for longer. He was about to give up when the speaker crackled into life.

"Hello?" came a woman's voice.

Nigel and Jenny exchanged glances.

"We've come to see David," said Nigel.

"I'm afraid he's away."

"Oh. Do you know when he'll be back?"

There was a pause at the other end of the conversation.

"Why are you looking for him?"

Nigel considered this for a moment, then spurred on by a look of encouragement from Jenny, he kept going. "I'm his cousin, Nigel."

There was another pause, then a buzzer sounded as the door was unlocked.

"Come on up," said the voice.

When Nigel and Jenny reached apartment 3c, the door opened to reveal a woman of average height, in her early thirties, with dark curly hair, brown eyes and glasses. She looked at her two visitors, then down at a framed photograph she was holding. Eventually, she spoke.

"Family wedding?" she asked in a quiet, refined voice, turning the picture around so Nigel could see.

He stared at the smiling faces of himself, David, their grandmother and a handful of others. It was the same as one he had on his wall at home.

"Our cousin Peter," he replied with a smile.

At this, the woman held up a second photograph, this time showing her and David together.

"My name's Liz," she said. "I'm David's fiancée."

Nigel was stunned. He didn't know his cousin was engaged, and he suspected their grandmother didn't either.

"What can you tell me?" asked Liz. Her voice trembled as she spoke, although hearing it without the crackle of the intercom, Nigel realised she sounded quite posh. A bit like newsreaders of old[22]. Her whole body was tense though, and she was undoubtedly anxious about something.

"We were hopin' ..." began Nigel, uncertainly.

"You see, we didn't know about you," continued Jenny, "and Gran hasn't heard from him in a while, so we were hoping he'd be home."

Liz burst into tears.

Jenny looked at Nigel, then without hesitation reached out to

---

[22] The BBC denies ever having had pronunciation guidelines for its presenters, and claims the story probably arose because most pre-war announcers used *Received Pronunciation*. This is an unusual accent, as unlike all others in the UK, it's defined more by social class than region, and some claim it's actually accent-free. This is, of course, crazy.

Liz. "Tea," Jenny mouthed to Nigel, gathering Liz into her arms. "Strong, sweet tea."

Nigel edged past the two women and headed for the kitchen. Jenny, meanwhile, guided Liz through to a cream, 3-seat sofa, above which hung a print by Tamara de Lempicka.

"I'm so sorry," said Liz, sniffing as she did, and taking off her glasses. "Whatever must you think?"

"I don't think anything," replied Jenny. "You get yourself together while Nigel's making tea. Then we can talk."

"Thank you," replied Liz mechanically.

Jenny pushed a stray hair from her eyes and looked around the room. It was light, airy, with white walls, and had a similar feel to her own home, albeit with the addition of a few male touches. On one wall, was a long line of cupboards, above which were row upon row of shelves. They held mostly books, and generally hardback at that. In contrast to Jenny's own tastes, they were predominantly non-fiction.

On the top shelf that meant animal behaviourism, and to the side of a line of textbooks were various academic papers, all authored by one Professor Elizabeth Benning. *So that's who she is*, Jenny might have thought. The books were too far away for her to read the spines though, so she and Nigel stayed in the dark on that for the time being. On the next shelf down was an impressive collection of cookery books. *Feed me vegan* by Lucy Watson, Ella Mills' *Deliciously Ella*, *Oh my goodness* by Levanen and Halberg ... the titles went on and on. The third shelf down was different again, and Jenny rightly guessed this was where David's tastes came in. As a result, *The Architecture of the City* by Aldo Rossi, and Lance Armstrong's *It's not about the bike* rubbed shoulders with the likes of *Catch-22* by Joseph Heller. On each shelf, all the various topics were separated by either academic awards or one of David's triathlon trophies. Below all this, on the top of the cupboards, were family photographs, a carved wooden bowl holding a mound of remote controls and off to one side, a few CDs. *How very quaint*, thought Jenny.

As she finished absorbing all this, Nigel reappeared with three mugs of tea. He and Jenny waited while Liz composed herself.

"You're looking for David?" she said at last. Her voice had lost some of its uncertainty but still sounded flat, as if all the emotion had been stripped out of it.

Jenny nodded. "Gran hasn't heard from him in weeks, and you know what he's like, so we thought ..."

"... that I might know something. I was afraid this would happen."

"Sorry?"

"I was afraid his gran would find out. I didn't like to call her as we've never met, but I figured as he hasn't rung me ..."

"How long's it been?"

"Only a few days, but as you said, it's not like him."

"And you've tried callin'?" asked Nigel.

"Of course, I just get voicemail."

"Sorry, I don't understand," chipped in Jenny, "we thought he lives here?"

"Well yes and no. We bought the apartment together eighteen months ago, but David's not been here since his latest posting." She brightened slightly at the sound of his name, but it was only for a second.

"So, he's left Weston?" asked Nigel.

"Wyton. RAF Wyton, but yes. It's only about 40-minutes' drive from here, and I work in town, so this was ideal for both of us. Then a few months back he was posted up to Lossiemouth."

"Blimey, that's in the north of Scotland, isn't it?"

"Almost as far as you can go."

"Could it be that?" asked Nigel. "New job and everythin'?"

"I doubt it. He still rang me every day for the first few months, or if he couldn't, he'd text."

"And nothin' since when?"

Liz paused as she went through the days in her mind.

"Last Thursday, so it was odd not hearing from him on Friday, but that happens sometimes, and I didn't worry until Saturday. He always rings on weekends you see. It's one of our things."

By now, Liz appeared to be on the verge of tears again, and Jenny reached out a hand to her. A look of understanding passed between them, and several minutes later, it fell to Jenny to break the silence.

"Have you thought about going up there?"

"Oh, I want to, but it's not like I can just drop in for a coffee with his job. And I know it sounds pathetic, but I never have much luck with long journeys."

Jenny hesitated while Nigel finished his mouthful of tea. "What if we all go up? The three of us."

Nigel spat out what little tea he had left and stared at Jenny. This look was different to when they'd been with Gran though and was more about Jenny than his own dislike of travel. He'd never understood why she didn't speak of her childhood in Scotland, and he'd always sensed something of a barrier there. Their eyes met, and to Nigel's surprise, Jenny's face seemed to say that it would be OK.

"Well everyone's so worried about him," she continued, "and

I've got holiday I can take, so ... well, we could all take a trip. Share the driving maybe."

"But it's got to be 500 miles!" Nigel was horrified.

"531," chipped in Liz, a hopeful tone creeping into her voice.

"531 miles. That'd take ..."

"9 hours 23 minutes, according to *Google Maps*. Thing is, it's ..."

"Don't tell me," interrupted Nigel with annoyance, "it's so unlike him."

"Exactly."

As the two women carried on talking, Nigel quietly panicked at the prospect of a road trip to Scotland. Something else was bothering him too, which he sensed had to do with when Liz had last spoken with David. He couldn't get his head round it though, and as his mind fluttered back to the coming journey, something else occurred to him. *What if Jen wants me to do some of the drivin'? If I'm a passenger, at least I can sleep most of the way.* He shuddered inside, and becoming aware of Liz's now enthusiastic voice, he looked up.

"That would be fantastic. As long as you can spare the time ..."

"Absolutely," replied Jenny with a smile. "I need to make one phone call."

She took her phone from her bag, scrolled through the contacts and dialled. It was a somewhat one-sided conversation, and after only a couple of minutes, she hung up.

"We're all set," she announced.

"Didn't your boss mind?" asked Liz. "It being such short notice I mean."

"Oh no, he was fine about it," replied Jenny. "I've only taken over from him recently, so I expect he'll enjoy covering my job *the bottom line is that your own conclusions are correct. We did find one anomaly though, so I'm hoping we can sort it out between us and have sent you a meeting invite to talk it through this afternoon.*

Speak later, Grant

Steve sucked in his breath and opened the enclosed report. It was divided into four sections: *Executive summary, Hardware diagnostic, Software diagnostic, Conclusion.* He flicked straight to the last of these.

In conclusion, the sensor is operating within normal parameters, and the data you sent is in line with a survey of an undisturbed area of ground.

This is at odds with the conclusions drawn from data automatically uploaded to us over the past six months, which showed the presence of ground disturbance in line with mole tunnels.

As a result, we have a contradiction in the data, with evidence of tunnels being present on one day, and not on the next. We can't explain this without further information.

Steve stared at the screen. On the one hand, he was pleased he hadn't missed anything. On the other, it felt like he'd sent off some grass for analysis, and received a report back saying nothing more than that it was green.

"I wonder what else they found," he whispered to himself. "What have they left out?"

He checked his inbox for the meeting invite. It was for 5:00 p.m. British Summer Time, Noon Eastern Daylight Time.

Patience had always been one of Steve Guthrie's strong points, for a few days. Show me how it should be done."

"So, what now?" asked Liz, a hint of a smile starting to play at the corners of her mouth.

Jenny thought about this for a moment before replying. "We should probably go in two cars ..."

"But ..."

"Not all the way," soothed Jenny quickly, "but I need to go home to sort my cats out first, so maybe we could meet up partway. Somewhere near the border, perhaps?"

"Tebay Services," said Nigel with surprising authority. "Should be three or four hours for each of us and the food's nice there."

"Tebay it is!" grinned Liz. She was going in search of David.

Luckily for Steve Guthrie, he'd only spoken with Seismic Dynamics a few days before, so he knew Grant and the team would be in the office over the weekend as they had a big project on. Even so, time zones being what they are, it was afternoon before an email dropped into Steve's inbox, where it joined the usual mix of faculty messages and spam. It was all there ... Invitations from holiday companies, offers of grants for solar panels, and several pleas from attractive Romanian women who apparently couldn't wait to meet him. He was looking out for *the* email though, and within minutes of it appearing, he was absorbed.

Hi Steve

It was good to hear from you, and many thanks for the package. We've completed a diagnostic on the sensor you sent and compared the data to previous readings. The full results are in the enclosed, but

but even so, the afternoon passed like treacle[23] on a cold day, and he was dialled into the conference bridge with five minutes to spare. Right on time, the familiar tone sounded, and Grant's lazy southern drawl came on the line.

"Hey, Steve. How y'all doing?"

"Fine thanks? Y'all?"

This was their standard greeting, although Steve had struggled with Grant's accent to begin with. What with that and the American's slowness of speech, he'd wondered whether Grant was up to the job. Steve quickly learnt he most definitely was though, and a firm friendship had developed between them. At the same time, Grant had got used to the Englishman's preoccupation with the weather, and whenever Steve asked what it was like in Raleigh, he took the opportunity to roll out one of a dozen colloquialisms. Steve's favourites were "It's been hotter'n a goat's butt in a pepper patch," and it's opposite, "It's colder than a penguin's balls."

"I was better before I got your email," laughed Grant.

"Don't say I never send you anything interesting."

"I wouldn't dare. This one's a doozy though."

"Come on then. What did you miss out of the report?"

"You read it?"

"Of course."

"And?"

"You're the experts, but if I had to guess, I'd say you found something in the sensor logs that accounts for the change in the readings."

"So you contacted us, why exactly?"

---

[23] In some countries, Treacle is known as *Molasses*, that thick, sticky syrup made from partially refined sugar which can't be poured fast even if you try, especially in cold weather, so I suggest you think of it as the snail of the syrup kingdom.

"You did then."

"Not right away because you didn't mention it, but yes. The sensor you sent had undergone a hard reset."

"But that's not possible. I know Benning did a soft reset, but she wouldn't know how to do one on the hardware. It's not as if she could even do it by accident either."

"Still the bane of your life, eh?" chuckled Grant.

Steve grunted. "You could say that."

Grant laughed.

"So, what now?"

"Are there any electricity cables running by the site?"

Steve thought about that for a moment, recalling his time there. "I don't think so," he said at last. "And the nearest overhead lines must be ... I don't know ... half a mile away?"

"Nothing underground?"

"I doubt it. This is farming land we're talking about."

"This is where it gets weird then, because in our experience, the only thing that can cause a spontaneous, hard reset is a strong, nearby power surge."

Steve considered this and took a minute to reply.

"Weird is the word," he said at last. "I guess I can ask the Prof' to check with the farmer she rents the site from. He should know if there are any buried cables."

"Sounds good."

"And if the answer's no?"

"Then we talk again."

Steve mused on this after he put the phone down, then true to his word, he rang Liz. The call went to voicemail, so he didn't go into detail. He just mentioned the possibility of some interference with the sensors and asked her to find out if there were any power cables nearby.

When Liz picked up Steve's message, she rang the farmer's number, and the line only rang once before his gruff voice sounded at the other end. It was only an answering machine though, so she left a message asking him to call her back. What she didn't know was that his liking of technology was akin her own, and the machine was hidden away in a hall cupboard, where various coats had long since fallen down on top of it. The advantage of this was that the coats were nice and warm when anyone wanted to wear them. The disadvantage was a very real risk of fire. That, and the fact that the message light was now blinking quietly to itself under a mound of hats, scarves, and waterproof jackets. Consequently, it was several days before anyone saw it.

The first time it happened to TC, her last memory from before was of sitting in her room at college, looking at a photograph. You can guess who it was of, and as she stared at it for the umpteenth time, memories rolled down her cheeks. She took a sip of tea, nibbled a slice of cake and folded her arms on the desk in front of her. The emotional exhaustion of the previous weeks was catching up with her, and as she leant forward to rest her head, she closed her eyes.

When she opened them, TC was lying under a tree on a hillside overlooking a small town. She let out a yelp and snapped her eyes shut. A minute or so later, she opened them again, only more slowly this time. Giving a shiver, she pressed her back against the tree, as if trying to back away from what was in front of her. It wasn't scary in itself, but it wasn't *his* photograph, and her eyes widened as they darted back and forth across the landscape.

TC trembled, as a feeling of disorientation started to creep up her spine. The tree she was under was pleasant enough, and the town appeared to be as nice as anywhere can from a distance, but it wasn't her room. What's more, she had no memory of getting wherever she was. She was shaking now, as disorientation turned to panic and fear. Then she blacked out.

The next time she came round, TC went through the same gamut of emotions as before. Now though, rather than blacking out, she pulled her legs towards her and hugged them tightly against her chest. Her brain was in overload, and she quickly shut her eyes again. Sitting like that she could almost convince herself everything was normal. Only *almost* though, because even if her eyes were deceiving her, the traffic noise she usually heard in her room was gone too. Instead, there was only birdsong.

"I've lost it," she said under breath. "I've gone crazy."

She hadn't, but put yourself in her place. TC had been in mourning for almost two months and had barely left her room in that whole time. Now she was outdoors somewhere, when half a second before she'd been sitting at her desk. She opened her eyes again, and for the first time, she actually looked around. Not in a panic now, but slowly and deliberately, taking in as much as her brain could handle. Where the hell was she? She had to close her eyes from time to time, as her mind buffered what she saw. At last, she could both see and process the scene at the same time. As she did, she realised to her surprise that the town below her wasn't unfamiliar after all.

The first thing she recognised was the church spire in the centre, and as she stared at it, she blinked. Surely it couldn't be. As her gaze moved on, she realised she knew the street pattern too. Next, she spotted the green roof of the town library, and alongside it, the Victorian bank building that was now a wine bar. After that, her eyes scanned rapidly across the place, and the more she looked, the more it came back to her. It was the town she'd grown up in.

All of a sudden, she spotted a massive housing estate on the outskirts, and she frowned. Something about it rang a bell, but something wasn't right. She shrugged and turned her attention to the surrounding countryside, but her eyes kept going back. Then she remembered, but what came back to her, made no sense at all.

It had been during her first year away at college, and she remembered her father telling her about a campaign against the estate being built. There'd also been something about a town meeting, but mostly she recalled him telling her the planning application had been turned down. So what had happened? She had a vague recollection of hearing the builder had opted for a smaller development instead. But that had been on the other side of the town, hadn't it? And yet there it was.

As never seems to happen in movies, her stomach chose that moment to rumble, and she realised how hungry she was. It was almost six o'clock, which given the time of year, meant dusk. She was also becoming aware of a brisk Autumn chill creeping through her fleece. She wasn't dressed for the outdoors, so with her panic now reduced to a dazed sense of confusion, she stood up and started down the hill.

Before long she came to a gate which she found she remembered from years before. She unlatched it and walked through, then looking back up towards the tree, she realised even that now felt familiar as well. She followed the footpath downhill for another ten minutes before coming to a bridge over a river. Once on the far side, she passed through a short alley between two buildings and found herself standing in a busy high street. People streamed past her on their way home, to the pub or wherever. Some were chatting with friends, some were simply in a rush, and others had their heads bowed down to their mobile phones.

They were a blur to TC though. The bridge, the river, the high street; she remembered them all. She started to relax. She still had no idea how she'd got there, but at least she knew where she was.

Familiar shop fronts shone in the early evening light, and with them, the familiarity of it all began to sink in. Then with an ease borne of memory, TC walked a few more yards and pushed open the door to *McDonald's*.

She knew instantly that something was wrong. It was too quiet, and there was no familiar smell. Her eyes focused, and she saw to her surprise that she was in a bookshop. She frowned, stepped back outside, and looked around. *McDonald's* was across the road, next to the wine bar. If TC had really been paying attention, she'd have seen there was something wrong with that too. It was still a bank and had never been converted after all.

"Weird, I could've sworn *McDonald's* was on this side of the road."

She crossed over, and after queueing for a minute or two, ordered what appeared to be the healthiest option on the menu. She was about to say "Regular coke" to the question of what drink she wanted when she noticed *Root Beer* on the menu.

But I've never been able to get that in the UK before, she thought.

In the circumstances, it might seem an odd thing for TC to get excited about, but it was one of her favourites, and she'd never seen it in *McDonald's* outside of the US before. As she opened her wallet to pay, she saw the photo. It was a smaller version of the one she'd been looking at in her room before.

Before what though?

Photo aside, what she didn't see in her wallet was any money, and without thinking, she pulled out her credit card. She went to use contactless, but there was no machine. No chip and pin keypad either. The server took her card from her, placed it into an old-fashioned, manual imprinter, and slid the top back and forth. It made that odd, *kerchunk-kerchunk* sound she vaguely remembered from childhood. Next, the assistant handed TC the flimsy, multi-layer receipt and a pen. She stared at them, uncomprehending for a moment, then she signed.

What on earth?

As TC started her fries, some of her earlier disorientation returned. *Where was she?* It was home, only it was different. Familiar but somehow not. The housing estate, the bookshop, the Root Beer ... it was like a different version of the same place.

And there she had it. It was indeed a different version of the same place; a parallel version of it. A parallel world, in fact.

Her thinking didn't extend that far though, and for the time being, whatever thoughts she had were tinged with a nagging feeling that none of it could be real. And if not, what? A dream? Or was she really in a padded cell somewhere, wearing a straitjacket?

Wherever she was, she was still hungry, and after finishing her salad, she went back up to the counter for coffee and cake. They helped, and sitting by the window, she started to relax again. Watching the people flow past outside was like watching waves follow each other up a beach. Mesmerizing. Calming. Hypnotic even.

She looked at her watch. It was a little after seven. Where had the time gone? Suddenly hunger was replaced with tiredness, and she knew she needed to sleep. But where? With a renewed sense of panic, her eyes scanned the room as if searching for something. Then she had it.

Walking up to her childhood home, a few streets later, felt strange. It was over a year since TC had gone away to college, during which time she'd only come back a couple of times. Sure, she missed friends and family, but she'd caught the travel bug from her boyfriend, and the rest had just happened. Her parents' compensation was the knowledge that she was happy, and a growing collection of smiling photos from around the world.

Even after her boyfriend's death, TC had stayed away, and now, with one hand on the garden gate, she paused. She wasn't sure she could stand the outrush of emotion she knew she'd get from her mother. The idea mushroomed in her head, and she was about to turn and run when the front door opened, the porch light came on, and her mother's voice broke into her thoughts.

"You came home. What a lovely surprise!"

TC blinked her eyes open, and there was her mum. She was walking towards her, wearing an apron and a smile. She sounded completely normal - no tears, no false jolliness, nothing of her recent manner at all.

"Come on in dear, I'll put the kettle on. Your dad will be so pleased to see you."

TC followed her mother into the house, and as the kettle boiled, they chatted about all manner of things. Her mother did most of the talking and didn't seem to notice TC was running on automatic. The ease of it all was soothing yet disconcerting. It was wrong, yet so normal. There was even cake.

They went through into the living room, and it was exactly as TC remembered, except for one thing. Everywhere she looked, there were photos of her as always, but unlike the ones she remembered of her and *him*, these only showed her. Her mother hadn't cut him out or anything like that, and they showed precisely the same scenes TC remembered. It was just that instead of them showing two people, they showed one. Even the shot of Machu Picchu from when the two of them had walked the Inca trail the previous year, now only showed TC. Disorientation nudged at her mind again, and with it, a fresh wave of panic washed over her.

"Look, Mum, I'm sorry to bail on you, but I'm exhausted. Do you mind if I go to bed? We can talk in the morning."

"Of course, dear, I always keep your bed made. Your father will be sorry he missed you though. He's down the driving range this evening."

When TC woke up the next morning, she was back in her room at college.

Finding out, Covering up

Monday, September 13th

At 8 a.m. the third alert from Crianloch flashed up on two screens, only this time, neither was in the dark, circular room. Instead, it went straight to the offices of both the UK Secretary of State for Defence and the head of Operation Carter, aka the Director General of MI5. It was sent as a priority message, and within minutes, the two men were on the phone with each other. Then as per protocol, a call was put out to the commander of Crianloch's nearest RAF base, which was in Lossiemouth. The minister and the director wanted an on-the-spot report but didn't want to involve the local police until they knew more. By 8:25, a video conference had been convened for twenty minutes later.

So, at a quarter to nine on the Monday following the incident, the seniors convened. The Defence Secretary, the DG, and Group Captain Finch, commander of RAF Lossiemouth. Sitting in front of their respective video screens, it fell to the Defence Secretary to open the meeting.

"Good morning, gentlemen. Director?"

"Thank you, Minister. The last contact we had from Crianloch was at 13:32 on Friday. The first alert was therefore raised at eight a.m. on Saturday, the second one 24 hours later, and the third, 45 minutes ago."

"Why's it taken three days for us to find out?" demanded the Defence Secretary in his usual impatient voice.

"It's the nature of the facility and the reporting chain I'm afraid, Minister. Weather stations aren't considered crucial to national security, so they're not monitored as closely as other facilities."

"Aren't crucial ..." exploded the Defence Secretary. "But Crianloch isn't ..."

"If you remember Minister," interrupted the DG smoothly, "we agreed Crianloch would be treated as an ordinary weather station for the most part."

"I know, but surely a comms failure is serious whatever?"

"Not necessarily, although it's for situations like this that we agreed to handle any third alert from Crianloch as being proper to Carter. To be on the safe side."

The DG's voice was more forceful as he said this and didn't give the Defence Secretary anywhere to go. When the latter spoke, he'd regained much of his composure.

"Well, we are where we are, I suppose. What do we do next?"

"Group Captain?"

It was Finch's turn to speak, and when he did, it was with the world-weary voice of someone who'd rather have been out on the golf course. He was a year away from retirement and had taken the post at Lossiemouth fifteen months before, primarily to indulge his passion for the game.

"To be honest gentlemen, I'm not sure why I'm here. I've not been read in on the situation either, so perhaps we could start with what's so special about this weather station. And who this *Carter* is."

It's hard on a video conference to get a sense of two people looking directly at each other, but the momentary silence told its own story. It was followed by a slight nod from the Defence Secretary, and after taking a sip of water, the DG began. Once he'd finished, Finch stayed silent for a moment as he absorbed what he'd been told.

"So what do you think now?" demanded the Minister.

"Well I understand the need for the RAF's involvement, so I'll send some people to investigate the site. We should probably involve the local police as well."

"Is that wise at this stage?"

"I believe so," answered the DG. "We need to keep a lid on this, and that will mean liaising with the public, which is a job for the local police rather than the RAF."

"Very well. You'll arrange that I take it, Group Captain? And I'll have a daily video call set up for later today."

The Defence Secretary didn't wait for either of the others to reply, and the call ended.

A little afterwards, there was a knock on Finch's office door.

"Come in," he barked.

Two officers entered, stood to attention and saluted.

"At ease. What I'm going to tell you is *Top Secret*," he said without greeting. "You're both aware of Crianloch?"

"The weather station, sir?"

"Turns out it's rather more than that," said Finch with a smile. "I wondered why Marston took the posting, but it makes sense now."

"Sir?"

"Take a seat. This is going to take some time."

With all the comms down, time was something that everyone in Crianloch Station had plenty of. The scientists continued to analyse data, their various experiments stayed running, and the air conditioning kept on doing its thing, without once being tempted to freeze everyone again. Life in the station, therefore, changed while staying much the same. Even the differences had a familiar feel to them. The station's runners, for example, who previously did circuits of the perimeter fence, now ran around the maze of underground corridors instead. Inevitably this caused a few collisions with some of the more absent-minded scientists, but as most of them rarely left their laboratories, it wasn't a big problem. After all, a few of them hadn't even realised anything had changed, and some of the others actually welcomed the lack of comms, as it gave them a chance to get on top of the growing mass of data. In fact, in the sort of ironic twist that *Fate* thrives on, it was trawling through the backlog that provided the answer everyone wanted.

When Jessica Williams made the discovery, mind you, she didn't know what it meant at first, but she knew it meant something. It wasn't obvious though; it was small and annoying, which was also how Jessica's manager thought of her. Young, brilliant and a bit too sure of herself to be likeable. It's been said though that an idea is one of the hardest things to kill, and that was what this was. It just wouldn't go away, and neither would she, let alone her insistence that it was something they should investigate.

"But why, Jessica?" asked her manager.

"Because it's not right!"

"Look. We're all in new territory here, so ..."

"But it's only data ..."

"And you have your own projects to focus on, so ..."

"But it's our job to be curious isn't it? It's not like I'm saying we've been invaded by creatures from the jelly dimension or something!"

Her manager let out a deep, frustrated sigh. Jess was known for her analogies, but this one was bizarre, even for her.

Living on the shores of Loch Ness, *bizarre* was part of everyday life for the residents of Drumnadrochit. Routine exists everywhere though, and in the town's Police Station, Detective Inspector Diane Hendricks was busy with paperwork when there was a knock on her office door.

"Come in."

"Sorry to disturb m'm. I've got someone in the interview room I think you should see," said her duty sergeant.

She raised an eyebrow.

"Local milkman, m'm. He's got quite a story. I think you should hear what he has to say."

Hendricks tilted her head as if to ask a question. Then, knowing her sergeant wouldn't disturb her without good cause she got up from behind her desk and followed him down the corridor.

So, picture the scene, and just to check, are you imagining a run down, stone police station that looks like it's not been redecorated since the 1950s? Or alternatively, one built with ash wall cladding, recycled insulation, and a curved turf roof that blends seamlessly into the landscape? An award-winning building with excellent green credentials which is the envy of other police forces?

Yes, you've got it, and as the officers entered the dank, dismal room, they could almost hear the paint peeling off the ancient ceiling. Add to that the gentle murmur of condensation dripping down the walls for a chat with the rising damp, and you've got the picture.

After introducing herself, DI Hendricks asked her first question. She had a light yet decisive voice that gave away her birthplace on the east coast of Scotland. The milkman, on the other hand, came from a large city in the north-west of England. He looked across at Hendricks.

"_____," he said

Hendricks threw a confused glance at her sergeant.

"Liverpudlian, m'm. He said he wants to report a missing object."

Hendricks raised both eyebrows. The Liverpool accent is one of the most distinct in the UK, and she wondered how the milkman and his customers ever understood each other[24].

"What do you want to report as missing, sir?"

"_____," replied the milkman.

Hendricks understood this ... "The research station?" she blurted out in surprise.

The man nodded.

"What do you mean it's missing?"

"_____," replied the milkman.

Hendricks looked at her sergeant again. "What was it made you notice the station was ... no longer there?"

---

[24] Actually, they didn't always, and most had resigned themselves to using sign language, writing notes, or simply getting the wrong order. It also explained the great chocolate-milk incident and the strange case of the disappearing yoghurt.

"_____," replied the man, cheerfully.

Hendricks turned to her sergeant yet again. It was fortunate he'd worked down south in the north of England at one point ... "The milk, m'm."

"What about the milk, sir?"

"You asked what made me notice the station wasn't there, and it was the milk."

This wasn't what Hendricks heard of course, but by now, the duty sergeant was instantly translating everything the milkman said.

"I'm sorry," Hendricks said patiently. "What I meant to ask was, what was it about the milk that made you notice the place had ... well, gone?"

"There was too much of it," replied the milkman via his translator.

"You delivered too much?"

"I did not." said the milkman indignantly. "That was a lie ... or it wasn't proved anyway."

Even without translation, Hendricks could tell the milkman was now upset about something, so she decided to take a different approach.

"Calm down, sir, I'm not concerned with any of that. You said there was too much milk, so I'm trying to understand why that was."

"Oh, right. Well, I kept on delivering it."

He seemed almost proud of this and Hendricks paused, looking at the man on the other side of the table. She'd recently bought a new fridge, and the customer survey afterwards had asked for a single word to describe the salesperson. With the milkman, the word would have been *Frayed.*

He was wearing a green turtle-neck jumper that was more

pulled threads than not. His jeans were snagged from the attention of numerous dogs over the years, and the lapels of his jacket were fuzzy from decades of being tugged up against the cold. The jacket itself looked like it might have once been the same colour all over, and his bootlaces had long ago been replaced with garden twine. The salt and pepper stubble on his face completed the look. Definitely frayed.

"You kept delivering the milk?"

"I did."

"You left it at the entrance?"

"By the guardhouse."

"But no-one took it in?"

"Well they used to, else I'd have noticed before."

"Of course. So, you've been delivering milk there for ..."

"A few months now."

"You've been delivering milk there for a few months, and they always took it in until last week."

"Yep."

"And how many days did it stay like that before you thought something might be wrong?"

"Over the weekend and today. Three days."

"So that was what? Three days of milk at ... how much a day?"

"Six crates."

"Meaning?"

"24 litres each."

Hendricks screwed up her eyes as she did the sum in her head.

"So, you waited until you'd delivered eighteen crates at twenty-four litres each ... That's 432 litres[25] of milk before you

---

[25] It's a peculiarly British quirk that we still talk in terms of miles per gallon for cars, but we buy fuel in litres. We also buy milk in litres but beer in pints. So, 432 litres? That's 95 UK gallons or 114 US gallons, although why US gallons

called us."

The milkman didn't answer. Hendricks, on the other hand, counted to five in her head.

"Why didn't you get in touch straight away?"

The milkman wriggled uncomfortably in his seat. "I didn't like to."

"Why ever not?"

For the first time, there was a note of annoyance in Hendricks' voice, but again the milkman said nothing.

"OK," resumed Hendricks in a resigned sort of voice ... "So, what do you think has happened then, sir?"

"Well, it's gone, hasn't it?"

Hendricks slowly closed her eyes, took a deep breath, and signalled to the duty sergeant to take the milkman away. She stayed quiet for a few minutes, considering whether to drive out to Glen Crian there and then. The prospect of her waiting paperwork finally made up Hendricks' mind for her, and a few minutes later she was making her way to the police Land Rover, lapping up her daily quota of local gossip on the way. It was part of living in a small community, and if she hadn't relished it, she wouldn't have transferred from Edinburgh.

That was where Hendricks started with Police Scotland, and she'd enjoyed her time in the city well enough but had always yearned for the sort of life she'd grown up with. As a result, barely two years after her promotion to Inspector, she'd applied for, and got the position in Drumnadrochit. Strictly speaking, she was based out of Inverness, about fifteen miles to the north-east. But as most of her colleagues preferred city life, they were happy for her to handle the rest. She therefore rarely made the journey

---

are smaller than UK ones is anyone's guess, when everything is allegedly bigger in the States.

north, and today was no exception as she was headed in a different direction entirely. West towards Crianloch.

It was a pleasant, leisurely drive through a succession of broad, green valleys. After half an hour, Hendricks passed over a bare outcrop and dropped down towards the small, ragged body of water that was Loch Crian. On its north shore sat Crianloch village. It was typical of the area with its small stone houses, pub, a combined shop and Post Office, and by the T-junction in the centre, an ancient granite church.

Hendricks turned left at the junction, and a few minutes after leaving the village behind, she took an unmarked turning on the right. This was where the Land Rover came into its own, as from there on, the track was just gravel.

As she crested the last of several hillocks, Glen Crian lay ahead of her. The mounds had been left behind by the last glaciers to cover Scotland and off to one side was the small, playful stream that had cut through them centuries ago.

She stopped the Land Rover, got out, and surveyed the landscape. Then like you do when you lose your car keys but keep looking for them in the same place, she scanned the valley once more. She'd never visited Crianloch Station, and one of the few things she remembered from the news at the time, was its minimal impact on the landscape.

There's minimal and minimal though, she thought, especially when she'd been expecting the milkman to have imagined things. He hadn't though, and her state of mind could now best be described as a mixture of confusion, shock and disbelief. Or to put it another way, *What the hell?*

She got back into the Land Rover and drove down into the valley below. At the end of the gravel track were eighteen crates of something, only some of which was still recognizable as milk.

"Lazy sod. He could at least have taken them away this morning."

Shrugging, she loaded the crates into the back of the Land Rover, then went around to the cab and picked up the radio handset.

"Hendricks to Drumnadrochit. Come in."

"Drumnadrochit here. Over."

"I'm at Glen Crian but don't know what's going on yet. I'll take a walk up the glen and will be out of radio contact for half an hour or so. Over."

"Roger. Do you have any mobile signal? Over."

"Only one bar at the moment Sergeant, so don't bank on it. I'll radio in when I'm back at the vehicle. Hendricks out."

She took her all-weather jacket from the rear of the vehicle and put it on, not that she needed it. It was a cool but sunny day, so the only weather she had to cope with was a light breeze, and whether she would find anything to report. In other words, as someone who loved the outdoors, and whose job was paying her to take a walk in the highlands, she was having a good day.

She followed the stream up the glen for maybe twenty minutes, turned, and looked back the way she'd come. Crianloch Station should have been between her and the Land Rover. Instead, all she saw was gorse, heather, and a few boggy patches of grass.

Over the years, Hendricks had attended plenty of crime scenes where things hadn't been as expected, but that was the nature of the job. Murders, missing persons, thefts … they all had their peculiarities. None of them could compare with this though. In fact, how could you even categorize what *this* was? She pondered that as she walked back to the Land Rover, and taking out her phone, she took a series of photos. After the promised radio call to Drumnadrochit, she started the engine and drove off.

"London?" queried the duty sergeant.

He actually had no idea where the Meteorological Office had its headquarters, so this was a guess, and he spent the next few minutes googling the answer. As he did, DI Hendricks started on the paperwork. In reality, it was their crime reporting site, and right away, she ran into a problem; there wasn't an option for vanishing weather stations.

She briefly considered *Theft*, but decided against it and chose *Report something else* instead. That brought up a screen with twelve more options, and none of them fitted the bill either. Falling back onto *Other*, she completed the simple form and sat back in her chair. After a minute, she picked up her mobile and called her boss in Inverness. Evidently, he had her programmed into his phone.

"Hello, Diane. To what do I owe the pleasure?"

"It's a tricky one, sir. In fact, I'm not sure where to start."

"You intrigue me," said the jovial voice at the other end of the line. It was a trait Detective Chief Inspector Croft was known for, and one which had lulled many a suspect into revealing things they shouldn't. It relaxed Hendricks.

"It's like this, sir ..." She paused. "You're familiar with Crianloch Station?"

"The weather research place?" he queried.

"That's right, sir. Well, it's ..." She hesitated. "The thing is ..."

"Come on, Diane, spit it out."

"It's gone, sir."

"What do you mean gone?"

"I know it's hard to take in, sir, but ... it's vanished."

There was silence as DCI Croft absorbed this.

"Well, you'd better tell me about it," he said, opening his notepad to a new page.

Over the next ten minutes, Hendricks outlined the milkman's story, then went on to describe her own visit to the site. As she did, her voice regained its usually confident tones.

"So you're seriously telling me that the whole place has disappeared into thin air."

"That's right, sir."

"What was it like?"

"Like any other highland glen, sir."

"No, I mean before. The research place."

"I never visited it, sir, but I've checked online, and it was almost entirely underground, so there was never much to see anyway. Just a short runway and a few buildings for lift access and the like."

"Oh yes, I remember now. Personnel?"

"Around 2,000, sir."

"Good grief. What have you done so far?"

"I've filed a standard crime report, sir, and stationed a constable on site. I was going to get SOCO[26] out next and notify the Met Office, but I wanted to brief you first."

"Who else knows about it?"

"My sergeant, sir, the milkman, and the newspaper boy from the village."

"Good. Well, seems it's my turn to share some information."

---

[26] Rather than being part of Police Scotland itself, Scene of Crime Officers (SOCO) there come under the *Scottish Police Authority*. In some ways, the role of a SOCO is akin to the CSIs of TV fiction, although what they actually do is often quite different.

"Sir?"

"I had a call earlier from a Group Captain Finch at Lossiemouth. Evidently, Crianloch has been out of contact since Friday."

"Why on earth weren't we notified?"

"I don't know yet, but I've got a video call with him and some others this afternoon, and apparently a couple of his people will be over to see me in the morning as well."

"What do you want me to do in the meantime, sir?"

"The priority has to be to get a lid on the situation before anything gets out."

"I have an idea on that, sir."

"Go on."

"We could call a community meeting, sir. Be upfront with the locals, tell them of the need for secrecy and so on. There are only about 300 people in the village, so it shouldn't be too hard to arrange."

"Come clean about it all."

"Precisely, sir. In a place like Crianloch, I'd be amazed if it wasn't already common knowledge anyway."

"Good point. Very well, you organize the village meeting and leave the rest to me. I don't suppose you know where the Met Office is based?"

"Exeter, sir. Would you like the number?"

As soon as Hendricks put down the phone, she called the duty sergeant into her office.

"Who's in today Sergeant?" she asked.

"Everyone, ma'am. You, me, Fergus, and the ALO."

"Get them all in here would you please, Sergeant?"

Minutes later the sergeant returned with the station's

Agricultural Liaison Officer, and Fergus, its only constable.

"You're each aware of the interview I conducted yesterday?"

There were nods all around.

"Well there's no easy way to say this, but what the chap said is true."

"But, m'm ...?"

"I know it sounds unlikely Sergeant, but the weather station at Glen Crian isn't there anymore."

The three men stared.

"You mean it's been blown up or something, m'm?"

"No constable, I mean it's simply vanished. Take a look for yourself."

Hendricks laid her phone on the desk, and turning it to face the three men, she flicked through the photos.

"It's the glen all right." ... "Well, I'll be damned." ... "Nice shot of the Land Rover."

They were convinced.

"What are we going to do, m'm?" asked Fergus.

"The priority is to contain the story. So, I've spoken with the Chief, and we've agreed to hold a village meeting tonight. We'll come clean about everything, be completely open with them, and make it clear they mustn't tell a soul."

"That'll be easier said than done, m'm."

"Possibly, but let's take one thing at a time. What about the village hall as the venue?"

"Right you are, m'm, I'll get onto that," said the sergeant. "And you two," he continued, turning to Fergus and the ALO. "Put together a leaflet, get over there, and stick one through every front door. Leave some in the General Store, the Post Office, the pub, and any Bed & Breakfast places you come across too."

"I think the Post Office and General Store are one shop in Crianloch."

"Well, that'll make it easier for you, won't it?" said Hendricks briskly, "let's say 7:30 tonight for the meeting."

It's almost a two-hour drive from Lossiemouth to Glen Crian, so DI Hendricks was long gone when a blue SUV rolled to a halt at the far end of the gravel track. The man got out of the vehicle first, followed by his colleague, their RAF uniforms making an incongruous sight in the highland glen. They scanned the area for life. The tally should have been fourteen guards around the perimeter, with two more by the utilities building in the centre of the site. In reality, it was one kestrel, a handful of small birds, seventeen rabbits and two sleeping owls. It was disappointing, to say the least.

"Well, that explains a lot," said the woman.

Once she and her colleague had mobile signal again, they put in a call to Group Captain Finch. As his phone rang, he was grumbling to himself that he could have been out on the links if it wasn't for Crianloch. Even with his minimal level of interest though, he had to admit that three days of silence couldn't be good. A terrorist attack, perhaps? Or maybe some freakish act of nature? Either way, the other thought that refused to leave his brain was the feeling that neither could be the case. After all, surely terrorists would have claimed responsibility by now, and even it was just a nasty thunderstorm or a few scared sheep, the locals would have noticed something? It's hardly surprising then, that when he heard what his officers had to say, he was both surprised and not.

"That's right, sir," responded the airman. "The gravel track still leads off the main road as you said. Except now, there's only countryside at the other end."

"Did you try the local police?"

"Yes and no, sir. We stopped in Drumnadrochit on the way back, but the station was closed up. It was weird actually as there was no-one there at all. Just a sign on the door saying to dial 999 in case of emergency."

"Hm."

"What do you want us to do, sir?"

Finch paused for a moment, as he eyed an advert for a revolutionary new putter.

"Stay there."

"Sir?"

"I've spoken with a Detective Chief Inspector Croft in Inverness. He's in charge of the Crianloch area, so I have a call with him later, and he's expecting you both at nine in the morning."

As he said this, Jenny's old VW pulled into Tebay Services, just south of Penrith. She and Nigel were ready for a break. In Nigel's case, this was partly because his and Jenny's musical tastes had only coincided once every fifty miles or so, and he wasn't sure how much more he could take. Then a familiar guitar riff had come on, and seconds later they were both belting out their own version of Queen's *Crazy little thing called love*. It was an old habit, and on quieter roads, other drivers had been known to turn round to see where the awful noise was coming from. Neither was a good singer you see, but they didn't care, as for different reasons, it was a song they both loved. Nigel, because he'd always been a fan. Jenny, because her parents had played it incessantly throughout her childhood. It had been the first song they'd danced to at their wedding, and they were determined everyone else would like it too.

Jenny scanned the car park, but there was no sign of Liz. Half an hour passed before she tried calling, but it went to voicemail. After another 40 minutes, her finger was hovering over Liz's number, when a large yellow, recovery-truck pulled into the car park. On the back of it was Liz's car.

"I told you I don't have much luck with long journeys," she said, clambering down from the lorry's cab. She appeared to be in much better spirits than the day before, which in the circumstances was remarkable.

"Whatever happened?" asked Jenny.

"Something electrical, I think."

"Don't look at me," interjected Nigel. "I know where the petrol, oil an' water go. That's it."

Just then the recovery driver joined them, and after a brief discussion, he reluctantly agreed to unload the car and leave it there, in the car park.

"Quick coffee, then get going?" asked Liz after he'd gone.

The others agreed, and they all headed inside. As they drank in tea, coffee, and the view across to the Lake District, Nigel was struck by how vast the landscape was. He'd visited the area once before, so part of what he was seeing was a memory as the mountains were still only in the distance. That would change as they headed further north though. And by the time they reached the Scottish Highlands, the scenery would be grander than any of them had seen before.

Forty minutes later they were transferring Liz's luggage to the camper van, and after refuelling, they were off again. Their first stop was to be the small town of Moffat, where they'd arranged to stay over and break the journey.

As they were checking into their hotel, four offices around the UK echoed to a series of beeps, indicating the start of Croft's first video call with Finch and the others.

"Good afternoon, gentlemen," began the Defence Secretary.

"Good afternoon, Minister," came the replies.

"Thank you for joining us Detective Chief Inspector. You've spoken with Group Captain Finch of course, and I expect you recognize the Director General and myself."

"Of course, sir. It's a pleasure to be here."

"Well, I'll get straight down to it. We have a situation with a community within your jurisdiction, and we need your help."

"That'll be Crianloch I take it, sir." It was a long-established tactic of Croft's to open conversations in such a way as to throw others off guard. Judging by the sharp intake of breath from the Defence Minister, it succeeded.

"What do you know about it, Detective Chief Inspector?" asked the DG calmly.

"I know it's not there anymore, sir."

"I see. We were hoping news of it hadn't got out."

"Well, it hasn't as such, sir. A local milkman alerted us to the situation this morning, so one of my officers has already visited the site, since when we've had a constable on duty there."

"Excellent. What about the local community?"

"As the milkman and a newspaper boy from the village had known about it for several days, sir, we felt it likely that word would have already got around, so DI Hendricks is holding a village meeting there this evening. Explain the situation, stress the importance of keeping quiet, you get the idea."

In Crianloch village, Fergus and the ALO had leafleted everywhere with a letterbox, and by six-thirty, they'd set out rows of chairs in the hall. It had meant evicting some disgruntled badminton players, but needs must. So, what with that, and the fliers through every door, the villagers were more than a little intrigued when half-seven came around. They thought they had a good idea what it was all about though, and when Hendricks took to the stage at the end of the hall, the place was packed. The room was silent as she spoke, and it didn't take her long to go through everything. As agreed with Croft, she finished with a polite but firm insistence that they tell no-one anything, then asked if there were any questions. She didn't expect many, but she was still surprised when only two hands went up.

The first was from a farmer who wanted compensation for his sheep having been frightened, the second from the landowner who sold Glen Crian to the MoD, asking if he'd have to give the money back. The other farmers in the hall paid close attention to the answer to the sheep question, but no-one seemed to care much about the other.

In short, by the time Hendricks closed the meeting, she was starting to think the containment exercise might work. Before she left the village, she put in another call to DCI Croft.

"How was it, Diane?"

"It went very well, sir. As we thought, most people already knew. Plus there are no tourists in town this week, so we could be in the clear."

"Excellent. Any questions?"

"A couple, sir, but nothing significant."

"They understand they mustn't say a word."

"They do, sir."

"Very good. So, what next?"

"I could do with three more people to maintain the watch on the glen, sir. We only have one constable in Drumnadrochit."

"Of course, I'll have them sent over first thing."

"Thank you, sir. And SOCO?"

"You're the officer in charge here Diane, so please get them out in the morning. Anything else?"

"I'm curious to know what happened on your video call, sir."

Croft paused before replying ... "I can't tell you much I'm afraid, as it turns out this is a lot bigger than we realised, but I can say the government is involved ... and the security services."

"As well as the RAF?"

"Indeed. I don't suppose you took any photos of Glen Crian by any chance?"

"I did, sir. I could email them over if you like?"

"Yes, please. Well, goodnight, Diane. Keep me in the loop."

It minus 11 years

 For TC, finding herself back in her own bed wasn't as reassuring as you might think. After all, she'd just been in her own bed, only that was the one in her parent's house, whereas now she was back at college. She looked around. Not with the same confusion as when she'd woken up under the tree, but it was still enough to shake her.

She needed cake.

Not most people's breakfast of choice perhaps, but as TC was starting to realize, she wasn't most people. After raiding the kitchen, she sat back down at her desk with a coffee, and a slice of the lemon drizzle cake she'd made the day before[27]. She loved baking and had always found it relaxing, which in the circumstances was a bonus. After scoffing down the first slice, she cut herself another. As it is for many people, doing something normal was comforting, and after finishing her coffee, with what ended up as three slices of cake, TC ran over the last few hours in her mind. It had been quite a dream.

As she thought about it, a whole new wave of emotions washed over her. It was as if the dream had broken through to her in a way that nothing else had since *his* death. Maybe what she needed was some fresh air; it had undoubtedly felt nice in the dream. Freaky perhaps, but

---

[27] TCs lemon drizzle cake
- Heat an oven to 180°C/356°F, Fan oven 160°C/320°F, Gas mark 4.
- Take 1½ eggs, 90g flour, 90g caster sugar, 90g butter, 4g baking powder, and some lemon zest. Beat together until smooth.
- Move to a baking tin lined with greaseproof paper and bake for 40 minutes or until it's golden brown and pulling away from the sides.
- Mix 50g granulated sugar with the juice of half a lemon, then pour over the cake while it's still warm and leave to cool until you can't hold back any longer.

it had. TC pulled on some jeans, a t-shirt, and an old Snow Patrol hoodie, then gazed at herself in the mirror. She smiled for the first time in months, picked up her keys and left the room.

It was far from cold outside, but far from warm either, and the crisp autumn air felt good on her face. Some trees were already changing colour, and the nearby beech hedges were already brown. Summer was her favourite season, and she couldn't stand winter, but she'd come to appreciate spring and autumn. The one for its sense of newness. The other for its colours, and the promise of a hot chocolate at the end of a long walk. She caught her breath, and a tear spilt out. That had been one of *his* things.

She pulled her hood up, and stuffing her hands deep into her pockets, she set off at a brisk pace. In one pocket were her keys. In the other was an open packet of mints and what felt like a scrap of paper. She pulled it out. It was scrunched up, but judging by the shiny feel of it, it was a till receipt. She smoothed it out between her fingers and stopped dead in her tracks. It was dated the day before and was from the *McDonald's* in her home town.

TC peered at the date. It wasn't clear, but no matter how hard she tried to make it say something else, it still stubbornly read as the day before. She looked at the items listed.

1 x Crispy Chicken Salad
1 x Regular Fries
1 x Medium Root Beer

Disorientation crashed over TC like an avalanche. How long she stood there for she'd didn't know, but when the world came back into focus, she was still where she'd stopped. She looked at the receipt again. It was evidence of something utterly impossible, and her brain was having a hard time reconciling that.

"But I don't remember getting there!" she muttered with rising panic. "I can't remember the drive or anything. And why was I by that tree? I really must be going mad."

Moving purely on instinct, she started walking again. Then reaching into her back pocket, she took out her phone. She paused for a moment before dialling.

"Hello, Mum."

"Oh, hello, dear, it's lovely to hear from you. How are you feeling?"

"I'm OK, Mum. I've come out for a walk actually."

"Oh, that's nice. Are you feeling a little brighter today?"

"A little. Thought the fresh air might do me good."

"What's the weather like?"

Her mum's voice held that concerned, almost patronizing tone TC remembered from before. It was the tone of someone desperately trying to sound normal, and which hadn't been in the dream. TC hesitated as she steeled herself to ask the question.

"Mum?"

"What is it, dear?"

"This may sound crazy, but ... but did I visit you yesterday?"

"Visit? What here at home?"

"Yes."

"Are you feeling all right dear?"

"Did I Mum?"

"Well no, you've not been home since ... Well, not for ages."

"Oh ... OK ... Thanks, Mum."

Her voice trailed away, and after she rang off, they were both left worrying for her sanity.

Over the following months, TC spoke with her parents every week or so as they always had. Sometimes TC made the call, sometimes it was them, and gradually the memory of the dream started to fade. As time passed, TC even managed to push all thought of it to the back of her mind. She'd pinned the receipt to the cork board in her room at college, but she rarely looked at it.

In fact, by Christmas, she'd all but forgotten, so after much thought, she decided to bite the bullet and go home for the holidays. As you can imagine, her parents were delighted, and she was especially looking forward to spending time with her father. It went really well too.

As expected, she sometimes struggled with her mum's over-attentiveness, but she understood why she was like it. And Christmas Day itself was lovely. Just the three of them for lunch, then they had neighbours over in the afternoon. They even played charades as they'd done when TC was a child, and the familiarity of it all was bliss.

On the 26th she woke up and went downstairs to find her father in the kitchen as usual.

"Morning, Dad."

"Oh morning love, your mother's round next door. What would you like for breakfast?"

"Just some granola and coffee please, Dad."

"Granola? I don't think we've got any. Will porridge do like yesterday?"

TC went to speak, and as she did, she noticed something over her father's shoulder. The kitchen cabinets were oak instead of white. Then her ear caught the sound of a cat flap opening, and a small, black kitten strolled in like it owned the place.

As she watched it, she felt her mind falling.

Last time it had been the location of *McDonald's*, the root beer and her mother's sunny attitude. Now it was the breakfast, the kitchen and the cat. *Oh god, I'm somewhere else again*, she thought to herself as the all too familiar feelings of confusion flooded her mind.

Where this time, though? It's got to be a dream. It just has to be! She ran upstairs to her room and winced as she dug her fingernails into the palms of her hands, but it didn't make any difference. She thought back to the *McDonald's* receipt in her room at college, and she swayed on her feet.

"I'm off out to get my paper," called her father from downstairs. "I won't be long."

The sheer normality of his words sent a fresh shiver down her spine, and she dropped slowly onto the edge of the bed. She stayed there for maybe twenty minutes before the world cleared. Then she went back down to the kitchen and took a photograph of it with her phone. She took one of the cat too.

The rest of the week passed with its usual sense of familiar unfamiliarity, and the day before New Year's Eve, she found herself alone in the house. Her parents had gone to a golf event, so she was relaxing on the sofa with a cup of tea and the last of the Christmas cake. They'd had a big lunch, and sinking back into the cushions, TC felt sleep creeping up on her.

You know what happened next.

Travelling north

Tuesday, September 14th

When Jenny woke up and looked around the hotel room, her first thought was one of confusion. Her phone read 08:13 when there was a knock on the door, followed moments later by Nigel's familiar voice. She remembered where she was.

"Good mornin' madam, this is your personal wake-up call. Breakfast will be served shortly in the executive dinin' room. As you know, this doubles as our bar, so you'll be pleased to hear we've had the carpet cleaned following last night's *incident*. This is part of our ongoin' commitment to excellence, an' we look forward to servin' you shortly."

She smiled.

"For your drinkin' pleasure, we offer a choice of individually wrapped tea bags, instant coffee or somethin' that passes for orange juice. It *has* been watered down rather though, so you may want to give it a miss. Toast is available in either white or ... well just white actually, and with it, you can have marmalade ... or not. You can also have a cooked breakfast if you wish, but if that is madam's preference, I suggest an early arrival, to maximize the ratio of food to grease."

She smiled again. "OK, Nige."

She'd have been surprised to know that out on the landing, he smiled too. After two and a half years, he was getting used to her name for him. He was a slow learner.

Forty-five minutes later, Jenny walked into the dining room. Nigel was sitting at a table by the window, and Liz was by a centre counter. She was filling a bowl with a mixture of grapefruit, muesli and Greek yoghurt.

"Sleep well?" she asked as Jenny walked over.

Jenny said she had, and helped herself to some cereal, toast, and a glass of the translucent orange juice.

When she joined Nigel, he was fighting with an individual tub of butter and had just managed to take hold of one corner of its peel-back top. As Jenny watched, the small, plastic carton slipped from his fingers and flew across the room. Luckily it didn't hit any of the other diners. Unluckily, it landed on the carpet half a second before a smart young man in a navy suit placed his foot on precisely the same spot. He didn't stay there for long, and as the butter squelched out, his foot slid out from under him. Jenny gasped, as in what seemed like slow motion, the man's tray of tea, corn flakes, and toast flew skywards. She shot a glance at Nigel, then at Liz, and in the commotion that quickly ensued, they made their exit.

In the corridors of power, something was stirring, and it wasn't just the Defence Secretary's morning Darjeeling. As he added his customary two drops of lemon juice, the familiar greeting tone sounded from his laptop, and the face of MI5's Director General appeared on-screen. A second tone sounded, and there was DCI Croft. A third, and Group Captain Finch joined too.

"Good morning, gentlemen," began the Defence Secretary.

"Good morning Minister," responded the others.

"So Detective Chief Inspector, how did the village meeting go?"

"Very well, sir. We were right about the majority of people already knowing, and I gather none of the villagers were even that interested."

"Excellent news," smiled the Defence Secretary, his usual annoyance at life temporarily diminished. "So now we've contained the situation, what else do we know? For a start, what exactly is it we're containing?"

There was a momentary silence before Finch spoke.

"I had two officers visit Glen Crian yesterday, Minister, and I know this is hard to take in, but Crianloch Research Station has vanished into thin air. I'm told the glen appears to be absolutely untouched, with no evidence of anything ever having been there."

"Well, yes and no," added Croft. "Bear with me, sir, and I'll share my screen."

Moments later, one of Hendricks' photographs appeared on the video conference.

"Where's that?"

"It's Glen Crian yesterday, sir. And this ..." he said flicking to the next photograph "... is a photo showing the base when it was first built. You'll see they were taken from virtually the same spot and both have the same track leading up from the main road."

"Interesting," said the DG softly. "The track was gravelled

rather than being tarmacked, so it blended into the landscape better and helped maintain the station's anonymity. And it's still there?"

Croft nodded, and it fell to the Defence Secretary to speak next. He was almost calm.

"What do you think, Director? Operation Carter?"

"I'm not aware of anything that could cause this."

"Even so ..."

"Yes, you're right, of course. I'll speak with the station's liaison officer at RAF Wyton. Find out if there was anything I wasn't aware of. In the meantime, we'll be sending some people up to examine the site, and I'd like to involve local SOCO as well. Detective Chief Inspector?"

"Of course, sir. DI Hendricks is the officer in charge from our side, and she's speaking with SOCO this morning anyway, so my only ask is that your people put everything through her."

Not long after the call ended, the buzzer sounded on DCI Croft's desk, and his assistant announced the arrival of the RAF officers Finch had told him to expect. The man and woman were shown in, and once they were seated, Croft looked at each of them in turn before speaking.

"I assume you're here about Crianloch?" he began, as he had on the previous day's call. The difference now, was that rather than being deferential as he'd been then, he was now geniality itself. The questions that came at him were more or less the same though.

"So, if the milkman saw the base was gone last Friday, why did he wait until Monday to report it?" asked the woman.

"I gather he didn't like to say anything," smiled Croft. "It's quite a closed community by all accounts and our sense is the locals felt it simply wasn't any of their business. Coffee?"

His affability was palpable, and the two officers gratefully accepted. Neither would have admitted it, but they'd both been thrown by recent events and felt a little out of their depth. Now though, the man started to relax a little. Not the woman, mind you, although she wasn't tense, so much as excited. Unknown to her colleague, she was something of a conspiracy nut and was having the time of her life. In fact, her mind had already gone to all sorts of off the wall possibilities ... Alien abductions, invisible force fields and time travel for starters.

When Croft re-entered with the coffees, he asked the question he'd been preparing the ground for from the start. He already knew part of the answer, of course, but he wanted to know what they'd be briefed to share.

"So why's the RAF interested? I'd have thought this was a matter for the Met Office."

The woman only paused for the tiniest fraction of a second, but Croft spotted the hesitation.

"As you probably know, sir, they're headquartered on the south coast. And with the base being headed up by one of our officers, it made sense for us to take a look."

Plausible, thought Croft. "I was going to ring the Met Office myself, and in the meantime, we've put constables on round-the-clock duty in Glen Crian."

"Excellent. We wondered about something like that ourselves, sir."

"Well, anything involving the civilian population is our responsibility, so we'll naturally be taking the lead here."

The woman hesitated again. "As you can imagine, sir, we need to report back to Lossiemouth, so may I call you after we've done that?"

"Of course. Thank you for coming in. I look forward to us working together."

They shook hands, and once the two officers had gone, Croft sat down. He was smiling, and as he often did when thinking, he raised a hand to his chin and started stroking his beard. It was a subconscious habit he'd picked up years ago, and he only knew he did it because his sister had pointed it out once. The thing was, it had always annoyed her, so when she discovered it could be interpreted as a sign of deception or lying, she just had to say something. Croft had never married you see, and with his sister being the pushy one in the family, she'd always seen her role as being to help his career. The habit was too ingrained for him to change by then though and rather than stop doing it, he deliberately started incorporating it into his questioning and negotiation techniques. After all, if his sister was right, he figured it might confuse others. Maybe even give him an edge.

This time though he hadn't needed to put his visitors off their guard, as they were plainly uptight enough already. They were genuine though, he was sure of that, and it really was good to have them on board. Even so, he could have sworn the woman's eyebrows had twitched when he'd mentioned the Met Office. Then there was her pause when he'd asked why the RAF was involved. And the fact that she'd referred to the weather station as a *base*. Was that just habit from talking about airbases most of the time? He wasn't sure.

He sat thinking about this for a minute or two, then picked up the phone.

"Diane? There's something I'd like you to do for me."

~~

After the earlier video conference, the DG had also gone straight into another meeting, this one being with three scientists he'd had summoned into Palmer Street[28]. Minutes later, they were being driven to RAF Northolt, where politicians and members of the Royal Family fly from. The waiting plane didn't hang about either and took off almost straight away.

The flight itself took less than an hour and a half, and when they landed at RAF Lossiemouth, the three scientists were greeted by a driver. After transferring several crates of equipment to the car, they all set off towards Crianloch.

Almost two hours later, they pulled into the car park of *The Shepherd's Arms*, which serves as a pub and restaurant for the community, as well as offering rooms for visitors. It was, therefore, here that they'd been booked into for their stay.

The hotel's owner didn't show any emotion as they checked in, but just handed over room keys as anyone in his position would. The car was unmarked, the RAF officer was out of uniform, and the scientists looked normal enough, so why wouldn't he? Country folk aren't as stupid as fiction sometimes likes to make out though, and the proprietor knew something fishy when he saw it. As soon as the four of them had gone to their rooms, he picked up the phone.

"It's them; they've come."

"More police?"

"Don't think so. One's RAF I reckon, and two of the others seem normal enough, but the last one ..."

"What about him?"

---

[28] Confirmed in April 2019, Palmer Street is GCHQs London base, tucked away in a side road near St James' Park tube station.

"Definitely some kind of scientist. Little guy, about 5' 3", big mop of grey hair and thick-rimmed glasses. Looks like Einstein got left out in the rain and shrunk."

His mate chuckled. "How long are they staying?"

"A week they reckon."

"Nice money. You charge 'em tourist rates?"

"Of course. Booking came through normal enough, but there was something funny about it, so I figured why not?"

"Government."

"Right."

"Let me know what happens, Terry. I'll tell the village."

And he did, for the hotel owner had phoned AGB, or Alexander Graham Bell to give him his full nickname. He'd acquired the name after the inventor of the telephone[29] as he was a genius at getting news around Crianloch. Some might have called him a gossip, but that didn't come close to doing him justice.

The thing was, when the villagers had seemed uninterested at the community meeting, it had just been a front. They'd long suspected there was something odd about the weather station, and they were intrigued. They wouldn't tell anyone mind you. Not because Hendricks had asked either, but because this was *their* secret and that made it all the juicier. Now the visitors had come, the rumour mill stepped up a notch.

It needn't have bothered though, because when the driver and the scientists set off for Glen Crian a short while later, they were

---

[29] I realise there are some who dispute this and throw in names like Reis, Gray and Antonio Meucci (who looks spookily like Bell's twin brother by the way). But seeing as Bell was from Scotland where much of our story is set, I'm sticking with that.

followed by three SOCO minibuses. They didn't have their lights flashing, but the chequered, blue and yellow markings and the Police Scotland logo on the sides were a bit of a giveaway. Secrecy was no more.

Arriving in the glen, the first thing the team saw was the blue and white *Police Line - Do Not Cross* barrier tape, set up across the valley by the two duty constables. It looked out of place flapping in the breeze; it was such a vast site. It was protocol though and not the only aspect to be observed either, as despite the constables recognizing some of the SOCO team from previous investigations, they quickly set about checking everyone's credentials.

With that done, everyone changed into their white, hooded, scene-suits, complete with safety wellington boots, particulate masks and secure-fit glasses. Even the boffin did the same, although in his case, he declined the face mask and the protective goggles. He knew from experience that they always made his glasses fog up.

The scene of crime officers were used to conducting fingertip searches, and scouring even a wide area was fairly standard. All the same, combing half a square mile for clues to explain the disappearance of an entire building was something new. They were a well-oiled team though, and with their site manager calling the shots, the six officers got started immediately. The first step was taking accurate measurements of the site, and as five of them did that, the team's photographer unpacked her gear. Then with the help of a bundle of crime scene marker cones, she started recording key features of the surrounding landscape.

While they did that, the boffin and the two London scientists set up a laser grid, not unlike the one Liz had used. The difference was that here, the *Transmit/Receive* units were mounted on extending tripods to take account of the terrain. With that done, the two scientists unloaded their equipment from the car and started taking a variety of readings across the landscape. The boffin did the same, carefully unpacking a large, padded crate, in which was a Geiger counter. It looked like a handheld vacuum cleaner, with the addition of various dials and controls. It also had a pair of headphones attached to it, and unsurprisingly, as the boffin went to put them on, he sent his glasses flying. Muttering apologies to no-one in particular, he bent down to pick them up. Then, ignoring the tuft of heather they'd acquired, he put them back on and set off between the first row of tripods.

As he did, one of the constables noticed how slowly he was walking. This was evidently something not to be rushed. The boffin was muttering too, and scribbling things in a notebook as he walked, adjusting the Geiger counter's various dials as he went.

From Moffat, Liz, Jenny and Nigel's journey was long but spectacular, passing to begin with through the Scottish Lowlands, then around the southern edge of Edinburgh and across the Firth of Forth. As they drove over the A9000, they all looked to their right to catch sight of the iconic Forth Railway Bridge. Huge, orange and star of John Buchan's *The Thirty-Nine Steps*, it dominated the estuary.

An hour later they stopped for coffee in Perth, before carrying on towards the Cairngorms National Park. It was worth the wait too, as the scenery was incredible. Mountains on either side, acres of forest and at one point, off to their left sat the *Dalwhinnie* distillery. Under other circumstances Nigel for one would have been happy to stay there all day. As with his library trip though, he was on a mission and wanted to get to Lossiemouth as quickly as possible. It was ironic then that in heading straight there, they went nowhere near Crianloch, and the nearest they got was 60 miles east of it.

At that point, they still had well over an hour to go to their destination, and eventually, over five hours after leaving Moffat, Jenny, Liz and Nigel finally approached RAF Lossiemouth. The first clues were signs reading *Restricted access - No admittance* and other such greetings. Next came a glimpse of runways beyond the wire fence on their left and shortly after, they came to a small, grassy roundabout. On it was an understated blue sign reading simply *Royal Air Force Lossiemouth.* They turned left into what felt like a business park with an array of warehouse-like buildings spread out on either side of the road.

It wasn't at all what Nigel or Jenny had been expecting. There were barriers across the road right enough, but it was only the sight of the RAF Regiment gunner[30] waving them to a parking space that hit home.

"Wish me luck," murmured Liz as she got out of the car.

She walked over to the approaching airman and began talking. In response to one question, Nigel saw Liz produce something from her wallet. It was her civilian identity card from RAF Wyton, and with the preliminaries over, the two of them walked back towards Nigel and Jenny.

"Good afternoon," said the gunner in a light Scottish accent. "I gather you've come to see Group Captain Marston."

"My cousin," chipped in Nigel.

"Quite the family outing. Is he expecting you?"

"Well," said Liz with a hint of uncertainty in her voice. "Not

---

[30] If you think of regular members of the army as being called *soldiers*, the equivalent term in the RAF Regiment is *gunners*.

specifically."

The man raised an eyebrow, but Nigel came to the rescue.

"The family hasn't heard from him for a while, an' we've not been able to reach him on the phone, so, we thought we'd try in person."

As he said it, Nigel realised what was missing. Gran would probably only have called David's mobile rather than the airbase. Maybe Liz had?

"I see. I take it you called the base?"

"Of course," replied Liz. "I spoke with someone in public relations, but they couldn't tell me anything."

As she spoke, Liz subconsciously pushed her glasses up the bridge of her nose.

She's holding up remarkably well, thought Jenny.

"I see," repeated the gunner. "Stay here, please. I'll see what I can do."

With that, he turned and strode smartly away towards the low, red-roofed building up ahead. Most of the windows were mirrored so you couldn't see in, and Nigel rightly guessed it had been built more for security than approachability.

They were beginning to think they'd been forgotten when the side door opened, and the man reappeared.

"Hello again," said Liz in her brightest, friendliest voice. "Any luck?"

"I've spoken with my duty commander, and he's going to send someone out to speak with you."

"Sounds ominous," said Nigel.

"Not at all, sir. We have our protocols, and you'll appreciate we can't allow members of the public beyond this point. It's perfectly standard practice."

"Even me?" asked Liz, "with my identity card, I mean." She

adjusted her glasses again.

"I'm afraid so miss. It *is* for a different base, after all. I'm sure you understand."

With that, he nodded politely to each of them and retraced his steps. As he did, Liz's shoulders slumped. She didn't faint, but Jenny's hand was instantly under her elbow, and the two stayed like that for a moment.

"I'm fine," said Liz, a little brokenly.

"Sure?"

"I will be ... I just need to know."

There was a hint of desperation in Liz's voice, and she was clearly struggling to keep herself in check. That was the trouble with being in touch with a loved one multiple times every day. You got used to it, and whereas people from another generation might not notice if a week went by without contact, it had taken Liz less than a morning. From then on, it had slowly got worse, up to the time of Jenny and Nigel's arrival. Knowing now that David's grandmother was worried too, only added to the stress.

Ten minutes passed before anything else happened, and when it did, it was in the shape of a blue SUV which rolled to a halt on the far side of the security barriers.

"I gather you're looking for Group Captain Marston."

These words, spoken in flat, official tones, came from a uniformed RAF officer who'd arrived in response to the call from gate security.

"That's right," replied Liz as confidently as she could muster. "Can you help us?"

"May I ask your interest in him?"

"I'm his fiancée," said Liz.

"And I'm his cousin," added Nigel as before.

"Oh yes," replied the airman, looking at his clipboard. "I see it now. When did you last hear from him?"

"A few days ago."

"Could you be exact, please?" He had a cold, business-like voice, and Liz could felt her hackles rising.

"Last Thursday. Why?"

"And yet you drove up here in person."

"He's usually very reliable," she replied testily.

"I see. How frequently did you normally speak with him?"

"What's with all the questions?" she snapped. "We came for answers, not the other way around."

"Of course, Miss. My apologies. I take it you tried calling him?"

"Yes, I tried his mobile, I texted, and I rang here." Her voice was now like a parent who was failing to keep their temper with an unruly child.

"Oh, really?" The airman flicked through the papers on his clipboard again. "Ah, yes. Well, I hope you've not come far."

"Why's that?"

"He's not here, Miss."

"Well, where is he?" she demanded angrily.

"I'm afraid I'm not at liberty to say."

"You're not at liberty ..."   "What does that mean?"

Liz and Nigel had spoken simultaneously and exchanged a quick look. As they did, Nigel also caught sight of Jenny over Liz's shoulder. She appeared not to be paying any attention at all.

"It simply means I'm not able to say where he is."

"You don't know, or you won't say?" challenged Liz.

"I'm afraid I can't say."

"Can't say much, can you?"

"I'm sorry, Miss, but that's just how it is."

"And what about her?" asked Jenny, pushing back a strand of hair as she turned towards the others.

"Miss?" asked clipboard-man.

"What about the woman in the car. Is she at liberty to say?"

Jenny pointed at the blue SUV the airman had arrived in. His female colleague was sitting in the front passenger seat. The man shifted his feet very slightly before replying. "I'm afraid not, Miss."

"Well you're very polite I'll give you that," chimed in Nigel. "But you're not much help, are you?"

"I'll be happy to help you however I can, sir."

"So, to be clear, his 86-year old grandmother is worried sick about him, and so's his fiancée here, but you won't help us."

"I'm afraid I can't, sir."

"So, what next?"

"Miss?"

The anger was back in Liz's voice, only now it had an icy, sarcastic edge to it, which demanded a response … "It's a simple enough question. I want to speak with my fiancé and so does his grandmother, but you won't help, *sorry*, can't help, so what do we do next?"

"I'm afraid you'll have to be patient Miss. I'm sure Group Captain Marston will be back in touch when he can."

"You're sure? That's quite a statement from someone who can't tell us anything." Her voice was like steel.

"I'm …"

"… afraid that's all you can say," jumped in Nigel, finishing the man's sentence for him.

"And if we're not willing to wait?"

"In that case, you can raise a formal query by going to our website, miss. This is the address."

The man handed Liz a card, and before she had a chance to say anything, he turned and walked off. This was evidently the end of the discussion.

"What just happened?" asked Liz in a dazed voice.

"We were given the brush-off," said Nigel, equally as stunned. "Very politely, but we were definitely given the brush-off."

"Amazing." Liz's voice had fallen to its lowest point.

She and Nigel looked at each other.

"Well, no point in hangin' around I suppose," said Nigel, forcing a smile. "We might as well go into town an' get a spot of lunch. Decide what to do next."

"Yes, why not," sighed Liz.

"Want me to drive Jen?" asked Nigel.

Jenny didn't reply. She had her eyes fixed on the retreating SUV.

"Jenny?"

"Sorry?" she said with a start.

"Do you want me to drive?"

"You? Drive?"

"Yeah. Just for a change."

"Wonders will never cease."

On their way into Lossiemouth itself, they passed the golf course, a sign to Duffus castle (not pronounced doofus), and a man walking either a large dog or a small horse. There was also a hastily scrawled board on the roadside, advertising a local burger bar which boasted *THE BEST Irn-Bru Battered Butterballs in Moray*[31]. They ignored that though and were soon sitting in the

---

[31] Irn-Bru (pronounced Iron Brew) is a fruit soda that outsells even Coca-Cola in Scotland. Battered butterballs, on the other hand, are made by coating frozen

Happy Lobster Café overlooking the North Sea. The café was in a converted, dockside warehouse, and the vaulted brick ceiling gave it a warm, welcoming feel. It didn't help their mood though.

"I've never seen polite and useless rolled into one like that before," said Liz angrily.

"So, what now?"

"I'll tell you one thing," said Jenny, "I'm too tired to turn around and drive straight home."

"So we stick around?"

"I'm not sure we're done here anyway. Think about it. David's based here, and the RAF can't tell us how to contact him? It doesn't make sense."

"Yes, I get that," said Nigel, "but what are we going to do? It's not like they're going to start talkin' to us just cos we're here."

"What about the woman in the SUV?"

"You looked at her more than us, Jen."

"I was intrigued. Half the windows were blacked out, and she was in the passenger seat."

"So?"

"In movies, the one in the passenger seat is usually the more senior."

"And it was the guy who both drove and spoke with us."

"Like he was ordered to."

"What about the card he gave you, Liz?" asked Nigel. "Any use?"

Liz picked up her bag, took out the business card, and handed it across.

"It's a standard contact site."

"Worth a try, I guess."

---

cubes of butter with Irn-Bru mixed with batter, and then deep-frying them. Some feel there should be defibrillators near chip shops selling these.

Nigel took out his phone and looked around the café. On the wall behind the till, between two watercolours of the North Sea, was a small blackboard. It read: *Our Wi-Fi password is The_Hidden_Cave*. He typed it into his phone and waited.

"What's the URL?"

"raf.org.uk/contactus."

When the page opened, he had five choices: *Careers*, *Media*, *Complaints*, *MoD*, *Other*.

"Other?"

The two women nodded, so Nigel tapped the link. It opened a blank email, and at the sight of it, Liz held out her hand. It was an unspoken request, and Nigel handed her the phone. After a moment's pause, Liz started typing, and when she was done, she took a laminated card from her purse, photographed it and clicked *Attachment*. She ran her eyes over the result and read it aloud.

Dear Sir or Madam,

I'm writing regarding the whereabouts of my fiancé, Group Captain David Marston, and enclose a photo of my RAF civilian ID as proof of his, and my identities. He recently transferred to Lossiemouth, and as he's not been in contact for over two weeks, his relatives and I are very concerned. I, therefore, visited the base today and was met by an officer who was unable to help, hence this email. I know the RAF takes the well-being of both its employees and their families very seriously, so please contact me as soon as possible at the number below.

"The friendly approach. I like it."

"Not entirely true, but worth a try."

"Well, you never know. Send?"

Nigel and Jenny nodded.

Liz tapped the screen, and nothing happened. She swore and thrust the phone at Nigel. He did exactly the same as her, and it worked first time. Technology is like that sometimes. If it doesn't think you're friendly, it does what it wants - a bit like cats.

After this, the three friends lapsed into silence, each absorbed in their own thoughts. In Liz's case, these were focused exclusively on David. *Where was he? Why couldn't the guy at the base tell them anything? Would the email do any good?* Suddenly a new thought crystallised in her mind.

"I don't think he knew."

"What?"

"The chap at the base. He said he couldn't say anything, so ..."

"He said he *wouldn't* help." interrupted Jenny.

"No, he didn't," said Liz with growing excitement. "Nigel asked him why he *wouldn't* say anything, and he said he *couldn't*. I don't think he knew any more than we do. I mean it's not like we're dealing with some secret organization or something ..."

"True enough but ..."

"... and they're good with personal stuff."

"So, if the chap really didn't know ..."

Nigel stopped in mid-sentence as Liz let out a small groan. The idea of the man not knowing more than them had been appealing at first, but now ...

"Oh god, David's had an accident."

"We don't know that," said Jenny, putting her hand over Liz's.

"He's had some sort of accident, and they don't know whether he's OK or not."

"You can't say that. It could be anything."

"Like what?" challenged Liz, fear and frustration now bubbling up in her voice.

"I don't know, but if they really don't know any more than us, we can't assume anything. You could go mad thinking like that."

"And no news is good news," added Nigel, regretting the platitude as soon as it left his lips.

For a moment, Liz looked as if she was going to yell at him, then her face cracked, and a smile appeared.

"My mum always says that."

Nigel smiled in return, and Jenny squeezed Liz's hand.

"Thank you ... thank you both," she laughed. "And to think, we didn't know each other three days ago."

Their laughter broke the tension, and with it, they each drifted off into their own thoughts again. In contrast to Liz, Jenny's weren't just about David, but Nigel, her cats, and for some reason, the moles. *Why do they keep popping into my head?* she wondered. Nigel, on the other hand, ever one to be different, was wondering why the choices to have on top of gammon and chips, were either fried egg or pineapple. *OK so they always are, but why*[32]? he wondered. *It's like ordering corn flakes and being given the option of asparagus or ice cream with them. It's just too weird.*

He had no answer though, and as Jenny was the first to emerge from thought, she got up and went over to the counter.

"How was the food?" asked the owner.

"Excellent thanks. Are you on TripAdvisor?"

---

[32] Urban myth has it this is a 1970s thing whereas it really dates back to the 1490s when Christopher Columbus found remote Caribbean islanders using pineapples to soften up visitors to be human sacrifices. Why eggs are an alternative is anyone's guess, but you didn't have to risk getting eaten to find out, so don't complain.

"Sure. Search in Lossiemouth, and you'll find us easily enough."

"Will do. Look, I wonder if you can help us with something. We're on a bit of a road trip and need somewhere for the night."

"Well, there are a dozen or so hotels and plenty of Bed & Breakfast places. What sort of thing do you want?"

"Bed & Breakfast would be fine."

"How many rooms? Two? Three?"

"Three."

"OK, bear with me."

He picked up a small address book and started flicking through it. Stopping at *P*, he muttered a phone number to himself and dialled. A voice sounded in his ear.

"Hello Sally, it's Peter at the Happy Lobster. Look I've got some folks here who need somewhere for the night. Have you got three rooms?"

There was a short silence as the woman at the other end spoke. Then the owner of the *Happy Lobster Café* thanked her and put the phone down.

"You're all set," he said. "Mrs Pascoe at the *Waterview Guesthouse*. Go out the front of here and turn left. It's four doors down."

Jenny thanked him, paid the bill and the three of them headed outside. Fifteen yards later, they rang the doorbell to number 23, and before its chimes died away, the door opened. Mrs Pascoe was a slim woman with tied back blonde hair and a big smile. She looked at each of them in turn, weighing them up.

"Come on in," she said, "three rooms is it?"

Jenny answered for them all, and their host showed them upstairs. All three rooms lived up to the name of the guesthouse.

How long it usually took for emails like Liz's to get a response is anyone's guess, and in this case, as she and the others were settling into their rooms, the officers from the blue SUV were already on their way to Group Captain Finch's office. They were expected, and his assistant waved them right through.

"What have you got?" he snapped, hurriedly closing his laptop to hide the copy of *Golf Monthly* hidden inside.

"They don't appear to know anything, sir," said the man.

"Good. So nothing to worry about."

He was about to open his laptop again when the airman coughed. Finch looked up with annoyance.

"There may be something, sir. The man is his cousin, and one of the women is his fiancée."

"Hm. And the other?"

"Friend of the family I imagine, sir."

"She took quite an interest in me, sir," said the woman.

"How so?" asked Finch reluctantly.

"She couldn't take her eyes off me, sir. Didn't look to be paying attention to the other conversation at all."

"And when she did, she asked about you," said the man.

"Did she indeed? Now that's interesting. What did she say?"

"I said I couldn't tell them anything, and she asked if you could."

"So, what next?" asked Finch testily. He'd had enough of this conversation and wanted to get back to more important matters. Frankly, he could have done without the whole business.

"If they are who they say they are, sir," responded the woman, "we have a duty of care towards the fiancée at least."

"I gave them a card with the standard *Contact Us* address on it, sir," added the man. "We could wait. See if they try that."

There was a pause as Finch considered this.

"Fine. What about DCI Croft? I assume you saw him earlier?"

"Yes, sir. He knows the base has gone, so the local force has advised the locals to keep things to themselves and have someone on site 24/7."

"Anything else?"

"He wanted to know why we're interested, sir, so I gave him the standard line about us being nearer than the Met Office."

"And he bought that?"

"He seemed to, sir. He also indicated he believes he has jurisdiction over the whole business."

"True enough. Let me fill you in on a few things."

With this, Finch explained about the video conferences, and once the two officers had left him in peace, he happily reopened his laptop and went back to the article he'd been reading. It was about *The Old Course* at *Moray Golf Club* where he was a member, and he was so engrossed in it when his assistant came in forty minutes later, she had to cough twice to get his attention.

Located at the northern end of the Great Glen, where the rivers Ness and Moray join forces, sits Inverness. A lovely, cosmopolitan city, with a fabulous castle, cathedral, theatre, art galleries, and contemporary shopping mall ... In fact, everything you could ask of a modern city with a historic past.

In the offices of the *Northern Echo* (*Bringing world and local news to the people of the Highlands*), Erica McBride was scouring the web. Fair skinned, dark-eyed, and with hair the colour of an old-fashioned phone box, she was looking for weird stories to fill her weekly column. So far, she wasn't having much luck.

The previous week had been a good one with the piece about the tangoing penguins, and although she didn't know it yet, the following week would be incredible. But not so much the one in the middle. In fact, with a copy deadline to meet, she'd had to fall back onto an old favourite; strange things found on *Google Earth*.

Fortunately, images of alleged alien markings always went down well with her readers, not to mention the ever-popular, rude-shaped rock formations. That was all old news though, and this week's column, which she'd called *Marketing to Martians?* featured company logos that are visible from space.

She loved the freedom of doing *Erica's oddities*, not least because of its contrast to what she'd been recruited to do. That was covering births, marriages and deaths across the Highlands, and it had given her the start she needed in the newspaper business. Only the start though, and she'd suggested her own column just a few months after joining the *Northern Echo*. She was young, keen, and had snuck in *Erica's Oddities* as the column's title before anyone noticed. By the time she'd been told off for that though, readers were already responding in droves. The way she looked at it, the ordinary had started her off, and the extraordinary could help her take the next step.

The irony was, despite her career ambitions, she was one of those rare people who'd never wanted to leave her home town. In fact, apart from her honeymoon the previous year, she never had. In contrast, her wife had always been a keen traveller, and Erica was surprised at how much she was now looking forward to sharing the other's adventures. In fact, she was daydreaming about Bali and wondering *Where next?* when the email pinged into her inbox.

I say *the email* rather than *an email*, because unlike most, it was one of those few that make you sit up and pay attention. You know the sort of thing ... Maybe you got the concert tickets you wanted, your exam results came in, or perhaps you were accepted onto that fish-juggling course you'd applied for. Whatever generally counted as big for Erica though, this one was more than that. She didn't know it yet, but this one was going to change her life.

It was ironic then that she didn't spot it at first, and when she did, she only opened it out of habit. It was from the newsfeed her colleagues used to stay abreast of world events. Unlike them, her keywords were *Bizarre*, *Strange*, *Peculiar*, and *Custard*, although that last one had been put in as a joke by one of her co-workers the previous Christmas. Even so, with some of the hits she got from it, she'd wondered for a while whether she should expand her own search parameters. Especially after missing the story of the *Munich cheese disaster*. Still, there never seemed to be a shortage of weird stuff going on in the world, and she was generally happy with what came her way.

Today was no different either, as she knew the company logos would go down well with her readers. As she started to read the new email though, she wished she hadn't already submitted her copy. This was so much better.

The moles, you see, were getting used to their new environment, which, if you remember, was no longer in the East of England. Quite the opposite in fact, as they'd somehow managed to relocate 205 miles west, to the tiny island of Lundy[33].

---

[33] Only 3 miles long, and half a mile wide, Lundy sits in the Bristol Channel, 12 miles from North Devon and twice that from South Wales. All three are lovely places, but even so, it's hardly where you'd expect moles to go on holiday. Then again, moles don't generally get out much, so it's probably as good as anywhere.

Its size is irrelevant, mind you, because it has ten times as many puffins as people, and puffins are one of the coolest birds around.

They're cute in a clownish sort of way, with bright orange beaks and feet, both of which contrast nicely with the stylish black and white of their plumage. OK so their large feet make it hard for them to land on a breezy day, and their over-sized beaks are a bit of an issue in crosswinds, but nobody's perfect.

Puffins aren't alone on Lundy either, as it's well-known for being a sanctuary for wildlife in general. Even so, the island's warden had been amazed when molehills started appearing across the landscape. Nowhere near as surprised though as the island's pygmy shrew population. After all, with moles growing to over six inches long, compared to a pygmy shrew at under two, from their perspective, it was as if the island had been invaded by tunnelling hippos.

Erica read the article with growing interest and hadn't finished the first paragraph before she was picking up the phone to call her editor.

"I'm sorry, Erica, but it's already gone to print," was his reply. "It'll wait till next week, won't it?"

After the long drive north, not to mention the disappointing visit to the base, Liz, in particular, could have been forgiven for wanting to take a nap. Like Nigel and Jenny though, she felt the need for fresh air instead, and after only a few minutes to drop their bags off, they all stepped back out into the sunshine.

Liz and Jenny headed into town, and as they set off, they fell into an easy conversation. Jenny had been looking for an opportunity to talk with Liz since their first meeting and Liz was happy to chat. Soon they were engrossed, discovering quite how much they had in common.

Nigel, meanwhile, walked east towards Lossiemouth's two marinas. He'd liked the look of the town as they'd driven in, and as he wandered through the narrow streets, it grew on him more and more. The pale, granite buildings had a friendly feel to them, and their dark slate roofs added to the effect.

Next, he passed a handful of shops and finally found himself walking across the low, wooden footbridge to the East Beach. It was fabulous. Wide, deserted, hardly any breeze, and with a sky that was simply huge. The temperature seemed a little milder now as well. He could forget moles, cousins, and everything else in a place like this. Not Jenny though, and when his phone woke him a while later, it was her usual friendly tones on the other end.

"Where the hell are you?"

"What? Eh? Oh sorry, I was just ... No, wait a minute," he stammered as wakefulness slowly returned.

"You were asleep, weren't you?" she asked in a softer voice.

"Maybe," he answered sheepishly.

"Where are you?"

"On the East Beach, it's fabulous. Why don't you come over? It's only a twenty-minute walk."

"What time's sunset?"

"Dunno. Half seven-ish?"

"Alright, we'll be right over."

He ended the call and lay back on the sand. As he did, the rustling of the marram grass and the gentle murmur of the waves filled his mind again, and it wasn't long before sleep returned.

A while later he became aware of familiar voices nearby and came half-awake long enough to give a grunt of welcome before he dropped off once more. He might have been prone to insomnia at night, but daytime napping was yet another of his core skills, and in a place as relaxing as this, it was easy.

The three of them had the beach to themselves until almost dark when they walked back into town. Halfway back to the guesthouse, they stopped outside an Indian restaurant and scanned the menu. It looked nice enough, and pretty cheap too, so Jenny pushed open the door, and they went in.

They were greeted by the sound of raucous laughter from a birthday party at a long table on their right. As they went to sit down, the other thing they noticed was the decor, which unlike the dark, patterned wallpaper of many such places, was surprisingly light and contemporary. The seats were comfortable too, and they were soon dipping popadoms into the usual array of sauces, as they waited for their entrées to arrive.

While they ate, they revisited the question of what to do next. The consensus was that there was nothing to be gained from staying in Lossiemouth for the sake of it. Even Liz agreed with that, although she still couldn't completely silence a nagging thought about the email. *What if they left, and then she got a reply?* As Nigel pointed out though, by that logic, they could stay there forever.

 This time, when TC woke up back at college, she knew immediately where she was. She also knew exactly what to do next. She pulled out her iPhone, opened *Photos* and there they were ... Oak units in one picture, and a black kitten in the other.

And that was how realization began. TC didn't understand it yet, and still had a feeling she might wake up in an asylum at some stage, but that wasn't the point. Whatever was happening, it didn't need her to understand it in order to keep going, and by the look of things, it wasn't going to stop anytime soon.

How many other worlds are there? she wondered one day the following summer. *The one with the tree and the root beer ... The one with the cat and the oak kitchen ... Were there others too?* There were, of course, dozens of them, but she remembered some more clearly than others.

Then a couple of months later, everything changed again. The first giveaway was that her bedroom had different wallpaper. The next was that her dad had a beard, and the third was that the cat was now a dog. A large friendly one, but a dog nonetheless. Oh, and the kitchen was a different design altogether.

Luckily, by now, she no longer got as freaked out as she had the first few times. Even so, realizing she was in yet another world was always disorientating. As it happened though, *Fate* had a less devious sense of humour in this one, and she'd not been up long before the doorbell rang. When she answered it, there stood Sue.

"Oh wow what a lovely surprise," said TC happily, pulling her childhood friend towards her.

"That was nice," smiled Sue when they eventually pulled apart. "You wouldn't think we only saw each other last night."

"Oh yes, well ..." began TC as she rapidly pulled her thoughts together. "I'm just pleased to see you."

Sue smiled. "Are you ready?"

"Ready?"

"Shopping ... Our girly shopping day?"

"Oh, of course," replied TC, hoping she sounded convincing. "I'll get a coat."

Forty minutes later they'd parked and were heading for the first shop of the day. Sue was looking for a dress for her and Simon's anniversary meal on the weekend. Over the next few hours, they wandered around a succession of clothes shops, until needing a break, they headed for a little coffee place they both liked. Latte in hand (with cake for TC of course), Sue ran through the dresses she'd liked. The ordinariness of the situation was comforting, and TC was starting to feel at ease when the question came.

"Are you all right babe? You don't seem yourself today."

"Yes, I'm fine," said TC a little too quickly.

"Are you sure?" persisted her friend. This time TC paused before answering.

"I'm OK. Just a little out of sorts."

"Oh, you should've said. I bet the last thing you need is to be dragged around the shops."

"No, it's nice to get out."

"Well as long as you're sure ..."

"I am," said TC decisively. "So come on. Which one are you going to get?"

"The blue one, I think."

"The strappy one in the first shop?"

Sue laughed at this. "Don't tell Simon. He always says I walk the whole High Street before ending up back where I started."

They laughed, and two days later were back in town with five other friends at a small Italian restaurant. It was six years since Sue and Simon had got together, although the two women had been friends for much longer than that. As the evening came to a close, Sue took TC on one side, and giving her a goodnight hug, she whispered in her friend's ear ...

"Thanks ever so for coming babe. I'll be round in the morning, and you can tell me all about it."

First answers?

Wednesday, September 15th

In Whitehall, Westminster, Lossiemouth and Inverness, four video-conference screens beeped and blinked into life. It was 8:30 and time for the daily call.

"Good morning, gentleman. Where are we, Director?"

"We've taken a big step forwards, Minister. We now have three specialists on site, six local Scene of Crime Officers and a Crime Scene Manager. Plus two police constables to keep prying eyes away."

"You're happy with all that I take it Detective Chief Inspector?"

"Very much so, sir. The whole thing has come together well, although, with all the activity, some additional people would help keep the situation under wraps. Perhaps the RAF officer in the village could assist?"

"Group Captain?"

"Actually, I've had to recall him, but I can send over a replacement if you want."

"Two would be better."

"Fair enough. I'll send the officers you met yesterday, and your people can liaise with them directly."

The investigation was gathering pace.

Meanwhile, underground, it was time for David Marston's daily meeting with his top team.

"Doug?"

"Thank you, sir. First of all, I want to express my thanks to the engineering teams for getting us to where we are. We've got power, lights, and internal comms, so we're operating largely as normal."

"Quite right too" ... "I agree" ... "Yes, excellent work" chimed the others.

"As we know though, external comms systems are still down. I've had teams working on them round the clock, and there's no easy way of saying this, but we're still stuck for answers."

All those present knew how hard Doug's team had been working, and although his statement came as no surprise in itself, it was unusual to hear anyone in that forum say something so final.

"What next, then Doug?" asked Marston calmly.

"As you know, sir, we've got dedicated comms circuits coming in from Inverness, and a duplicate of the same capacity via satellite, so we can keep everything running even if one route fails completely. Plus we've got the public 4G network as well, which by itself could keep us running at about 75% of normal. With me so far?"

There was a murmur of assent around the room.

"Well we've checked everything, and electrically it's all OK.

The question is, why can't we communicate outside?"

"And what's the answer."

"There you've got me I'm afraid, sir, but with the lockdown over in a few minutes, we can do five things. We can test the landlines, the satellite circuits and the mobiles. We can also turn the Air Traffic Control cameras back on, and we can go outside. I confess, comms aside I'll be pleased to get some fresh air if nothing else."

"I know what you mean," smiled Marston. "I take it you've got all that ready to go?"

"We have, sir. I just need your OK."

Marston looked at his watch; it was 8:58.

"Make the call Doug."

Doug Smoke hit the familiar pattern of keys on the conference phone. The call had barely connected when Jim Waynes' voice came on.

"100 seconds and counting Jim," said Smoke. "Send everything at zero nine hundred as planned."

"Right, sir, I'll come back to you."

The line went dead.

"He really is brisk," smiled Marston. "I guess all we can do now is wait."

Waiting wasn't one of Erica McBride's strengths, and although only a day had passed since she'd found out about the moles, she was keen to get on just the same. Which is why on this particular day she was busy gathering background to take to her editor. She aimed to convince him to let her run an exclusive article.

One of the things Erica liked most about her job was the way she could do it from anywhere with Wi-Fi. Despite that, she rarely did so from home because her wife worked shifts as a paramedic, and when Erica didn't fancy the office, she generally headed for the city's covered Victorian Market. It was a place she'd always liked, partly because of the fond memories she had of her father taking her as a child. Then, the attraction had been the old-fashioned sweetshops, with their rows of glass jars, whereas these days, it was the artisan jewellery stores where she tended to loiter. So much so, she and her wife had bought their wedding rings in one of them the previous year. On days like this though, her destination was the small café at the end of the market where it joins into Academy Street.

She often went there because she liked the quiet buzz of the place, and best of all, it had fast, free Wi-Fi. She set her coffee down on a window table and slung off her backpack. Inside were her laptop, a few loose papers, a spiral notepad and some pens. In a side pocket were five pear drops that had glued themselves together since she'd last looked. She opened the laptop and the notepad.

The next thing she did was to check for any updates about Lundy. There were none. She was surprised the story hadn't made its way into the national press as a funny filler for one of the inside pages. This was ideal for her though because if it stayed that way, she could break the news herself. As a journalist, she had a great many skills, and her specialism was tracking down every detail of even the most obscure stories.

She put on her headphones and turned on her music. For some reason, when she was researching, it was almost always to the accompaniment of Michael Bublé, and today was no exception.

It didn't take many tracks before she found what she was looking for; the name of the warden on Lundy who had reported the moles. She jotted it down along with his email address, and phone number. After a few more minutes research, she dialled the number, and just as she thought it was going to voicemail, it answered.

"Hello Landmark Trust, Lundy Island," said a slightly breathless voice.

"Oh hello, is that the warden?"

"Speaking."

"Oh, great. Look, my name's Erica McBride, I'm a journalist, and I'm interested in a piece I've seen about moles appearing on the island?"

"Really? I wouldn't have thought it a big enough story for the national press."

She didn't correct him, and over the next few minutes, asked question after question until she found out what she wanted … The moles had first appeared on the island on Friday the 10th of September."

"Well, that's Lundy," she said to herself once she'd put the phone down. "The next thing is to find an expert on moles." She googled *Mole expert*, and after refining the search to get rid of hints about skin conditions, she scanned down the list of options. Most were for exterminators, but after a few minutes, she came across a link that looked promising … *Cambridge University, Faculty of Biology.*

Skimming through the site, she tried the *For students* page first, then on a side menu, she spotted a link to *Specialist areas.* At the top of the list was Professor Elizabeth Benning, and her specialism was listed as: *Burrowing habits, and behaviour prediction of true moles.*

She wondered what true moles were as opposed to ordinary ones. It sounded like some sort of religious cult. There was a contact number for the faculty at the bottom of the page, so Erica picked up her phone again and dialled.

It rang a couple of times before an automated message cut in saying the call was being diverted. A few seconds later ... "Hello, this is Professor Benning. Please leave a message after the tone."

Erica hadn't planned what to say, so she kept it brief: "Hello Professor Benning, my name's Erica McBride. I'm a journalist in Inverness, and I'd be grateful if you'd give me a call when you can please."

She left her number and left it at that.

As she did, DI Hendricks' Land Rover drew up alongside the two constables on duty in Glen Crian. Ranged across the valley were nine figures in white and one in a muddy version of what had once been white. The boffin had been arguing with the landscape, and was already on his second pair of wellington boots, as he'd lost one of the first pair in a boggy patch.

The SOCO team was well into its task by now too and had already finished going over much of the terrain with a metal detector and a multi-filter crime-lite. They'd also filled numerous evidence bags with soil and vegetation specimens from across the site, as well as taking two samples of the stream water, one from the northern end of the site and one from the southern. Each container had then been secured with its own numbered tag and placed into one of the Croc boxes they'd brought along. They'd also made a cast of a section of the gravel track. It showed where the track ended and was still in its casting frame while the plaster dried.

"Afternoon gentlemen," said Hendricks, getting out of the vehicle.

"Afternoon, m'm."

"Everyone's looks busy."

"Yes, m'm. Seven of ours and three up from London."

"And the folks from the RAF?"

"The new ones arrived a little after 11 o'clock, m'm, and stayed until midday, so I imagine they're back at the hotel."

"Thank you, Constable. When are you both on until?"

"Nine tonight, m'm."

"Do you need anything?"

"No, we're fine thank you, m'm."

"Well, keep up the good work."

With that, she drove back to Crianloch, where she found who she was looking for in the bar of *The Shepherd's Arms*, having a late lunch. The waiter recognised her from the community meeting, and she ordered a cappuccino. While it was being made, she walked over to the two officers and introduced herself. She explained she was there in her capacity as the overall officer in charge and sat chatting while she waited for her coffee to arrive. They all hedged around the subject of the glen for a while before Hendricks decided to take the bull by the horns.

"Look, I know my boss is talking with your boss, but mine won't tell me anything more than that, so what about you?" This was a lie of course, but Finch's laissez-faire attitude hadn't endeared him to Croft, and he'd asked Hendricks to surreptitiously find out as much as she could.

"I'm afraid we're bound by the *Official Secrets Act* not to divulge anything," said the man, for whom being unhelpful was clearly a speciality.

"As am I," said Hendricks evenly. "But we're working on the same case, so I thought some low-level information sharing might be in order."

The man looked at his colleague. She pursed her lips and nodded.

"What do you know?" asked the man.

"I know there used to be a weather station up the road and there isn't anymore. I also know the village is a buzz of speculation about you lot. So why is the RAF interested?"

The woman stepped in with her stock answer, and unlike DCI Croft who had noticed a slight pause, DI Hendricks was struck by how quickly the reply came. Too quickly? Hendricks wasn't sure, and after mulling over the question for a minute or two, she concluded that either they didn't know any more than she did, or they were very talented at hiding things. Something told her it was the latter, and on the drive back to Drumnadrochit, two words kept rattling around in her head. The words were *Conspiracy* and *Cover-up*.

As these words took root in Hendricks' mind, Nigel, Jenny and Liz were already well past Tebay Services, heading south. In an unusually kind twist of *Fate*, Liz's car had started first time too. There was some debate about whether it was wise for her to attempt the journey after the previous one, but Liz preferred the risk to waiting for another service truck. So there they all were, none the wiser from their trip to Scotland, and having to retreat for the time being.

Luckily Liz's car didn't misbehave, and stopping in on David's Gran meant she had a slightly shorter drive than going straight home, so it all worked out. Even so, it was still almost eight in the evening by the time she got to Wensbridge. It had rained the whole way too, so had been especially tiring. She also couldn't shake the feeling she'd somehow let David down by leaving Lossiemouth.

It wasn't the way the two of them had talked of her first meeting with his grandmother, but these were strange times, so Liz had to make do. Plus, Nigel had promised Gran that Liz would drop in, so she had to go through with it. Liz turned off the car engine, locked the doors, and walked up to the bungalow. She rang the bell and half a second later, the door was flung open. Gran stood there, smiling.

"That's the last time you ever do that," said the old woman by way of greeting, pulling Liz into her arms.

What she meant was that her door was always unlocked, and she expected family members to walk straight in. As the two of them stood locked in a warm embrace of welcome and understanding, Liz somehow sensed that. Once they let one another go, they each took a step back.

"David's done all right for himself," smiled Gran, brushing the back of her hand against Liz's cheek. "Come on in dear, you must be exhausted."

"I'm so sorry we didn't find out anything," said Liz when they were seated in the lounge.

"Don't be silly. You want to know what's happened to him even more than me I expect. I just hope you understand an old woman being worried."

"Of course, Mrs ... err? I'm sorry, but what do I call you?"

"People generally call me Gran, so how about you do too."

"Thank you," smiled Liz.

"Well come along, dear. I'll make us some coffee, or is it tea?"

"Coffee please, Gran."

"Coffee it is. I'll bring some biscuits too. I want to hear all about it ... and all about you. I can tell you my news too. You're not my first visitor about David today, you know."

She left that statement hanging as she walked towards the doorway.

"Not the first?"

"Oh no, I had a delightful lady from RAF Wyton come to the front door this afternoon."

By the time the others reached Penmound, they'd been on the road for well over ten hours, and Jenny was beyond exhausted. They, therefore, parted company on her driveway, and as Nigel walked home, he occupied his mind with thoughts of the dinner he was going to cook for Jenny the following evening. It was his way of thanking her for not making him drive.

As he walked into his cottage, the first thing that struck him was the amount of post he'd accumulated. The second thing that struck him was the oak beam above the kitchen doorway. It was the perfect height for him to crack his forehead on, and he swayed backwards.

"Blast!"

Plainly, people had been a lot shorter in the 17th century. Then again, it was his own silly fault for buying the house in the first place. Rubbing his head, he ducked down and went into the kitchen to make some tea.

Finding a packet of fruit shortcake biscuits that were only a little out of date, he took his tea through to the living room and started sorting through his post. One DIY catalogue, two double-glazing fliers, several holiday brochures, three letters addressed to *The Occupier*, an assortment of other junk and a free sample of shampoo. Not exactly a bumper crop. He threw it all away, pondered briefly on the fate of the rainforests, and looked around the room.

He brought up the *Sonos* app on his phone and selected *Born and Raised* by John Mayer. As often happened, he heard it start playing in his study upstairs, so hurriedly changed the room settings, and sat down. He leant back in his armchair, and as he did, he felt a wave of tiredness wash over him. The next thing he knew, it was half-past two in the morning.

"Oh, not again," he muttered.

Turning off the music and the lights, he headed upstairs to bed, carefully missing all other beams on the way. Out of habit more than anything else, he even avoided the pile of washing, which still sat stubbornly on the landing. In the shadowy darkness, it seemed to be daring him to do something about it.

When Jenny got home, hers was a different, and much shorter, routine, starting with checking to make sure her neighbour had left enough food out for Tommy and Tuppence. She had ... and some. With that done, and now feeling thoroughly shattered, she went upstairs. It was lucky she had a recurring alarm set on her phone, as she fell asleep the instant her head hit the pillow.

In contrast with either Nigel or Jenny, Steve Guthrie's evening had been somewhat unusual, as not having heard from Liz, he'd decided earlier in the day to take things into his own hands. He'd therefore blocked out his calendar for the following day as *On-site*, made a short visit to the university's archaeology department, and set off for Effington.

When he pulled into the car park at *The Spotted Pig*, the first person he saw was Dot. She was watering the hanging baskets outside the pub.

"Do you do everything around here?" he asked cheerily,

getting out of his car.

She turned around.

"Oh hi, Steve, what brings you here? You know Liz isn't around don't you."

"Yes, I've got some stuff to do out at site myself. I don't suppose you've got a room for the night, have you?"

"Sure. Give me a chance to finish off here, and I'll be right with you."

Steve took his bag from the passenger seat and followed her in. As he entered the bar, a game of darts stopped, and he became aware of four heads turning to look at him. He'd seen a re-run of *An American Werewolf in London* a few weeks before and remembered the scene where the pub fell silent as the two strangers walked in. Thankfully, the eyes on him now were more curious than wary. Plus, there aren't any werewolves in this story, so he was safe enough.

"The one night, Steve?" asked Dot, interrupting his thoughts.

"Yes please, Dot. Dinner if you can too please."

As quickly as the locals had turned to look at him, they lost interest and went back to their game. Evidently being on first name terms with the landlady eliminated him as an object of suspicion. What it also did, was open him up to more friendly scrutiny, and as he re-entered the bar after dropping his bag upstairs, he was greeted by one of the darts players.

"Steve, is it?"

Somewhat taken aback, Steve answered in the affirmative.

"You play?"

"Sorry?"

"Darts."

"Oh. Not very well, I'm afraid."

"S'alright, we ain't that great, 'cept Old Charlie there."

Old Charlie, it turned out, was in his mid-30s, and Young Charlie was almost 80. That left the man who'd welcomed him, who was in the middle somewhere, and a lad who didn't look old enough to be allowed in the pub. Ages aside, darts turned out to be a bonding experience, and apart from when Steve stopped for dinner, they played until well after closing time.

By that time, they were firm friends, and the other players went so far as to invite him to join their team. He declined on the grounds of distance, but that didn't stop them from insisting, and if anything, they seemed even keener. Steve was touched, although if he'd understood why, he might not have felt so flattered. Why? Because the rules of the local league stated that if a team repeatedly had to field four rather than five players, its handicap improved. So, whether Steve was there or not was OK with them. He didn't know that though and went off to bed smiling. Before dropping off, he checked his email and sent an update to Seismic Dynamics.

Hi Grant
I've not heard back from the Prof' yet, so I'm visiting the site myself.
I'll be there in the morning and will send you an invite for a call later in the day, so we can discuss findings.
Cheers, Steve

 TC hadn't known what to think when Sue said she'd be round the following morning. What did she know? How could she know anything? These and a dozen other questions whirled around TCs mind as she had breakfast, and when ten-fifteen came, the doorbell rang.

Her parents had gone out by this time, and TC led Sue through to the kitchen. She put tea bags in two mugs and absent-mindedly poured cold water over them. Then with a small, embarrassed laugh, TC refilled the kettle and tried again.

Sue was TCs oldest friend unless you count 76-year-old Jean in the newspaper shop, so being nervous was silly, but she was. They went through to the living room, sat down, and after an obligatory bite of cake, TC began.

"About what you said last night ..."

"I thought that might be playing on your mind, babe."

"Well, I wondered ..."

Sue reached across and took her hand. "Oh, you're trembling. Whatever's the matter?"

"It's nothing."

"Come on, how long have we known each other?"

"I don't know, sixteen years?"

"Since the first day of kindergarten, we were both three."

"Eighteen then."

"Look, I know you, and something's not right. You've not been yourself since we went shopping the other day."

Interesting, thought TC. *So I was OK before that? But I wasn't here before that!*

"TC?"

"Eh?"

"You drifted off somewhere."

"Oh, sorry."

TC hadn't drifted as such, but she'd suddenly realised how much she needed to talk about everything and was wondering what to say next. Sue had reached out to her though, so how hard could it be? She took a deep breath ...

"What was I like before we went shopping, Sue? The day before, say?"

"What do you mean?"

"Humour me, Sue. What was I like?"

"You were you," shrugged Sue.

"But what is that? What am I like normally?"

Sue stared at her friend and frowned. TC was sounding increasingly anxious, and she was obviously being serious, so Sue decided to indulge her.

"Well, you're a smiley, not a care in the world sort of person. Glass is half full, that kind of thing."

Now TC's expression reflected Sue's from a moment before.

"And recently? The last few months say?"

"Same as always. Look, what's going on?"

TC thought about that for a minute. Part of her felt her best option was to keep saying everything was fine. Another part of her was wondering whether she should come clean, even though that would patently be a bad idea. As her brain told her that though, her mouth decided the opposite, and she started to speak.

"The thing is, I don't belong here."

"Whatever do you mean? You love it here."

"It's not that. I just belong somewhere else."

"Sorry, you've lost me."

"I should be at college."

"Oh babe, I thought you were over all that. You never went because your mum wasn't well. But she's fine now, you're happy at work, and you've got great friends. I just need to set you up with a boyfriend, and you're sorted."

TC burst into tears.

Sue didn't know what to say, and when she reached out, TC fell into her arms. *What on earth prompted that?* wondered Sue.

Some minutes later, TC stopped crying and dried her eyes. She couldn't face Sue again yet though, so she stood up and went over to the window. She gazed unseeingly through the glass at her mother's prize roses, now cut back to nothing for the winter. TC started to speak, and Sue stayed quiet as the floodgates opened, only this time as much out of shock as concern.

TC told her about her own world, the death of her boyfriend, and about the dreams she'd been having. She told her about the *McDonald's* receipt, the photographs, the changing kitchens and everything. Once she'd said it all, she turned and walked back to the sofa.

"So, this is all like a dream to you?" asked Sue at last.

"Everywhere feels totally real when I'm there, so I don't know. I think I'm losing my mind, Sue."

Sue pulled TC to her again. She didn't cry this time, but simply rested her head against her friend's shoulder, and as she did, a thought started to form at the back of Sue's mind.

It was an impossible thought, and as it took shape, Sue began to doubt herself. *It couldn't be. That was crazy!* The idea wouldn't budge though and what was more annoying, was that she couldn't remember where she'd heard it. Was it something Simon had told her? Or had she picked it up from one of the science programmes he was always watching? She thought it might be the latter, but she wasn't sure. Maybe a podcast?

Sue took her phone from her bag and rang Simon's number. Then giving TCs shoulder a reassuring squeeze, she walked through the kitchen. She didn't want her friend to overhear the conversation.

"Hey Hun," she began. "Sorry to disturb you at work but I need your help with something. I'm with TC, and we got into some science stuff when ..."

Simon obviously interrupted at this point because Sue stopped in mid-sentence. He'd repeatedly tried and failed to interest her in his favourite subject over the years, so his reaction was hardly unexpected.

"Yes, I know love," resumed Sue, "but tell me about parallel worlds."

Judging by his exclamation, this touched still more of a nerve, as even from the other room, TC could hear the excitement in his voice.

Sue spent the next few minutes calming him down, and while she still had him on the hook, she moved on to persuading him to come over. He protested a first, but she slowly won him round, and 45 minutes later, the doorbell rang. Sue answered it, leaving TC on the sofa. She could hear the two of them whispering in the hall before they came through into the lounge.

"Hi, TC," said Simon. "I gather you've become something of an inter-dimensional traveller."

She looked at him. He was obviously taking the piss.

"Don't be flippant," glared Sue. "This is serious."

"Sorry, love. It's ..."

"It's alright," said TC in a quiet voice. "I know I must seem crazy to both of you."

"Of course not, babe. Look, if you're up to it, how about telling Simon everything you told me?"

So TC did. She told him everything she'd told Sue and more besides.

"The receipt and the cat photos?" he asked when she'd done.

She took out her phone and showed him.

"Even the kitchen's different."

"I really think I'm losing it, Simon."

"Well that isn't like you at all," he replied kindly.

"You believe me?" she asked incredulously.

"I can't say I do ... but I'm not sure I don't either."

"Simon," scolded Sue.

"I'm sorry love, but it's a lot to absorb."

He was unwilling to commit himself, while at the same time, he understood now why Sue had called him, and the seed of an idea was already germinating in his mind. Simon knew one thing for sure; he needed time to think.

"Oh, and I've never been to the same world twice," added TC.

"How many are there?"

"To be honest, I've lost count. Half a dozen? A dozen? Oh, I don't know."

TC's voice got higher as she said this, and instinctively, Sue took one of her hands in hers.

Simon, meanwhile, paused for a moment, then with a sudden decisive movement, he stood up.

"Either of you fancy another drink?" he asked.

"Of course," managed TC, wiping her nose and going to stand. "What would you like?"

"Let me," said Simon. "You two can chat. Both white coffee, no sugar?"

The two women nodded, and Simon left the room.

TC raised a questioning eyebrow.

"It's nothing personal babe," replied Sue. "It's just his way of getting some thinking space."

It was an interesting choice of words, as Simon might work for an insurance company, but at heart, he was a rocket scientist. Not literally perhaps, as he'd not had the grades for university, but that had only spurred him on, and these days his understanding of physics was impressive - Quantum physics in particular.

He'd read all the masters ... Planck, Bohr, Feynman, Heisenberg, Schrödinger and just for fun, Chad Orzel's brilliant *How to Teach Quantum Physics to Your Dog*. He'd even tried some of that one on his cat, but it hadn't been interested. After all, physics vs playing with invisible floaty things? I know what I'd do if I was a cat.

Anyway, as Simon made the coffees, he reflected on what he'd just heard. He'd always been a fan of Everett's many-worlds theory of parallel worlds[34], which was presumably why Sue had remembered it. And with what TC had said, the seed in his mind had taken root and started to grow. First, it was like a tiny shoot, then the size of something you see in a garden centre, and by the time the kettle had boiled, it was a fully-grown tree. A tree that stretched into the unknown, leaving the past behind in its roots, and reaching out its branches towards any number of possible futures.

Why was he such a fan of the many-worlds theory? Partly because it explained so much that others didn't. Partly too because it meant there were lots of versions of him running around the cosmos, and he rather liked the idea of that. Heck, there should even be one where he'd gone to university and ended up as a celebrity astrophysicist. There was a snag though. According to Everett, all parallel worlds occupy the same time and space as each other, and there's no way between them. So where did that leave TC?

He wasn't sure yet, but even Stephen Hawking's final paper had talked about multiple worlds, so Simon figured there had to be something in it. Admittedly, Hawking hadn't spoken of them in quite the

---

[34] Hugh Everett published his original hypothesis in 1957, and over the next two decades, it was popularised and renamed *Many-worlds* by Bryce Seligman DeWitt.

same way as Everett, but that last paper of his had still asked whether multiple universes might actually be a lot more similar than people had thought.

I paraphrase of course, but however you look at it, space is a funny old place. Impossibly big and absurdly weird, but also oddly familiar and strangely repetitive. It was for this reason that Simon had always been drawn to the many-worlds theory, and why, when TC described her experiences, it had felt so right.

When Simon finished making the coffees, he took them through to the others. They looked at him expectantly, and in the silence that followed, he explained Everett as best he could. He wasn't sure it didn't all sound like something out of *Star Trek*, and by the time he finished, their coffees had gone cold. The silence had changed too, from expectant to stunned.

"What are you saying?" began TC. "That I'm somehow flicking between these different worlds? Come on, Simon."

"Well, it fits."

"It fits with you being off your head!"

"But what about the photographs?" asked Sue.

In the heat of the moment, TC had forgotten about them. She went quiet as she ran over the details of the different places in her mind again. *In her mind? Places?* She thought of that quote from Sherlock Holmes about after having eliminated everything that made sense, whatever was left had to be true[35].

"So, if I really am jumping about as you say, and I'm not saying I believe you; why's it happening? *How's* it happening for that matter?

Simon paused before answering.

"Well, the way I look at it; either you're real and your experiences

---

[35] The original quote, *Once you eliminate the impossible, whatever remains, no matter how improbable, must be the truth* comes not from one of the well-known Holmes stories, but from *The Adventure of the Beryl Coronet*, published by Conan Doyle in 1892.

are too. Or you're in a dream, which means Sue, and I don't exist, and I don't much like the idea of that."

"So, what if I'm really here, and all the other places are dreams?"

"We'd be back to the photos again."

"Oh, good point. So let's say they're not dreams."

"OK."

"But they're these parallel worlds of yours."

"Wait a minute," cut in Sue, "even if they exist, Simon said it wouldn't be possible to move between them."

"Yet here I am."

"And what about the *you* who was here until this week? What's happened to her?"

TC had never thought of that, and she suddenly felt a pang of compassion for this other self of hers. What if they'd somehow swapped places, and the other one had ended up in TCs world? Imagine waking up in self-imposed isolation after the death of a loved one you didn't know. She shuddered.

"So, ignoring the possibility that none of this is real ... the options are that one of the places I'm in is real and everywhere else is a dream ... or they're all separate versions of real which I'm somehow jumping between."

"Sounds kinda funky when you put it like that," said Sue with a smile.

"But how do I do it?" asked TC.

As responses go, Simon's "I've no idea," was an understatement along the lines of Apollo 13's "Houston, we've had a problem[36]. Mind you, if any of them had known how it was really happening, they'd never have believed it.

They didn't though, and by the following day, it didn't matter.

---

[36] Jack Swigert's famous quote, erroneously attributed to Jim Lovell in the film *Apollo 13*, is often given as "Houston, we have a problem," but that is actually a misquote.

This time was different too because rather than snapping back to her room at college as she had every other time, TC found herself in yet another parallel world. And that was only the beginning, for over the next eight years, she found herself jumping between hundreds of different worlds. Still, never the same one twice and all as alike as each other, yet just as different as the one before. People were similar, places were sometimes identical, and literature still followed the seven basic plots[37], but music ... music differed wildly. *Disco*, for example, existed everywhere. What we called *House*, on the other hand, sounded like something from the 1930s in one world, and *Punk* in another, sounded like what we call *Country*.

In fact, the only truly consistent thing was cake. It existed everywhere, and better still, it tasted the same everywhere. Indeed, it was about the only thing that kept TC sane. OK so Carrot cake always tasted a bit weird, and Battenberg always looked like it was imitating the side of a police car[38], but all the good things were there too. Like lemon drizzle cake and of course, raspberry and white chocolate muffins. Call it comfort food if you like, but you try jumping between parallel worlds for almost a decade without losing your mind if you haven't got something to hold onto.

In short, cake is important.

---

[37] According to journalist and author, Christopher Booker, there are only seven basic plots in the world, and these are used repeatedly in books, plays and films alike. They are: 1. Overcoming the Monster, 2. Rags to Riches, 3. The Quest, 4. Voyage and Return, 5. Rebirth, 6. Comedy and 7. Tragedy. Your homework is to work out which one this book is.
[38] Bizarrely perhaps, the high-visibility checkerboard designs on the side of UK police cars are called *Battenberg markings*.

The thing about coincidences
Thursday, September 16th

At a quarter to eight, Jenny woke from one of those dreams that feel so real you don't know where you are at first. In this case, it had the added annoyance of her not being able to remember any of it. This bugged her, and when her alarm went off, she hit *snooze*. The dream wouldn't come back to her though, and the more she tried to remember it, the more it receded into the distance. After snoozing the alarm for a second time, she reluctantly got out of bed.

On the way to work, she thought about her neighbour. The woman didn't believe in dry cat food and apparently felt that giving twice the quantity made up for its deficiencies. Jenny suspected she even put food out all year round, so the previous summer, she'd put a label on each cats' collar to discourage her. They read: *Please don't feed me, I'm on a special diet.* They still put on weight though, and the trip to Scotland had reminded her of all this, so with a grunt, she decided enough was enough. She'd buy an automated feeder.

In contrast, Liz's day started with a nudge, and as her eyes flew open, she let out a squeak.

"Oh, I'm so sorry." she blurted out.

"Good morning, my dear," smiled Gran.

"Whatever must you think of me?"

"I think you're a charming young lady who stopped in to see her fiancé's grandmother after driving all the way from Scotland."

"And you put a duvet over me too!" said Liz, looking down at herself.

Liz was lying on the sofa, with David's grandmother standing next to her, holding a cup of coffee.

"Don't make such a fuss, dear. It's nice to have a young person in the house, and I'd have hated for you to fall asleep on your way home."

"So I dropped off here instead. Oh, tell me you weren't talking at the time."

Gran smiled her most reassuring smile. "It was while I was in the kitchen fetching coffee."

Then it all came back to Liz. She hadn't told Gran anything at all and had fallen asleep within minutes after arriving.

"Anyway, time to get up, I think," continued Gran "and you can tell me everything over breakfast. I've put a towel out for you in the bathroom."

Liz fetched her overnight bag from the car and after a quick shower, joined Gran in the dining room. Then as she'd meant to the night before, she took her through everything that had happened so far.

"And you think the RAF doesn't know where David is

either?" asked Gran once Liz had finished.

"I'm not sure, but it does make an odd kind of sense."

"And it might explain my visit yesterday."

"Oh yes, I'd completely forgotten about that. What happened?"

"Nothing very much to be honest. An officer came to the door, nice lady too, and asked me some questions about when I'd last spoken with David. Then she left."

"Did she tell you anything?"

"Not a thing. She just gave me this."

Gran opened the battered old dictionary she used as a sort of filing cabinet and pulled out a business card. It was the same as the one Liz had been given in Lossiemouth.

For Nigel, the day started much more peacefully than it had for either Jenny or Liz. Tea came first, then breakfast, and after that, he went online in search of news about David. There wasn't any. He also looked for any updates on the moles, but again, nothing. What now? He tried to do some writing, but it felt odd being back home after their whirlwind trip to Scotland, and he couldn't settle.

He tried music, online *Scrabble* and yet more tea, then for want of anything better to do, he turned his attention to the packet of Hobnobs on his desk. Each biscuit contained 299kj/71kcal of energy, but how far would that take him? Downstairs? To the garage? Or was it only enough to scratch that itch on the end of his nose? Whatever the answer, it didn't help his mood, so he decided to go for a cycle ride instead. He enjoyed an occasional bike ride, but it meant braving the shed, which was never something for the faint-hearted. For a start, he wasn't keen on spiders' webs, and sod's law said there'd be even more than usual today. Plus, his bike was right at the back, behind the lawnmower, a birdbath and an inflatable Father Christmas. He eventually extricated it and set off.

Even by his own standards, the Defence Secretary was in a bad mood.

"What have we got Group Captain?" he snapped, without his customary "Good morning".

"My people are sharing duties with the police and the site is still secure, so nothing to report."

"*Minister.* Nothing to report, *Minister,*" corrected the Defence Secretary in a voice that mixed annoyance, frustration and indigestion. "Detective Chief Inspector?"

"Much the same, Minister. No news has leaked out yet either, so I'd say we're doing well. I gather the SOCO team is making solid progress too. Do you agree, Director?"

"I do. The local team has meshed well with the people I sent up."

"And?"

"Minister?"

"Well whatever happened, it was a week ago tomorrow, so what's the answer?"

"We don't have anything conclusive yet, sir. These things take time, you know."

"So we've not got anything?" shrieked the Defence Secretary.

"This is a painstaking forensic examination, Minister," explained the DG, using all his charms to haul the Defence Secretary down from the ceiling. "I doubt we'll have anything actionable until over the weekend, but you can rest assured we'll get to the bottom of things as quickly as humanly possible."

He was right of course, but that didn't alter the fact that an encrypted email would land in his inbox later that day, which would rock him back on his heels. The boffin was under strict instructions to send preliminary findings as soon as he had any, and when the DG read the word *Radiation*, the report would have his full attention.

Luckily for Steve Guthrie, his day started more like Nigel's than the DG's, and after a quick breakfast, he was soon back in his car, heading for Liz's research site.

The journey was different from before. Steve remembered the winding route well enough, only now he was watching out for power lines too, and he couldn't see any. When he reached the site and saw the nearest one was even further away than he'd remembered, he smiled.

He opened one of the car's back doors and slid out a large plastic crate, roughly the size and shape of a rectangular, guitar case. He lay it on the ground, flipped open the catches, and lifted the lid. Nestled inside was a long pole with an open, plate-like object on one end and a curved handle on the other. In a separate compartment sat a control box of some sort, and a pair of headphones with a neatly coiled cable. He plugged the cable into the handle, clipped the control box to his belt, and turned it on.

Steve had borrowed the metal detector from the folks in archaeology before so he knew what he was doing, and dropping his keys on the ground, he began the calibration process. There was a short, high-pitched whistle as Steve swept the coil across the keys, and he quickly turned down the volume. Next, he adjusted both the frequency and conductivity dials. Last of all, he gradually increased the volume again until the whistle normalized.

Sweeping the detector from left to right, he walked methodically along one side of the field. He was reasonably sure it was where he'd taken the sensor from that he'd sent to the US. To be sure though, he swept the other edge of the field too. He got nothing either time, so he expanded the search to cover the whole area. It took almost an hour, and still no beeps sounded in his ears. He walked the field for a third time, only now with the sensitivity turned right up.

"Bother."

As Steve sat in his car a few minutes later, he reflected on two things. On the plus side, his doubts about finding underground cables had been proven right. Unfortunately, this meant he and Grant were no further forward. He started the engine, and stopping by *The Spotted Pig* to leave a note for Dot, he headed back to Cambridge.

~/~

Nigel's cycle route was one he knew well. From his house, it passed through the market square, and out around the southern side of the town, before looping back again. It was gently undulating and neither hard nor easy for an occasional cyclist like him. He enjoyed cycling for the way his thoughts came together as he pedalled, and how even in the hubbub of the town, half-formed ideas fell into place as the world blurred past. Today's thoughts were about the trip to Scotland and about dinner that evening. There was also the matter of how he could incorporate a juggling lorry driver into his latest story. It was either that or a psychic weasel.

Halfway around the *four-miler*, as the locals called it, he stopped at the MiniMart and leant his bike against the sign advertising an array of local activities. The Easter eggs and Christmas cards were nowhere to be seen, and after only a few minutes, Nigel had bought everything he needed for later on.

When he got home, he emptied his saddlebag, made a revitalizing cup of tea and finally settled down to some writing. It went surprisingly well too, and several hours later, he went back down to the kitchen. He surveyed his shopping, raided both the fridge and the freezer, then started work on his signature dish ... Minced beef with mushrooms, onions and tomato puree. He always served it with rice, and up to that point, it might have passed for chilli con carné if it wasn't for one thing ... the week's surprise ingredient.

Because of it, some might have called him a bold, innovative chef, on a par with the likes of Heston Blumenthal. That would have implied planning though, and an innate sense of which flavours would go together, but neither of these traits were in Nigel's nature. Instead, he chose his special ingredient based on what was the first thing he saw when he opened either the food cupboard or the freezer. This week that meant spinach. He nodded in a satisfied kind of way. After the incident with the anchovies and the frozen garlic, he was now warier of the bolder choices.

The way he looked at it, his special ingredient added spontaneity to the meal, and Jenny liked spontaneity. Had he asked her, she'd have said she'd never thought of it in relation to cooking, but he hadn't. It wasn't long before his latest concoction smelled appetizing though, and he smiled. After all, no one had ever fallen ill from his cooking ... or not seriously ill. Plus, Jenny always kept indigestion tablets in her bag just in case, so he figured he didn't have anything to worry about.

Liz did though, as her phone had died on the way to Wensbridge the day before, and she was desperate to charge it up in case David had called. When she got home, the first thing she did was, therefore, to find a charging cable. Fortunately, she found one almost straight away, although why it had hidden itself among the TV remotes was anyone's guess. Liz plugged the phone in, and a couple of minutes of charge later, the screen blinked into life with its usual annoyingly chirpy *Ping*. She waited while it found network. There was one voicemail from a journalist in Inverness, and Liz's heart missed a beat. Inverness was only 40-odd miles from Lossiemouth. She dialled the number in the message.

"Hello, Miss McBride?"

"Speaking."

"This is Professor Elizabeth Benning. You left me a message."

"Oh yes, thank you for calling back, Professor. Do call me Erica."

"What can I do for you, Erica?"

"Well, I'd like to tap into your expertise if I may. Concerning moles that is."

"Oh," said Liz, her voice dropping with disappointment. "So, it's not about my fiancé? Or anything about the RAF?"

"I'm sorry, no. Why do you ask?"

"Just something you said," Liz replied quickly, not wanting to share with a complete stranger.

"Something I said?"

"It's not important. How can I help you, Erica?"

Erica had conducted enough interviews to know an

avoidance tactic when she heard one, so she launched straight into her first question.

"I gather you're held in high regard in the field of mole behaviour patterns."

"Kind of you to say so. What would you like to know?"

"Well I've googled moles, and I can see they're very widespread. But I wondered what sort of terrain they prefer."

"Any really. True moles are found across Europe, North America and Asia. Plus, they have some close relatives in South Africa and Australia, but they're not really moles."

"Not *true* moles?"

"Precisely. True moles are one specific family which the others aren't part of. A bit like koalas are often taken for bears when they're really marsupials."

"I didn't know that. So relatives aside, true moles can be found all over the world."

"Pretty much."

"What are they like? Their behaviour, preferred terrain and so on."

"Well, they're very solitary creatures, only really coming together to mate. So they need quite wide territories, but as for terrain, they're happy as long as the ground can be tunnelled."

"What about molehills appearing where there haven't been any before?"

"Oh, that's bound to happen. They're constantly digging fresh ones."

"And islands?"

"How do you mean?"

"Are moles found on any of the islands around the UK?"

"Oh, yes. There are colonies in the Orkneys, on the Isle of Wight, Anglesey, lots of places. As you said, they're a pretty common animal."

"What about Lundy Island? In the Bristol Channel."

"I'm not aware of any, but it's something of a haven for wildlife, so I wouldn't be surprised. What's all this leading to Erica?"

"Good question, and it's actually quite an intriguing story, so if you have a few minutes …"

"I'm sorry, but I'm already running late for something," said Liz without enthusiasm. "Perhaps another day."

Feeling the sting of the rebuff, Erica ended the call. She'd got her background, at any rate, so now she needed to write it up.

Given how the call ended, Erica would have been surprised to know that after they'd spoken, Liz hadn't been able to shake the conversation from her mind. So much so, that later in the day, a few minutes before five o'clock, Liz finally gave in and typed *Lundy moles* into her browser. After an article on cauliflowers, several on the island itself and a lot about puffins, she found it.

Sudden appearance takes locals by surprise
The 28 permanent inhabitants of Lundy have today been shocked by some new arrivals. Not tourists either, but a colony of moles which is believed to be the first of its kind on the island. Lundy is of course already well-known for its variety of wildlife, but local experts are at a loss to explain how these new visitors have got there.
Lundy island is a Site of Special Scientific Interest, England's first statutory Marine Nature reserve and a Marine Conservation Zone. It's managed by the Landmark Trust on behalf of the National Trust.

She read the piece twice, then picking up her phone, she scrolled through the day's calls and dialled.

"Hello, Erica McBride."

"Erica, it's Professor Benning, we spoke earlier."

"Oh, hello," replied Erica. "This is unexpected."

"Look, I'm sorry I was short with you earlier. I've had a lot on my mind recently, and with back-to-back meetings all day, this is the first chance I've had to call you back. I've googled moles on Lundy."

"So you know all about it."

"I know what the press release says, but what about you? I'm guessing you've found out something more?"

Erica paused before answering. This was interesting. Professor Benning had been polite and informative before, but she'd clearly not been interested. Only now she was. Erica decided to be open with her.

"Not a lot to be honest. I've spoken with the warden on the island, but he couldn't add much."

"What did he say?"

"Only that there weren't any moles on Lundy until last week."

"And since?"

"A few more molehills apparently, but nothing much. Why the sudden interest?"

"When did it start? Did he say?

"Friday the 10th. Why?"

"Have you gone to print on this, Erica?"

"No, not yet. The story came in after my weekly deadline."

"What are the chances of it getting picked up by the national press?"

"Hard to say. Why the sudden interest?"

Liz went quiet again as she debated how much to share.

"You remember how you said the Lundy story is weird, Erica?"

"Have you got an explanation then?"

"No, but I do have another story for you, and I'd say it's even weirder."

"About Lundy?"

"Oh, no."

"About moles."

"Uh-huh."

"Some others have appeared somewhere?"

"Not exactly ... Call me Liz."

Jenny's first day back at work was pretty easy. As she'd expected, her boss had enjoyed himself in his old department while she was away, and he was reluctant to leave. He'd even rearranged the varnishes and wood stains which she'd been intending to do herself, so what with that, and her time away, she was feeling nicely rested.

That lasted until lunchtime when the previous day's drive started to catch up with her. She was mixing paint for a customer when she first felt her eyelids drooping, and when her break came, she went outside to get some fresh air. A chill hit her the instant she stepped out of the staff entrance. It was odd it should feel so cold when they'd been 500 miles further north just the day before. It did though, and it did the trick, so what with that, and more than her usual number of coffees, she made it to the end of her shift. To be sure, the drive back to Penmound included having all the car windows open and singing along with London Grammar and Lana Del Rey. When she got home, she popped in for just long enough to feed Tommy and Tuppence before walking round to Nigel's.

As she let herself in, she was therefore wide-awake ... in a caffeinated, cold-air sort of way. Nigel was still in the kitchen when he heard the front door, so he poured the wine he'd bought earlier. He might have been scruffy and have a house that looked like it had been organised by a series of small tornadoes, but he knew how to be a host.

"I like the addition of the spinach," she said when they were done. "Great improvement on the shallots last time."

"Yes, they made the whole thing too oniony. Glad you liked it. Mince à la Nigel lives again."

"And I didn't need my indigestion tablets either."

"That only happened once."

"Once was enough. I hope aubergines have never darkened your door since?"

"Oh no. I learnt my lesson there."

At that moment, Jenny's phone rang.

"Hello, Jenny Stevens."

"Jenny, it's Liz."

"Oh, hi, how are you doing? Any news?"

"Well yes actually, although not really what we were expecting."

"OK, I'm intrigued ..."

"I had a call from a journalist in Inverness."

"A journalist? What about?"

"Moles."

"You mean ..."

"Exactly. Thing is I'm attending a conference at the NEC[39] tomorrow, so I thought I could drop in. Tell you all about it. You're not far from there are you?"

---

[39] The National Exhibition Centre near Birmingham, is the UK's largest venue for hosting exhibitions, shows, concerts and the like.

"No, not at all. You can stay over if you like."

"Just what I was going to ask."

"Fantastic. How was Gran by the way?"

Liz laughed ... "I'll tell you about that when I see you too."

"Well?" asked Nigel.

"She's coming over tomorrow. Going to spend the night too. Apparently, she has news."

After this, Nigel and Jenny settled into their usual easy conversation, but Jenny's coffee intake was already starting to wear off, and as nine o'clock approached, she was flagging again. Giving him a goodnight peck on the cheek, she set off home. It was only a five-minute walk.

As she did, it was exactly 36 hours since Marston had given the order to restart Crianloch Station. They'd then waited for barely a minute before he broke the silence ... "When will we know, Doug?"

"It should be almost immediately, sir."

Minutes went by.

At ten past nine someone coughed, and taking it as a cue, Smoke leant forwards. He pulled the conference phone towards him, dialled, and Waynes' voice answered.

"I think you'd better come down here, sir. You might want to bring the Group Captain with you too."

Smoke and Marston exchanged glances.

"OK, Jim, we'll be right down."

As they headed for Systems Control, Smoke was silent, wondering quite what had happened. Marston, meanwhile, was calmly humming AC/DC's *Back in Black*, which he'd had on his running playlist that morning. It takes a special sort of person to be able to hum heavy-metal numbers, and he was undeniably that.

When Doug Smoke pushed open the door to Systems Control, his team were again clustered around the table in the centre of the room. Unlike the scientists, they were all RAF personnel, as was everyone else involved in the running of the station. They looked up and came to attention.

"What's going on, Jim?"

"I'll take you through the data, sirs."

Jim Waynes picked up a remote and pointed it at the large plasma wall. The screens blinked once, then came to life, showing a complex series of tables. Smoke and Marston looked and absorbed. To be fair, Smoke absorbed more of it than Marston as it was more his area. Nevertheless, it was Marston who spoke first.

"If I understand loopback tests correctly, they should show figures for the outbound signal and the return."

"Just so, sir. A little like radar."

"And we've used them here on the landlines to check whether the problem is at our end, or somewhere out on the network."

"Correct, sir."

"So why are all the return signals at zero?"

Jim was impressed.

"That's the question, sir."

"And what's the answer?"

Jim involuntarily scratched the back of his neck.

"You don't know?" asked Smoke, his voice failing to hide his astonishment.

"I'm afraid not, sir. Not yet, anyway. The signals go out, but nothing comes back."

"And the satellite circuits?"

"The same. The 4G as well."

"You're sure everything is working at this end?"

"Absolutely, sir."

"Cable fault? Like some idiot sticking a digger through them or something?"

"If it was just the landlines, then maybe. But something like that couldn't affect everything at once."

"So where does that leave us?"

Marston's question hung in the air for barely half a second before Waynes answered.

"There is one explanation, sir, but you're not going to like it. Heck, I don't like it."

"Well?"

"It's like there's nothing on the other end, sir."

"Nothing ..."

"No far-end to generate any return signals, sir."

The three men looked at each other.

"You've run the tests twice?"

"Just about to do the second run, sir."

Marston puffed out his cheeks and exhaled.

"What else can we do?"

"Well, there are only two things we can do, sir."

"Turn the cameras on or go outside."

"Precisely, sir."

The three men looked at each other again. In any other circumstances, going outside would have been the most natural thing in the world. Today though it suddenly seemed like a very big deal. As ever, Marston was quick to decide, and after a brief internal call, he and Smoke left Waynes to re-run the tests. Their next stop was the armoury. This was an RAF base after all.

A few minutes later, each equipped with a standard issue automatic[40] they made their way to the pedestrian lift. This time they both walked in silence, and the air was now charged with tension rather than curiosity.

"Are the guns necessary, sir?" asked Smoke at last.

"I hope not, Doug," said Marston grimly, "but something weird's going on here, and I'm not taking any chances."

Two members of the RAF Regiment were waiting for them when they reached the lift. Both saluted, then one of them pressed the button marked S for Surface.

This meant a ride up three levels, and when the doors opened, they all looked out. They took a step forward and sucked in the fresh air.

"Seems normal enough," said Smoke, taking his mobile from his pocket. He held his thumb against the fingerprint scanner and waited. "No signal."

"Check the perimeter," ordered Marston.

The two gunners headed off in opposite directions as Marston and Smoke scanned the valley. It was no different to the one they'd last seen the week before. In fact, it was so normal, there was nothing to see. Casting an occasional eye at the other two men, they set off across the runway towards the guardhouse. It seemed eerily quiet, but that was probably just their imagination. Twenty minutes later, the gunners re-joined them.

"Well?"

"Nothing to report, sir."

"Same here, sir; everything looks perfectly normal."

"Except that," said Marston pointing at the ground.

The others followed the line of his finger. None of them got

---

[40] Glock 17 9 mm if you're interested. Actually, Glock 17 9 mm even if you're not interested.

it at first.

"I'll be damned. Sorry, sir, I didn't notice ..."

"That pretty much sums up my own feelings."

"Where's the track to the main road gone?"

As the question hung in the air, the four men stared at the ground, taking in what Marston had noticed. The station's tarmac roadway ended at the gates as usual, but beyond that, there was nothing. No gravel track, just rough grass, gorse and heather. They'd have laughed if they'd known about the reverse confusion felt by DI Hendricks and the milkman, but they didn't.

"What next?" asked Smoke at last.

Marston paused before answering. "We need to look further afield."

"The village, sir?" asked one of the gunners.

Marston nodded. "Change into civilian clothes, take one of the unmarked Land Rovers and check it out."

"Civvies, sir?"

"No point in making more of an impact than we need to."

The two gunners nodded and headed for the vehicle lift.

Several hours later, their Land Rover bumped back into view across the landscape where the gravel track was supposed to be. Marston and Smoke had stayed above ground and were sitting in the guardhouse as it did. They were well-placed to see the nervous glances the gunners exchanged as they stopped the vehicle and got out.

"Well?"

The two gunners looked at each other again. They'd played rock, paper, scissors for who would break the news.

"We drove to the village like you said, sir, and from there we went on to Drumnadrochit."

"Well, that explains why you were gone so long. What did you find?"

"The thing is, sir, it's not there."

"What's not?"

"Crianloch village, sir. It's now just a regular highland glen. Drumnadrochit is largely as I remember it, but Crianloch simply isn't there."

"But ..." started Doug.

"*Largely* as you remember it?" interrupted Marston.

"Yes ... well ... I've not been off base for a while, but when was the new police station built, sir?"

Marston frowned and looked at Smoke.

"Doug? You were dating someone there, weren't you?"

Smoke nodded. "There isn't a new police station, sir. It's still the old granite one that went up in the 1900s. Pretty run down. Looks like it needs a fresh coat of paint."

Marston looked at the gunner and raised a quizzical eyebrow.

"Ultra-modern looking place, sir. All steel and glass."

As TC jumped back and forth between worlds, it was the people who caught her out the most. It's not surprising then that she quickly got used to the glances that seemed to ask if she'd gone completely off her head. Humans are great at adjusting to change though, and as the years passed, TC slowly got used to it. That is to say, she got better at not making a complete arse of herself.

As she did, she started to relax a little. And as the enormity of what was happening slowly became commonplace for her, she began to enjoy some of the differences. New albums by bands she liked were a real treat, and new books by favourite authors too. Differences to world landmarks as well, like the twin towers of New York's World Trade Centre still standing on several worlds, and Paris having two Eiffel towers on one. In another, Apple's Cupertino HQ was shaped like the company's logo.

As she relaxed, something else happened too; she stayed longer in each world. It had been a couple of hours to begin with, then a few days, and one morning she woke up to realize she'd been in that latest world for almost three weeks. This was when the trouble started.

Why? Because three weeks is a decent length holiday in the UK, and after that, she'd have to go back to a job she likely knew nothing about. But what could she do? She figured her choices were either to risk it or run away. The trouble was, by that time she'd probably already connected with friends, possibly made new ones and generally started to integrate into the place. As she repeatedly moved from one world to another, she was also increasingly conscious of what Sue had said that day ... *And what about the you who was here until this week? What's happened to her?*

What *had* happened to her? Had they swapped places, and the other *her* had ended up in TCs world? Or did TC somehow replace her other self wherever she went? And would that mean that when TC wasn't in her own world, the other *her* was consigned to some sort of limbo existence? It wasn't a pleasant prospect either way and all things considered, TC decided it was best if she was swapping places with each of her doubles.

Now you might think it silly, but this is where cake helped. The fact that it existed in every world was comforting in itself, and tasting the same everywhere, was even better. It gave the universe a consistent, friendly sort of feel. That she enjoyed making her own helped still more, and in the fifth year of her travels, she even perfected how to make her favourite[41].

As you may have guessed though, cake was vital to more than helping TC feel at home, and here's where things get really strange. So let me start by taking you through a brief history of cakes.

Cakes you see, date back to ancient Egypt, where they were more like sweetened bread than anything we know today. Everything has to start somewhere though, and the next step came in ancient Greece,

---

[41] TCs raspberry and white chocolate muffins
- Heat an oven to 190°C/374°F, Fan oven 170°C/338°F, Gas mark 5.
- Mix 12g baking powder, 2.4g bicarbonate of soda, 100g caster sugar and 300g plain flour.
- Using a separate bowl, fork together 75g melted butter, 150g natural, fat-free yoghurt, 3 eggs, and 4.2g vanilla essence. Continue until mixed, then add to the above and fork together until mixed.
- Add 100g diced white chocolate, and 175g raspberries, then mix together.
- Spoon into muffin cases in a 12-hole cake tin and bake for 15-20 minutes or until golden and fully risen.
- Move to a wire rack and leave to cool for 10 minutes.
- Decorate with 50g melted white chocolate and ideally leave to harden before serving, although it's unlikely you'll be able to wait that long.

where they created a sort of cheesecake. Not wanting to be outdone, the Romans then invented fruitcakes, and I don't just mean some of their more erratic emperors. After that, things stayed much the same until the Middle Ages, when the Scandinavians created something called *Kaka*. It wasn't the sort of gingerbread you'd recognise nowadays mind you, as apart from anything else, it could stay edible for months. *Sell By* dates? Pah. I could go on, but to bring things up to date, it wasn't until the mid-1800s that cakes started to become the light, fluffy chunks of deliciousness we have now. As with anything though, some people liked them, and some didn't. I mean some people like celery, so there's no accounting for taste.

And the relevance of all that is …?

Well, in the thousands of years since someone in the Nile Delta had said "I fancy something a bit like bread, only with more honey," no one had ever lived exclusively off cake. To be fair neither had TC, but she was still the only person in the entire history of the universe never to have refused an offer of cake … ever.

Her first was a small piece of sponge cake when she was four months old, and after that, there was no stopping her. Gateaux, Angel cake, Torte, Coffee cake; you name it, she tried it. Throughout her childhood, she couldn't get enough. Then as she grew towards her teens, her parents noticed. It was a family joke, to begin with, and then came the day when Sue revealed the nickname she'd been given by the other girls at school. No one knew she was making history of course, and even if they had, they wouldn't have realised the consequences. All of which takes us to the truly weird part … The universe, you'll remember, likes to stay in balance. Not in each world perhaps, but across all the different ones. Consequently, when something odd comes along, it puts its nose out of joint. When something unique happens, it doesn't know what to do … and when a unique thing keeps happening, something has to give.

In TCs case, the *something* that gave was that doors started opening between worlds. Then by doing nothing more than eating cake whenever it was offered, she'd begun jumping from one to the next. None of the laws of physics were happy about this, and even *Fate* had to go lie down in a darkened room for a while, but what did they know?

Naturally, TC knew none of this, and the three-week deadline still bothered her, although ultimately that was taken out of her hands too. Not by jumping to any-old-world either, but by arriving in one that was entirely different to all of those she'd visited before.

Sure, the sky was still blue and all that stuff, and you could argue that for a parallel world to evolve without anybody she knew in it, was bound to happen sooner or later. Plus Elvis still held the UK record for the most weeks at No.1, and most Muppets were still left-handed[42], so it was broadly the same.

Broadly the same except for two key things, one of which was going to break TCs heart.

---

[42] Elvis had 80 weeks at No1 in the UK singles charts, and Muppets are generally left-handed because most of their operators are right-handed. Yes, I'm sorry, but they're not real.

Days 7, Answers 1½
Friday, September 17th

It was a week to the day since **it** happened, and after three days in Glen Crian, the SOCO team had gone back to Inverness to complete their analysis. The two government scientists had finished on site too, and no-one's data had yet to reveal anything to explain the station's disappearance. All of which left the boffin, and as he collated his findings in his room at *The Shepherd's Arms*, he realised that the radiation he'd discovered wasn't just an isolated reading. It was present right across the valley floor.

Anyone else would have been bouncing with excitement at this, not to mention advising the police to don protective clothing. But the man's vagueness was legendary, and it wasn't until he put the data into a modelling programme later, that he saw a picture start to emerge.

Literally, a picture, as the programme produced a map showing the various concentrations of radiation across the glen. The pattern it made meant nothing to him, although it would have done to anyone who knew the layout of Crianloch Station, and one such person was the Director General of MI5. Consequently, when the morning's video conference concluded, he asked the Defence Secretary to stay connected.

"Thank you for staying on, Minister."

"What is it? I've another meeting to get to."

"Radiation, minister."

"I beg your pardon?"

"One of our scientists has detected the presence of radiation in Glen Crian, and it appears to follow the outline of the base."

"Go on."

"That's all we have at the moment, Minister, but I wanted you to know, and felt you might not wish to include the others at this stage."

"Is it conclusive?"

"The presence of it, yes. What it means, we're not yet sure. I'll have the final report tonight, and the key scientists are flying back down in the morning."

"Carter?"

"We still don't understand how, Minister, but yes, it's Carter without a doubt."

"Very well. Keep me informed."

Contrary to her usual habits, Erica McBride had got up early, climbed into her trusty green Mini and set off towards Lossiemouth. She'd spoken with her editor after talking with Liz, and he'd given her details for a contact there who he thought might be useful. It was another lovely Autumn day too, and when Erica got to the village of Forres, she turned left. The detour took her off the main road and had two benefits. She was looking for an address on that side of Lossiemouth, and it meant she'd be driving the last few miles along the coast road. And given a choice, who wouldn't?

She didn't know Lossiemouth well, so she missed the first turning into Brander Street. Taking the second one, she followed it to where it became Shore Street and pulled over. The road was lined with warehouses, many of which had visibly seen better days. None of them appeared to have numbers either, but that was OK, as she'd be told simply to look for the fourth or fifth on the left. Her editor couldn't remember which, but he knew it had an orange steel door.

Erica walked the full length of the road but found nothing. She retraced her steps and was almost back at her car when something caught her eye. It was on the wrong side of the road, and the door was somewhat faded, but it was unmistakable.

The dilapidated building stood back from the road, between two newer warehouses, and yes, it had an orange door. As Erica approached it, she smiled. Her editor had also said to look out for the sign on the door and there it was … *All that we see or seem is but a dream within a dream*[43]?

She pulled on the chain alongside the door, and from deep inside the building, came the sound of a bell.

"What?" crackled the speaker alongside the chain.

"Oh hello; I'm from the *Northern Echo*. I think my editor told you I was coming?"

"No."

"Oh, I was sure he would."

"Why? You're not Eric."

---

[43] Completely irrelevant I know but to stop you having to google it, these are the last lines of Edgar Allan Poe's *A dream within a dream*, written in 1849. It also appears in an array of pop culture, like John Carpenter's *The Fog*.

"Ah no, sorry. The message must have got garbled. I'm Erica, Erica McBride."

The man grunted.

This is hard work, thought Erica as she waited for something to happen. Then a flap opened in the door, and she saw a pair of eyes on the other side. One was brown, the other blue.

She held up her Press card.

"Weird hair," said the voice.

"Weird eyes," she replied.

A warm chuckle came from behind the door, followed by the sound of bolts being drawn back, and a key turning in a lock. The door swung open to reveal not some crazy-haired hippy as she'd expected. Instead, there stood a well-groomed man in his early forties wearing a tweed, three-piece suit, a bow tie and of all things, a monocle. Despite the oddness of it, he looked perfectly natural.

So not an affectation, thought Erica

The truth was, he did almost all his business on the phone, with the result that he could dress however he liked, and when he did the occasional video call, he was careful only ever to show his bow tie. Anonymity combined with memorability. It was a neat trick.

He looked Erica up and down, then pursed his lips.

"Not what you expected, I imagine," he said.

"Likewise, given you were expecting an Eric."

The man chuckled again. "Come on in."

She followed him into what turned out to be a large, well-lit room. It was like him; a complete contrast to what she'd been expecting.

"Regular coffee, decaffeinated or tea? I have English Breakfast, Earl Grey or Lapsang Souchong."

Evidently, she'd passed whatever test he'd been putting her through.

"Regular tea, please. White, no sugar."

She watched as he boiled a kettle in the open-plan kitchen. She couldn't work out which was more incongruous. The interior of the building compared to its outside, or his eclectic fashion sense.

"You're wondering about my home?" he said, interrupting her thoughts.

"Well yes; the outside looks so ..."

"Shabby?"

"Yes."

"Makes it harder for them to find me."

"Them?"

"So how can I help you, Miss McBride?"

"Erica, please."

"Erica."

"What did my editor say in his message?"

"Just that you'd be visiting, and I should help you however I can."

"Well, I'm writing a story about moles."

"The Lundy appearance, I suppose?"

"That's right," she said excitedly. "What can you tell me about it?"

"Very little I'm afraid. I saw the story, but it's not really my area."

"Oh," said Erica, her voice dropping. None of this was turning out as she'd hoped. "What *is* your area?"

"Technology, government secrets, things that go bump in the night, you know the sort of stuff."

Erica was confused and was about to reply when a thought

occurred to her. She'd mentioned the moles to her editor the night before, so had imagined he'd given her the source because of that, but now she realised he must have done it because of her regular column. *Oh well*, she grumbled inwardly. *I may as well make the most of it while I'm here. He might know something about what Liz mentioned.*

"Anything that might interest me?"

"What here? In sleepy old Lossiemouth? All we've got in that line is the RAF base."

"What about it?"

"What would you like to know?"

"Oh come on, you must know what I'm asking, or my editor wouldn't have sent me." He'd piqued her interest now.

The man smiled again, took out a silk handkerchief and polished his monocle.

"Why do you wear that thing?"

"You want to know about my monocle or about RAF Lossiemouth?"

Now Erica smiled. The man continued polishing. He held the monocle up to the light, made a small grunt of approval and replaced it.

"I wear it because I have perfect vision in my left eye but am extremely short-sighted in the right. As for the base, I'm not aware of anything strange going on there."

Erica went to speak, but the man lifted his left forefinger, and she stopped.

"I'm not aware of anything strange going on *there*, but it's not the only RAF base up here you know."

"What? But Kinloss closed down in 2012, and apart from that, the next nearest base is down in Northumberland, isn't it? And what's that? 300-odd miles away?"

"That's certainly the nearest if you go by the RAF website."

"But there's another?" Erica was intrigued now.

"Did you know that the Met Office has over 200 automated weather stations across the UK? And eighteen of them are on RAF bases ... including one here?"

"I did actually."

The man smiled. "He told me you do your homework."

"So there's something strange about the weather station?"

"Have you ever heard of Crianloch?"

Erica frowned as a memory stirred.

"Or a Group Captain David Marston?"

Erica shook her head; she was more than intrigued now. This peculiarly dressed man obviously knew something, and her editor had suspected as much. What had he said? ... "If there's so much as a whiff of anything odd he'll know about it. You two should get along fine."

"How about the *Joint Force Intelligence Group*, or the *National Centre for Geospatial Intelligence*."

This time Erica didn't have time to shake her head before he continued.

"Let me tell you a story. It's about a weather station that isn't what it seems, an underground RAF base full of scientists, and all sorts of intriguing rumours about both of them. Are you sitting comfortably?"

Several hours later, Erica pulled off the A831 alongside a sign reading *Crianloch 2 miles*. Off to her left was the loch the town took its name from and in the late morning light, tiny waves sparkled and danced across the surface. She still couldn't get her head around everything she'd been told, but she knew sincerity when she heard it, even if she couldn't be sure of its accuracy ...

"High altitude balloons, night flights, helicopters ..."

"Well, you said it's a weather station," retorted Erica.

"Sonic booms ... Stealth aircraft ..."

Now he had her full attention.

"According to my sources they're painted in black and grey camouflage, and they always come in from the west. Not many places west of Crianloch."

"So no-one sees them you mean."

"And as the base has underground hangers, no-one ever does."

"How do you know all this?"

He nodded to his right where there was a wire cage the size of a small room. It was crammed with computer equipment, clustered around a single swivel chair.

"Faraday cage," he explained. "It blocks electromagnetic fields so I can do my research with a certain degree of privacy. No real need in this case though, as the plans are in the public domain ... Crianloch Weather Research Station. All very clever hiding in plain sight like that, but that's the government for you."

"Hiding what?"

"Did you ever used to watch The X-Files?"

"Before my time, but that was little green men, and all that nonsense wasn't it?"

"Scoff if you like, but I met someone in town recently who helped build Crianloch and some of the things he saw ..."

"Your source is some guy in a pub? Seriously?"

Her voice held a mix of annoyance, sarcasm and disappointment. He didn't react but calmly stared back at her. She relented.

"Alright, what did this guy of yours say?"

"Underground aircraft hangers, hundreds of laboratories, a server farm, massive generators ..."

"But surely a research station would have most of that. And you said yourself it was underground."

She was defiant, but her voice now held a note of uncertainty.

"All true, but it was the security that struck him the most. Particularly around the lowest level."

"Go on."

"Well, after the blasting was complete and they'd poured the concrete for the foundations, everyone had to leave the site for a month. When they came back, half the basement level was already walled up and roofed over."

"Meaning?"

"Meaning they brought in someone other than the regular contractors to do that part of the build, and whatever's down there, was put in without anyone else knowing."

"But someone ..."

"... must have seen something? Of course; here's their number."

Smiling a knowing smile, he'd handed her a slip of paper, and it was that which Erica now pulled from her bag. She dialled the number he'd written on it. It rang twice before a thick Scottish accent answered.

"Hello, my name's Erica McBride. I think you're expecting me?"

"Aye. Meet me by the track."

She knew from her contact what this meant, and ten minutes later she drew to a halt at the start of the track into Glen Crian. The man waiting for her was dressed in a long, waxed jacket with well-polished brogues and a wide-brimmed hat. He wore small, wire-framed glasses, and had a wind-tanned face that put him anywhere between 50 and 70. He got into the car and pointed up the track without speaking. After a few hundred yards, he uttered two words ... "Stop here."

She did as she was told, and he got out. Then gesturing to her to keep quiet, he set off. Not along the track, but up a low hill to the left. As they neared the crest, he signalled for her to hold back and dropped to his knees to move forward in a crouch. Once he was at the top, he peered past a small cairn of stones and beckoned to her to join him. She did as he had and found herself looking down across Glen Crian. She'd seen many highland glens in her life, and this one was remarkable for just one thing ... The dozen or so people standing around some vehicles at the far end of the gravel track.

She flashed a quizzical look to her left, and after a reassuring nod from her guide, pulled out her phone. She took a series of photos, then they retraced their steps, got back into the car and drove away.

Neither spoke until they were sitting at a corner table in the public bar of *The Shepherd's Arms*. She had the same million questions as DI Hendricks and the RAF officers before her. They hadn't asked AGB though, and he was able to answer questions they hadn't even thought to ask. Like the Chinook helicopters he'd seen fly in from the west while the contractors were off-site, each with colossal machinery parts hanging from their cargo winches. Then how he'd watched from a nearby peak as they'd been lowered into the bowels of the base.

He went back several times over the following weeks too, and by the time the station was finished, he was the only civilian with any idea of what had gone on. Not only that, but for once, he didn't spread the news around the whole village. He hadn't been sure why at the time, but sitting in the bar after Erica left, the bundle of £10 notes in his pocket told their own tale.

Erica's story though, was just getting started, and when she got back to the *Northern Echo* that afternoon, she emailed her photos to Liz, then called her editor. What with the moles and now Crianloch, she had two stories on her hands, and her ambition was starting to kick in. *Next career step here I come*, she thought to herself.

"You see, I've got two stories here," she began, "and I think either one of them would make a great lead. One's fairly local and has a real hint of mystery to it, whereas the other has animal interest and again, a bit of mystery. Plus, none of the national papers has picked up either of them yet, so I'd like to do a special."

"You would, would you?"

As always, her editor hadn't raised his head as he said this. It was a quirk of his that he rarely looked his employees in the eye, and instead, his deep, bass voice found its way to the world via his beard. It was an impressive beard too, which had started life during Movember a few years before, and had never gone away.

Erica waited while he thought.

"OK," he said, at last, finally raising his head and looking her full in the face. "I can't promise you the front page, but if you get me 1,200 words on the Crianloch story by Thursday, we'll fit it in this week. I'm glad my source worked out."

1,200 words thought Erica excitedly, *that's a full page when you add in photos*.

Smiling from ear to ear, she went back to her desk and turned on her laptop. She fetched a coffee while it booted up, and when she got back, she logged on. Like Steve, she had the usual mix of spam, and in deleting most of it, she almost missed her weekly update from the newsfeed. When she did see it, she thanked her lucky stars for her two stories, as there were only three items, and none of them looked particularly impressive.

- *Dogs invade Danish parliament*
- *Man spotted with pet brick*
- *French minister petitions to reinstate monarchy*

She scanned the three pieces. As often happened, the headlines were a lot more exciting than the stories, so she closed the email and filed it away for future reference. After all, there were only so many times she could fall back onto *Google Earth* for material.

As she did, Steve Guthrie's latest call with Grant was underway, and it wasn't going well.

"No underground cables I take it," said Grant.

"Not that I could find ... and like I said, the nearest overhead lines are about half a mile away."

"OK. Well, there's one other thing I'd like you to try, Steve."

"Sure, what's that?"

"Would you check the other sensors to see if they've had a hard reset too."

"Already done."

"They had?"

"Uh-huh."

Grant exhaled heavily. "I don't know. We've done some more research into similar incidents, and there are a few, but power spikes seem to be the cause every time."

"So there's got to be something else."

"I know. I'll keep on looking, but right now we're running out of ideas."

Steve liked Grant, and they had a good working relationship despite the distance, so he knew the guys at SD would do their best.

"When do you need to get back to Professor Benning?"

"It can wait till Monday."

"OK, I'll keep on it, and call you tomorrow night."

"Sounds good. Thanks, Grant."

"No worries Steve. I hope we find an answer."

Shortly before seven that Friday evening, Liz knocked on Jenny's front door and was surprised when it was answered by Nigel.

"You guys swapped houses or something?" she grinned.

"Lord no. Coffee?"

"I could do with something."

"Or wine?"

"Even better."

He smiled ... "Bad journey?"

"Just busy. Lots of idiots on the road."

"It's why I don't drive unless I have to."

"Can't put up with them?"

"No, I mean, why add to the number. You know me an' drivin'."

He grinned and pointed Liz to the living room.

As she walked in, Jenny was kneeling on the floor, making a fuss of Tuppence, while Tommy weaved around her legs like a small, furry koi.

"Hey, Jenny."

"Liz! I didn't hear the door."

"Nigel let me in. He said something about wine?"

"Absolutely. Red or white?"

"Wine."

"Red it is."

"Nigel not joining us?" said Liz, adjusting her glasses as always.

"He's doing dinner."

"Wow, you *have* got him well-trained."

"Oh I'm a rubbish cook, so I keep him plied with alcohol, and as long you're up for the odd culinary surprise, he's pretty good."

"You make a great couple," smiled Liz.

"Oh, we're not together like that."

"No? But you're so at ease with each other, and he cooks for you ..."

"Best friend I've ever had."

"Nothing more?" said Liz with a wink.

"Oh, he's great company in small doses, but he's as mad as a hatter. You've not seen his house either."

"Sci-fi figurines, I suppose. Dirty crockery everywhere? Out of date food?"

"Not that bad, but untidy. Oh my god. There are piles of books and clothes everywhere. I swear some haven't been touched as long as I've known him."

Liz laughed, and as Jenny handed her the promised glass of wine, Tommy and Tuppence sauntered back in. They'd left when Liz had come in, as they hadn't fancied the competition, but now they had access to two humans, they were going to make the most of it.

"Aren't they cute," said Liz, bending down to each of them

in turn.

It was a mistake, of course, as cats don't give up a new human lightly. So much so, it was only when Jenny went out to put some fresh food down for them, that Liz was able to tear herself away.

When Nigel appeared a few minutes later with that week's version of his signature dish, the three friends sat down. The food was almost identifiable as chilli con carné this time too. Admittedly it had a faint hint of sardines to it, but Liz didn't like to say anything.

"How did you get on with Gran?" asked Jenny after a minute or two.

"Oh she's lovely, isn't she? It was so embarrassing though ... I was knackered from the drive, and I'd hardly sat down before I keeled over and fell asleep on the sofa."

"You ..."

"I know. She put a duvet over me and everything. Woke me up with a coffee the next day too. I was mortified."

"I bet," laughed Jenny. "You'd better not do that tonight."

Liz considered that for a second, then after taking a sip from her wine glass, began by explaining what she did for a living.

"That's funny," said Nigel once she'd finished "I was reading a blog the other day about a mole expert in Cambridge."

"You read my blog? I thought only real geeks did that."

"And your point is?" said Jenny, shooting Nigel a grin.

"Hold on, but that was a Professor Elizabeth somethin' or other."

"And Liz is short for ...?"

"Oh, what? I'm so stupid. And *you* knew I suppose?" he said, glaring at Jenny.

She smiled, nodded, and Liz went to speak again, but Nigel

was already in full, puppy-mode … "So what's up with the moles? Have you found out what happened yet? Where they've gone or anythin'?"

"Possibly."

"What do you mean, *possibly*?"

Liz launched into a repeat of what Erica had told her, and how she'd realised her moles had vanished on the same day the ones appeared on Lundy.

"But you can't mean they moved?" asked Jenny.

"And on the same day as my brick!" added Nigel triumphantly.

"Your brick?"

"Don't start him off," interrupted Jenny, only to be wholly ignored by Nigel.

"A brick appeared outside my cottage last week doing all sorts of weird things, an' now it turns out it was on the same day as the moles vanished. You can't say it doesn't mean somethin' now Jen."

"I hate to admit it, but it does seem like too much of a coincidence."

"And the last time I heard from David was the day before that."

"I knew it!" said the puppy. "I knew there was somethin' about the date when you first mentioned it."

"So, what are we saying? That they're all linked somehow?"

"I *was* going to say simply that one colony vanished and another one appeared at about the same time. But now I wonder if that's all there is to it. I might have a way of proving the moles part though as I'd tagged some of mine and have talked myself into an invite down to Lundy."

"But if it is true …"

"I know. It'd be completely bonkers."

"What about the journalist you heard about Lundy from?"

"Well, that's the other interesting thing. She's based up in Inverness, which is only a stone's throw from Lossiemouth, so she's agreed to keep her ears open for anything strange going on in the area."

"So you told her about David?" asked Jenny.

"Not by name but I hinted that there might be some odd things happening, and she said she'd have a hunt around."

As this conversation was drawing to a close, the village of Crianloch was bursting with activity. It might not have seemed so if you're used to a big city, but for a community of 300, having a group of mystery visitors was big news.

AGB had done his job well too, and this Friday night, the Public Bar of *The Shepherd's Arms* was full. The landlord wasn't complaining of course, and with everyone wanting to get a look at the strangers, latecomers were lucky to find a seat.

Various villagers tried their luck at talking with the strangers but to no avail. The casually dressed RAF officers were saying nothing, the scientists were keeping themselves to themselves, and the boffin just looked too weird to approach. He'd sent his final report to the DG a little earlier and sitting in the bar now, he started to relax. He didn't get out much, and at first, the noise in the bar numbed him into silence.

Then the milkman approached him.

It was strange how alike they looked, with their worn clothes, and shared aura of dishevelment. The scientist had at least shaved, but other than that, and the less erratic look to the milkman's hair, they could almost have been related.

"_____," began the milkman.

The scientist stared at him and raised one eyebrow.

"_____."

The noise in the bar made the milkman's words strangely intelligible, and his statement that he'd been the one to discover that the station was missing got the boffin's attention. Having heard once that buying people drinks was a good way to start a conversation, he offered. This was new territory for him, but the milkman eagerly accepted, and soon, the whisky was flowing.

Sadly for the milkman though, the scientist's knees buckled partway through the third double, and that was the end of the free bar. It was lucky the place was so full because in an emptier pub the boffin might have hurt himself. Instead, he simply crumpled slowly to the ground.

Soon?

 It was an odd quirk, but whenever TC moved from one world to another, she always found herself in a version of her home town. Simon hadn't been able to explain why, any more than how she was doing any of it, but there it was. As she quickly discovered, though, it gave her two huge advantages. For a start, her parent's house was there, so she always had somewhere to stay. Plus, in an unusually helpful twist of *Fate*, many of her other selves kept their bank card in the same bedroom drawer. The signatures differed wildly of course, but she found people rarely looked closely. And the one time she *had* been challenged, a quick excuse about having a sprained wrist worked well enough. PINs were more of a challenge, but they didn't exist in every world, and if she had to, she could always rely on her parents ... although she didn't like to do that.

This time there was something different about the place though, and she felt it as soon as she came round. It was ironic then that when she did, she was lying under a tree, like she had that first time. It was dark this time though, and she shivered as she made her way into the town. The High Street was similar in every world she visited, and she'd long ago given up examining it closely as there were rarely any major changes. Sometimes a few different shops or maybe some new traffic signals, but it was always near enough the same. She turned into her parents' road and stopped. The house was in darkness.

Whichever world she visited, her parents were always very sociable people, so it wasn't unusual to find them out. But not to leave the hall light on was out of character.

They must be on holiday, she thought.

TC walked up to the front door and peered through the living room window. The furniture looked different, but that was no surprise. Bending down, she felt around for the plant pot where there was sometimes a key. It was there, so she turned it in the lock and pushed. The door didn't want to open. She pushed harder, and after a minute, she was able to squeeze in. Piled against the inside of the door was post; a massive amount of it. Mostly *junk mail* she imagined, but the hall light wasn't working, so she couldn't tell. There was a faint, musty smell in the house too.

She went into the living room and going by the glow from the street light outside, the furniture wasn't only different, it was covered with polythene sheets. There was a layer of dust on everything too, and the ceiling looked like a theme park for spiders.

She walked upstairs and pushed open her bedroom door. Dust sheets again, and the same layer of dust everywhere. A feeling of uncertainty had been building in her mind since she'd seen all the post, and now it started nudging at her consciousness. It had been a long day too, so with tiredness and a growing confusion washing over her, she crawled under the duvet cover and went to sleep.

She didn't close the curtains, and the next morning, she woke with a weak autumn sun streaming in through the window. As she moved under the duvet, a cloud of dust rose and danced in the air. She was still fully dressed from the night before, and as she went downstairs, the pile of post came into view. It wasn't the mountain she'd imagined, but it was impressive all the same.

"Mum? Dad?" she called. In the circumstances, part of her didn't expect a reply, and it was right.

She needed coffee, and she needed cake, but there was nothing in the kitchen. Even the fridge-freezer was turned off.

What to do next? She wandered back to the hall and dropped onto the bottom step of the staircase. The post stared up at her, and idly at first, she started sifting through it. Junk mail went onto one pile, everything else onto another. The second pile was much smaller, and when she went through it a second time, it also proved to be mostly junk, albeit masquerading as something useful. By the time she finished, the only real items she'd found were a utilities' statement, and a letter from her bank asking why she hadn't used her debit card in a while.

Unlike the disorientation she'd felt on her first few jumps though, this merely intrigued her. But what about her parents? Where were they? A wave of emotion washed over her. She closed her eyes and clenched her fists, digging her nails into her palms as she had once before.

By the time she looked up again, she'd made a decision. She'd go to the bank. Hardly an earth-shattering choice you might say, but she had to start somewhere.

The bank was the same one she used in her own world, although the inside was very different. Unlike the stained wood, old-world feel she was used to, it had an open-plan style with frosted glass cubicles along one wall. As she walked in, a smiling young assistant asked if he could help her with anything. She replied that she wanted to talk with someone about her account.

Minutes later, she was in one of the cubicles sitting opposite a junior manager. He wasn't quite as smiley as the greeter, but he was pleasant enough. In any event, she'd rehearsed what to say on the walk over, and hoped he couldn't hear the thump of her heartbeat over her otherwise confident words.

"I've been away for a while and have lost track of my finances," she began, "so I need to get a statement, and double-check the details you have for me. Is that possible?"

"Of course, Miss. Do you have your bank card with you and some other proof of identity?"

She produced the card she'd taken from the bedroom drawer, the letter about it and the utilities' statement. Evidently, *Fate* was particularly kind in this world, as the manager took them without a word, and said he'd be back directly.

Funny word that ... she thought ... *directly*. She looked around. Judging by the adverts for various financial services, banking was much the same here as at home. He came back.

"Everything seems to be in order, Miss. Although you've not used your account in so long, I'm afraid it had been marked as dormant."

"Oh, what does that mean?"

"It's nothing to worry about. I just need you to complete this reactivation form so I can check your personal details and signature against our records."

She leant forward, completed the various boxes, and signed where he indicated. She'd checked the back of the bank card before leaving home, so she was ready for this. It was too late to pull out now anyway.

He took the form and left her to sweat it out again. This time she had longer to wait, and her nerves were starting to get the better of her when the glass door opened.

"Everything's in order, Miss," he smiled. "You've been an excellent customer in the past, so we're glad to have you back."

"Oh, thank you."

"Just one question if you don't mind."

"Of course," she said calmly, wondering at the same time whether she'd be able to answer.

"You mentioned you've been away for a while and I see you haven't used the account for over six months, so I'm curious as to where you've been?"

"Australia" was the first word that jumped into her head and judging by his reaction, it was good enough.

"Very nice. It's on my bucket list, although my wife prefers the idea of New Zealand, so maybe both."

"Fantastic."

"Well, we'll see. Is there anything else I can do for you today?"

"Just the account balance please."

He handed her the folded slip of paper he'd brought in with him, and she almost lost her composure. She *was* a good customer.

So that was one mystery solved, and the next step was family and friends.

Then TCs world fell apart.

Truth emerges

Saturday, September 18th

In defiance of darkness and good sense, Liz's alarm went off at half-past five. Then, after looking uncertainly around Jenny's spare room, she got out of bed. The drive to North Devon took her a little under three hours, and as she pulled into the quayside car park, a nearby clock was chiming nine. She glanced around. Fifty yards away was a kiosk selling tickets for the crossing to Lundy. On her right was the River Torridge, and waiting silently by the quay, lay the MS *Oldenburg*. She walked over to the kiosk, bought a return ticket, and boarded.

As she walked up the gangway, she ran her hand appreciatively along the polished brass rail. According to the plaque set into the varnished decking, the ship had been built in Bremen in 1958, but it didn't look anything like that age. Glancing around at the navy and white paintwork, Liz smiled. *It could almost be new*, she thought.

It was a glorious day for a sea crossing too. There wasn't a cloud in the sky, and with the school holidays being over, there was plenty of room to sit out on deck. She settled down to read through her notes, and once the ship got underway, she headed down to the buffet. The smell of a past era greeted her as she went below deck. The furniture, the wood, the dark, rich carpets; it was like stepping back in time.

As she drank her first coffee of the day, Liz wondered why she'd never made the trip before. The warm, friendly surroundings would have been a great place to sit out the journey on a winter's day. Not today though, as she'd read about a pod of dolphins people sometimes saw on the crossing, and she didn't want to miss the chance of seeing them.

When the ship eventually docked at Lundy's South Pier, she was greeted by the sight and sound of hundreds of birds wheeling around the cliffs. The next thing she spotted was a man holding up a sheet of card with her name on it. She walked over and introduced herself.

"Welcome to Lundy, Professor," greeted the warden.

"Thank you. This looks like an amazing place."

"Your first time I take it. Good crossing?"

"Calm as a millpond."

"Excellent. Let's get going. You've got four hours before the *Oldenburg* goes back."

"OK, where to first?"

"You said you'd need a spade?"

"Yes please. Have you got one?

The warden nodded, pointed to a path that wound around the cliffs to their right, and they set off. After several minutes' walk, Marisco Castle came into view above them, and as they crested the hill where it sat, a stone building came into sight. It had the National Trust logo on one side. After collecting the warden's spade, they walked on to the square tower of St Helen's church and climbed over the low, stone wall behind it. Spread out in front of them was a field dotted with fresh molehills.

"What now, Professor?"

Liz slung off her backpack and dropped it unceremoniously on the ground. Undoing its various straps, she took out a pressurised cylinder and some lengths of rubber tubing.

"You're going to gas them?" said the warden in a shocked voice.

"It's only nitrous oxide, so it'll knock them out long enough for our purposes, and without any after-effects."

"Except for a bad case of the giggles."

"Exactly. And we should wear these ourselves, just in case." She passed him a face mask, and with it, a handful of ordinary party balloons.

"What are these for?"

"We need to block up any adjacent holes as best we can, so rather than disturb more soil than necessary, we'll put a balloon in each one and inflate it to fill the opening. It's not perfect, but it's quick and effective."

He smiled, nodded, and over the next few minutes they blocked up all but one of the nearest holes. Then Liz knelt down, poked one end of the tubing into the last remaining hole and sealed it in place with a few handfuls of earth.

"Ready?"

The warden nodded and pulled the mask up to his face. Liz did the same, opened the valve on the canister, and they heard a faint hissing noise. She kept it going for several minutes, and once she felt she'd used enough, she shut it off.

"Right, now we need to move fast to find the moles."

Liz had brought a camper's folding spade with her, and between the two of them, they quickly excavated the nearest molehill. Nothing. They put the soil back as best they could and tried again. No luck there either. They were running out of time.

Next though, they found two moles huddled together, and both had tiny plastic tags on their ears. As the warden gently lifted them out, Liz grabbed a small, yellow scanner from her backpack.

Moment of truth, she thought to herself.

She switched the scanner on, hit it, and scanned each of the tags in turn. When the screen showed a result, she looked for a moment as if she might faint.

"You OK?" asked the warden.

"Let's get them back into the tunnel," she said. "Cover it over and get rid of the balloons."

While he did that, she packed her equipment away.

"You sure you're alright?" said the warden when they were done.

"What? Oh yes, I'm fine thanks. Just the gas I expect."

"Well, you didn't seem to be seeing the funny side," he laughed. "Is that all you need?"

"That's it, thanks."

"Lunch? You've only got a few hours, and the tavern does nice food."

"Sounds good."

They stayed in the Marisco Tavern until it was almost time for Liz to leave, and back on the pier, she was about to board the *Oldenburg* when she turned and saw the warden wearing a quizzical expression.

"What?"

"You found something, didn't you?" he said. "Something you didn't expect."

"What do you mean?"

"Before. When you scanned the moles. You looked like you'd seen a ghost."

"Oh, I'm OK," she lied. "Just took my mask off too quickly and got a bit of a lung-full I expect."

And with a wave, Liz was gone.

It was six o'clock when she got back to Bideford, and after a day in the open, she was feeling tired. It was nearing sunset too, and the last thing she needed was the five-and-a-half-hour drive back to Cambridge. She hadn't thought about that in advance either, so hadn't arranged anywhere to stay ... and she'd need to eat at some point too. So, with the idea of finding somewhere on the way, she set off.

After an hour and three-quarters, Liz started to feel tiredness catching up with her, and at the next motorway services, she stopped for a break. As she sipped a double-shot latte, she opened the email on her phone. There were a handful of messages from exhibitors at the conference she'd attended the day before, and a few LinkedIn requests from people she'd met. She was about to give up and close the app when she spotted the email from Erica.

Hi Liz
I have news. Too much to go into on email so call me when you can, and I'll explain the enclosed.
See you soon, Erica

Liz opened the attachment. It was a zip file of six photographs showing a highland glen. It was picturesque enough, and there were some vehicles in a couple of the shots, but apart from that, it meant nothing to her. She dialled Erica's number, but it went to voicemail.

"Damn, where is she?"

Liz sat back in her chair and considered what to do next. The SatNav was saying it was still another three and a half hours to Cambridge, but only an hour and a quarter to Penmound, so the choice was easy. She called Jenny.

Unlike the darkness that had greeted Liz that morning, the final scientists in Crianloch had woken with the sun at about half six. The boffin, on the other hand, had only woken when one of them had knocked on his door, to be greeted by a faint, pained groan from within. He didn't feel at all well. When he did emerge, he only managed half a cup of coffee before they had to leave. If anything, it made him feel even worse, but they had a flight to catch at quarter past nine and were due in Whitehall before lunch.

Halfway to Lossiemouth, they made a brief stop for him to buy some water and painkillers, and for the few minutes they were outside, the fresh air helped. He also bought a box of travel sickness pills and some mints. If they'd had anything to make his complexion less pallid, he'd have got that as well.

Conversely, the DG's day had begun with a succession of early meetings. As a result, the flight from Lossiemouth was already well on its way to Northolt before he saw the boffin's final report. It wasn't a lengthy document, but it was dynamite, and even as he was still reading it, he called his assistant to have him pull together an urgent meeting with his top scientific advisors.

Half an hour later, he entered an anonymous meeting room and handed round the four copies of the report the assistant had made. His advisors started reading. He'd never known them to be the most demonstrative of people, so he was surprised to hear them mutter shocked expletives as they read on.

"Well?" he asked as the last one closed the file in front of them.

The two men and two women looked at each other.

"You're convinced this is genuine, sir?"

"You can meet the team who wrote it if you like, but yes, I am."

"And you know it's not possible."

"I do."

"Well we'd better meet them."

"My thought exactly. They flew into Northolt earlier this morning and should be on their way here by now."

When the DG's advisors entered the meeting room, the first thing they noticed was the contrast between the three visitors. The two forensic scientists were in their mid-thirties, smartly dressed, and obviously feeling slightly uncomfortable about being there. The boffin, on the other hand, was at his scruffiest and looked like he'd be dragged from his bed in the middle of the night, then pulled through a haystack. Odd socks, a tie that clearly had a long and close relationship with various kinds of soup, and hair that hadn't seen a brush in days. He was also still very pale.

The forensic experts were sitting at the table, talking quietly with each other, and the boffin was stirring a cup of coffee with the end of a pencil. All three stood up as the DGs advisors entered, two out of politeness, and the third because he'd just spilt his coffee.

"Can I get you a napkin for that professor?"

"No, I'm fine," replied the boffin, adding coffee to his tie's collection of stains.

"If you're sure. Thank you all for coming in. We've been reading your reports, and the DG has asked us to discuss your findings."

"Sorry, the DG?" asked one of the forensic scientists.

"The Director General of MI5."

"Oh!"

"Please take a seat."

The chairs were standard office issue, as was the table and the whiteboard. What set the room apart, was the portrait of the Queen on one wall, and the view down Whitehall. Downing Street was a few hundred yards away, and from the window, you could see the armed police guarding its entrance.

"So you're both in forensics," began the chief advisor, "and you're a physicist."

"Yes, so what?" The boffin's hangover had abated somewhat, and he was now just feeling grumpy instead.

"I'm intrigued. Do you know why you were assigned to this? It feels rather specific, sending a physicist before anything was known."

"My report speaks for itself, don't you think?"

"That wasn't really my point, but I expect we'll see. Let's start with the forensic side of things, shall we?"

For the next 45 minutes, the forensic scientists were quizzed on their findings and took it in turns to answer the advisors' barrage of questions. Theirs wasn't the report that had got the DGs attention though, and when the questions dried up, they were allowed to leave. Under escort, naturally.

That just left the boffin, who now had his head bowed over his phone, deep in concentration.

"Professor?"

There was no reply.

"Professor?"

"Hold on."

"We need to ask you ..."

"Hold on!"

They waited, and after several minutes he looked up.

"Right. How can I help you?"

"Important work?" asked the advisor, gesturing towards the phone.

"I've just reached level 1,100 of Candy Crush."

"You've ...

"What do you want to know?" asked the professor testily.

"We'd like you to take us through your findings."

"You've read my report?"

"Naturally."

"Which parts don't you understand?"

"We understand all of it professor; we simply find your conclusions rather hard to take."

The advisor opened the report to a map of Glen Crian. It was the one from the boffin's own modelling programme and was a standard topographical map, overlaid with an outline of Crianloch Station. The fence, the guardhouse, the runways and the central utility building; they were all there. At first glance, you might have thought it had been taken from the original plans, but if you looked closer, you saw there was something odd about the outline of the buildings. The contours of the landscape were shown in the thin, crisp, brown lines of any Ordnance Survey map. The outline of the base though was a strange, fuzzy green. Apart from the colour, it looked like a cross between an x-ray and a Lidar[44] image of some long-lost city.

"So, let's start with the outline of the base. Why are the lines so indistinct?"

"It's all due to the radiation. I thought you'd read my report."

"Bear with us please, Professor. This might be an everyday occurrence in your world, but we're having a bit of trouble believing it."

"I don't see why. The data is clear enough."

"The data which you claim indicates the presence of Hawking radiation."

"I don't claim anything, it does."

"But Hawking radiation is only emitted by black holes."

"So?"

"So don't you think it strange to have found that in a remote highland glen."

"I don't hypothesize on what I find. It is what it is."

With that statement, the boffin's head dropped back to his phone, and the DGs chief advisor realised where he'd heard of him before. He was notorious in academic circles. An absolute genius at data interpretation, but with no interest whatsoever in its implications.

~2

"Explain it to me again," said the DG a short while later.

"OK," began his chief advisor. "Einstein theorised that both mass and energy can bend the fabric of space and time, to the extent of cutting a portal from one place to another."

"A wormhole."

---

[44] Lidar is an aerial surveying method which measures the distance to objects by shining pulsed laser light onto them and measuring the reflected pulses. It's excellent at seeing through vegetation to ground formations beneath such as for lost cities in the Amazon.

"Yes. Think of it like an actual worm boring through an apple to get from one side to the other, rather than going around the outside."

"And wormholes are related to black holes."

"Yes."

"Which only occur in space."

"Yes. Although when the Large Hadron Collider was proposed, some claimed it could create a black hole capable of swallowing the Earth."

"Well, at least that didn't happen."

"Quite. But even some of CERN's own scientists predicted they'd find that forces like gravity could leak into other dimensions."

"Meaning?"

"Meaning maybe Crianloch found something."

"That's quite a leap of logic."

"I'm sorry, sir, but this is uncharted territory for all of us."

"Well, I can't take this to the Minister without anything to back it up. And if you're right, we'll need to involve the PM as well."

"The data's irrefutable, sir. The contentious part is what it means."

The DG reflected on this once he was alone in his office. Seemingly, the world was a very different place than he'd realised. Even so, what passed for normality had to carry on, so he picked up the bundle of papers on his desk and went about his day. It was therefore after lunch before he returned to his office, and as he walked in, he noticed a new envelope in his *In-Tray*. In his world, some things were still only trusted to paper.

He opened the envelope to find a note stapled to a sheet of

A4. It was from his chief advisor, and the covering note read *For your meeting with the PM*. He pulled it off and read the attached sheet.

> *You'll need someone to validate the findings, so I suggest either Steven Weinberg at the University of Texas (Nobel laureate for quantum field theory), Peter Harker at Cambridge, or Mir Faizal at CERN. You may find this quote of his interesting.*

Below this was a photocopied extract from a newspaper[45], and as the minister read it, his jaw literally fell open. At the end of the second paragraph, he sat down, turned his computer back on, and googled the source. It was genuine. Even though it talked about parallel universes, gravity leaking between them, and the possibility of CERN producing tiny black holes, it was genuine. It was too much for him to take in, and that was before the punch line where it mentioned Everett's many-worlds theory. OK so it dismissed it as philosophy rather than science, but where there's smoke ...

The article brought things home to the Director in a way that the pure facts hadn't, and he shivered. The contents of the boffin's report weren't merely astonishing, they were world-changing. He hesitated for a moment before picking up the phone and calling the office of the Defence Secretary. By a lucky chance, the minister had a free timeslot twenty minutes later, so gathering all the papers together, the DG left his office.

He walked along Millbank, through Parliament Square, and then down Whitehall, past the *Cenotaph* and the *Memorial to Women of World War 2*. As he did, he reflected on what past

---

[45] Read the original article in The Telegraph by Sarah Knapton, Science Editor (10:33AM GMT 23 Mar 2015) titled *Big Bang theory could be debunked by Large Hadron Collider*.

generations might have made of the conversation he was about to have. *Hell, what would the current generation make of it?*

"Good morning, Director."

"Good morning Minister; good of you to see me so quickly."

They shook hands and sat down on opposite sides of a large, leather-topped desk.

"What do we know?"

"I'll explain it as it was put to me Minister, but we're going to need to get some experts on it before we take things further."

"Further?"

"To the PM."

"Go on."

The DG laid out the map on the desk between them and took the other man though everything he'd been told. When he was done, the Minister blew out both his cheeks and sat back in his chair.

"And we're sure?"

"That it's Hawking radiation? Yes."

"Which is only known to occur as a result of black holes."

"Yes."

"So they accept it's impossible here."

"They're not offering any hypotheses, to be honest."

"Well, as you say, we need to get some more people on this. What about this Professor Harker your chap mentioned? I want to keep this under wraps as long as we can, so I'd rather use someone in the UK if possible."

"I agree. I suggest we get Croft to contact him."

"Good idea. Will you do the honours?"

"Is there an office I can use?"

The Defence Secretary pressed the intercom on his desk, and within seconds, his assistant was leading the DG to an office down the corridor.

"May I get you anything, sir?"

"A phone number please, for Detective Chief Inspector Croft in Inverness."

The room was comfortably furnished with a large desk, a swivel chair, and two leather armchairs, between which was a low coffee table. The DG sat at the desk, and a remarkably short time later, there was a polite knock on the door.

"Come in."

"The number you wanted, sir."

"That was quick."

"Thank you, sir. Will there be anything else?"

"What's the Minister's diary like today? I may need to see him again?"

"He has meetings all day, but I'm to make room for you, sir. You can reach me on Extension 23 when you're ready."

The DG nodded his thanks, picked up the phone and dialled Croft's number. His assistant answered and put the DG through.

"Morning, Detective Chief Inspector."

"Good morning, Director. This is unexpected."

"Quite. Look, we need your help with something."

With that opening, the DG quickly took Croft through the situation and why they needed Professor Harker's help.

"I'll contact the Cambridgeshire Police right away," responded Croft. "Can you tell me anything I can share with them?"

"Only that it's a matter of national security."

"They'll ask questions ..."

"... which you'll deflect. Get this Harker to Whitehall today. In police custody if necessary."

Croft put down the phone and looked at his assistant standing in the doorway.

"Would you get me the number for Detective Chief Inspector Gill in Cambridge please, Caroline?"

Two minutes later Croft was talking with DCI Cherry Gill. They'd been at Hendon Police College together and had always stayed in touch. As predicted, she had dozens of questions, and contrary to the DG's expectation, she wasn't easily deflected. Name-dropping worked in the end though, and mention of Croft's recent meetings with the DG and the Defence Secretary wore her down. She agreed to send a car to the university.

Before Cambridge, Professor Peter Harker had spent several years at the Swiss Federal Institute of Technology in Zurich, which earlier in its history had hosted the career of Albert Einstein among others. OK, so it's now ten places below Cambridge in the world physics rankings, but that just meant Harker had taken a step up when he'd moved from one to the other.

His was, therefore, a quiet, academic life, and to say he was shocked when two policemen entered his university rooms in response to his cheery "Hello" is something of an understatement. His shock increased when they insisted he come with them to London. It hit melting point when they said he could call the Ministry of Defence if he wanted to verify anything.

Less than ninety minutes later, the car carrying Harker swept around Trafalgar Square and pulled up at the MoD building on Whitehall. *Google Maps* gives 1 hour 48 minutes for the journey, and that's at 2 a.m. on a Sunday.

By the time a large, anonymous man escorted Harker into a meeting room, his brain was feeling decidedly scrambled. When the DGs advisor handed him the boffin's report and Harker started to read, his mind began to do backflips. When he finished it, he looked up. He was both shocked and annoyed.

"So I've been dragged all the way here to read someone's idea of a joke?"

Without a word, the DGs advisor passed across a second file. This one contained the raw data behind the conclusions, along with the name of the professor who carried out the work. Now Harker was quieter; he knew the name. After an hour, he'd read all the data three times, and the conclusions twice.

"You can see why we wanted your input now."

"But it can't ..."

"It'll save time Professor Harker if we both accept that the impossible may just have become possible. The question is, how do we prove or disprove it?"

Harker paused before answering, passing a hand through his mop of greying hair as he did.

"First of all, I'd need to go there; take my own readings."

"And if they bear out what's in the report?"

"One thing at a time. Where is this Crianloch?"

"The police car that brought you is outside with instructions to take you to RAF Northolt where a plane is waiting. It's only a short flight up to Lossiemouth and you'll be driven from there, so I take it you'll be able to get back to me this evening?"

"But I'll need specialist equipment." stammered Harker.

"All provided professor. Is there anything else?"

Harker dazedly shook his head. He was now thoroughly overwhelmed by the speed at which events were moving.

Barely two and a quarter hours later, Harker walked down the plane's steps onto the tarmac at RAF Lossiemouth. He was greeted by Finch's two officers who introduced themselves as his escort to what they referred to as *The site*. It was a brief conversation, and it rapidly became apparent that he wasn't going to get any more out of them. Resigned to whatever might happen next, he got into the back of the SUV, and they drove off. No-one said a word throughout the entire drive.

When they arrived at Glen Crian, they handed Harker over to DI Hendricks, who was waiting at the far end of the gravel track with two constables and a large, plastic crate.

"Welcome to Glen Crian, Professor Harker. I'm told you'll be familiar with this?"

She opened the crate, and he peered in. He grinned and lifted out the contents. Like the boffin before him, he put on the headphones and adjusted several of the dials. Next, he took a folded map from his inside pocket, orientated himself to it and walked off across the glen. He made the same slow progress as his predecessor, but at least he didn't have to cover the whole area. After all, he only needed a few data points to validate the original findings. After half an hour's work, he slung the headphones around his neck and went over to DI Hendricks.

"Do you have any plans of the er ... for the structure that used to be here? Architect's drawings, that sort of thing?"

DI Hendricks handed him the sealed envelope DCI Croft had couriered over. Harker looked around, located a rock in amongst the heather, and went over to it to sit down. Inside the envelope was an outline plan of Crianloch Station. There were also photographs of Glen Crian from both before, and after it's disappearance. He whistled as he absorbed the enormity of the place. Then comparing the photos to the landscape, he set off again.

When he reached what should have been the far side of the runway, he took another set of readings. What they revealed would have to wait until he'd done his analysis, but it was a start. So, with one last look around, he removed the headphones again and walked back to the police Land Rover.

"Thank you for the equipment and the plans Inspector. Do you know what's meant to happen now? I need to analyse the data, but am I supposed to do that here, or head back down south?"

"As I understand it, Professor, there is some urgency in the matter, so I'm to take you to the police station in Drumnadrochit where we have a desk set up for you."

"Fair enough. The results will take some hours to come through, so I'll need to stay over as well if you can suggest anywhere?"

"Already taken care of."

He smiled ... "Lead on Inspector."

An hour or so earlier, Steve Guthrie's mobile rang, and even before the first tones died away, he snatched it up off the table.

"Hey Grant," he said quickly, dispensing with the usual "Y'all".

"You must have been sitting on the phone." replied his colleague.

Steve chuckled. "Well, I'm dying to know the answer."

"I'm sorry to disappoint you then, because we've had everyone on this, and we've still only found six instances of spontaneous resets."

"All of which were put down to a nearby power surge I

suppose," replied Steve disconsolately.

"Pretty much."

This piqued Steve's interest ... "Pretty much? Meaning what?"

"Meaning five of the six have been, but the sixth hasn't been explained yet."

"How come?"

"Remind me when Professor Benning's sensors started acting up."

"A week ago yesterday ... Friday, September the 10th."

"I thought so."

There was a pause.

"Come on, Grant, what is it? Don't keep me in suspense."

"The sixth instance was reported by the British Geological Survey, and they contacted us on the same day."

"I'll be damned."

"Quite. I've emailed them, so with any luck, I'll get something back tomorrow. Call you in the afternoon?"

"Sure. What were they studying by the way? Not moles, I imagine."

"No, it's a joint seismology project with the Geology Department of the University of Aberdeen."

"Out of curiosity, where were their sensors?"

"Somewhere in the north of Scotland. A place called Crianloch."

When Liz got to Jenny's, the first thing her host did was to pour her a large glass of Malbec. It was almost eight o'clock, and since Liz had left that morning, she'd been on the road for 6 hours, taken two sea crossings and spent several hours on Lundy. She was exhausted.

"I don't suppose I could have a bath, could I?" she asked. "I'm feeling done in after the day I've had."

"Of course, I'll go and run it for you while you relax. Nigel has his writing group tonight, so I doubt he'll be round."

Fifteen minutes later, Liz was pouring some bubble bath when her mobile rang. Given her relationship with technology, even having it in the bathroom was a recipe for disaster, and *Fate* didn't disappoint. Liz had seen the caller's name too, and in her hurry to answer it, the phone slipped from her fingers and dropped towards the bath. For once though, it bounced off the edge, teetered on the toilet rim, and fell onto the bathroom mat. She snatched it up.

"Erica."

"Hi, Liz. You sound flustered, are you all right?"

"I dropped my phone."

"Well, I have news. Did you get my email?"

"With the photos. Yes, I tried to call earlier."

"Oh sorry, it's been manic."

"In a good way, I hope?"

"Oh, yes. It's nothing to do with your moles I'm afraid, but I've come across another story, and I thought you might be interested. This one's about an RAF base up here, and as you mentioned something about them the other day ..."

"Something about Lossiemouth?"

"Indirectly, yes. My editor put me in touch with a source of his there, and that led me to a village called Crianloch."

"Where's that?"

"You don't know it?"

"No, should I?"

"See what you think after I've told you what I've found out."

By the time Erica was done, she'd gone through everything

she knew about Lossiemouth, Crianloch and her visit to Glen Crian. Liz's disbelief was like everyone else's who heard the story, but Erica stood her ground.

"Sounds pretty far-fetched."

"I thought so too until I saw the glen."

"So, what's the connection with Lossiemouth?"

"Oh good question, hold on … Have you heard of the … the Joint Force Intelligence Group or the National Centre for Geospatial Intelligence?"

"They're based at RAF Wyton near me."

"Or a Group Captain David Marston?"

Liz's heart skipped a beat. She still wasn't ready to admit that to Erica yet.

"Look I'm sorry to cut you off, but can we talk about this tomorrow? I've been on the road all day, and I'm knackered."

"Of course, you should have said. Give me a ring when you're ready."

Liz hung up the call, and after putting her phone out of harm's way, got into the bath. They say you shouldn't, but five minutes later she was asleep.

She woke up once the water had gone cold, and although it wasn't late, she put on her pyjamas, along with the dressing-gown Jenny had left out for her. It was warm in the bathroom, but the water had chilled her, and going back downstairs, she gratefully accepted the hot chocolate Jenny had made for them both. Occupying a sofa each, the two friends settled down to talk.

"So, how was Lundy?" asked Jenny after a few minutes of chitchat. She couldn't wait to hear about Liz's day.

"Interesting."

"Oh do tell."

"They're my moles all right. We managed to catch two, and

they both had my tags."

Jenny gasped.

"That isn't the half of it either. Erica rang while I was upstairs. You know, the journalist I mentioned up in Inverness?"

"She found something?"

"She found something all right, but it's just more weirdness." Jenny listened attentively while Liz told her story, finishing with Erica's mention of David. When Liz said *Crianloch*, Jenny stiffened.

"Sorry, where did you say?"

"Crianloch. It's a few miles west of Loch Ness apparently. An hour or so from Inverness. Why?"

"Oh, no reason."

Had Hendricks or Croft heard this response, they'd have had a field day. Jenny's words were too hurried, too blasé and without question, a lie. Liz didn't notice though, so she pressed on.

"I'm sure David mentioned Joint Force Intelligence during his time at Wyton, but I've no idea what they do, let alone the other one."

"Well let's check them out."

Liz nodded, and reaching down to pick up her bag, she took out her laptop. The desktop picture was the one of her and David she'd shown to Nigel, only now it was hidden behind a mass of shortcuts, documents and other icons. One showed the familiar emblem of the RAF which David had put there as a link to their website. She clicked and followed the menu to RAF Wyton. Liz and Jenny both read the screen. It confirmed that the two groups were based there, but it didn't say much about either of them, let alone anything about Lossiemouth, David or Crianloch.

"How about the Ministry of Defence site?" suggested Jenny.

Liz nodded, and they spent several minutes hunting around it for information without much luck. Next, they tried the Civil Service site, where for the first time they found some useful details. After this, they fell back onto googling the names of the two groups, and after nearly an hour, they'd built up a picture of them both. As far as Liz could tell, they provided intelligence reports to groups like the MoD, other parts of government, the armed forces, and to what one website referred to as *international partners*. Something about helping to inform strategic and tactical level decision-making?

This was too much jargon for either of them to absorb, but at least they had a sense of things now. A sense of something very secret indeed. But how did David fit in? And where had Erica heard his name? They were both excellent questions, but by now, Liz was too tired to think about them.

Jenny meanwhile was wide-awake, and for once, it wasn't Nigel who couldn't sleep, it was her. Her mind was awash with memories that had last hit her on their trip north. The thing was, they were getting stronger, and she didn't like it one bit.

By coincidence, Jenny wasn't the only person having trouble sleeping, as deep underground in Glen Crian, David Marston was struggling too. Following Thursday's initial visits to Crianloch and Drumnadrochit, he'd sent out teams across the countryside, only to have them all come back with the same report. Some places were as they remembered them, others had a few different buildings, or maybe a new road layout, but none were exactly as before. The one consistency was the absence of any 4G mobile towers, so that answered part of the comms question. Then on the Friday, Doug Smoke had a team dig a trench across the route where the landlines came into the site, and like the tarmac of the roadway, the armoured cable simply stopped at the perimeter. On the base side of the line, the cable was there, and on the other, nothing. It hadn't been cut or anything either, it simply stopped. He'd half-expected it, but it was still a jolt. Which only left the satellite links, and there was no way of checking them. So, earlier this Saturday evening, Marston had called his top team together to discuss the findings so far.

"What's the explanation, Doug?"

"It's hard to say, sir, but I've met with the top scientists, and ... and they believe we've broken through to a parallel world."

"A parallel world," said Marston flatly.

"Yes, sir."

"I thought that wasn't possible."

"So did they, sir."

"So, what happened? And why didn't it set off any of the alarms?"

"They're working on that, sir."

"Hmm."

Marston grimaced. It was astonishing how easily one could lapse into talking about something so bizarre, and he wasn't happy. He'd known there were certain risks when he'd taken the post at Crianloch, but this wasn't supposed to have been one of them.

"When will they have a clear answer?"

Doug Smoke looked embarrassed as he replied. "They're working on that too, sir."

TC had never been one to delay when things needed to be done and knowing what she was going back to at the house, she'd bought cloths, surface cleaners and bin bags on her way there. It wasn't that she was especially house-proud, but things were clearly far from normal, and she needed to exert control over something. She bought a rechargeable vacuum cleaner too.

She started with her bedroom, moved to the bathroom, the spare room, and lastly for upstairs, the one her parents used. It always felt funny being in there by herself, but as with the other rooms, she soon had it dust-free and looking lived in.

Next, she vacuumed the stairs, then she tackled the living room and the dining room. The kitchen came after that, followed by the downstairs toilet, and finally, the utility room.

It was dark by the time she finished and having also bought some food on the way home, she microwaved a lasagne, poured herself a glass of Rioja and sat down. On a bookcase by the fireplace was a photo album she'd spotted earlier. She opened it, and, as she stared at the first page, all the colour drained from her face.

Two lives well lived

Below this heading were her parents' names, dates of birth and a single date for their deaths. Her glass slipped from her fingers, and the red wine splashed across the carpet.

She sat there without moving for an age. Then, over the next few hours, she forced herself through happy, smiling pictures of them in their twenties, thirties, with her as a baby, and finally, shots of the three of them on holiday together. Pasted in after the last page was a newspaper account of a car accident nine months before.

She didn't move from the sofa that night, and barely noticed when the sun rose the following day. It wasn't until lunchtime that she moved again, and only then because she needed the bathroom. It wasn't just the death of her parents. After all, this wasn't her world, so in real terms, they weren't even hers, and the baby photos were of a different TC. She felt for them all just the same … Plus it brought back memories of her long-dead boyfriend. What about her other self too? Her bank account was still there, and TC now felt terrible about using it, but there was no mention of her in the press cutting, so where was she?

That could wait though, and as if things couldn't get any worse, the next couple of weeks revealed that it wasn't just her parents who were missing from this world, it was everyone. There was no Sue, no Simon, no anyone. She was completely alone.

Consequently, the first time she saw *him*, she fainted.

When TC came round, she was surrounded by a group of concerned faces, none of which was his. She struggled to her feet, pushed frantically through the crowd, and looked all around her. There was no sign of him. It had definitely been him though, hadn't it? The man she'd loved and who she'd seen killed by a drunk driver all those years before.

As TC spun round to look, she almost collapsed again, and it was only the elderly couple beside her that stopped her. Supporting her under each arm, they helped her to a nearby bench. While one of them comforted her, the other rummaged in a backpack for a bottle of water.

"Here, drink some of this."

She took a sip, and another, then leant back on the bench.

"How are you feeling?"

She didn't answer straight away and just looked from one to the other.

"Did you see him?" she asked weakly.

"See who?"

"The guy in the *Inception* t-shirt. He was over there."

The couple turned to where she was pointing.

"Sorry, no. Was it someone you recognised?"

TC looked down at her feet. How could she explain? Obviously, she couldn't. It *had* been him though, hadn't it? Hadn't it? It was impossible; but what did that word mean anymore? So maybe it was possible. Actually, it was *more than* possible. After all, he hadn't been in any of the other realities she'd visited. Except now, she was in one with no one else she knew, so it almost made sense. No, it *did* make sense! It made perfect sense, and what with everything else she'd gone through, she felt the universe owed her one. Most importantly, somewhere deep in her heart, she knew it had been him.

"Hello? Are you still with us?"

"Sorry, yes it was someone I've not seen in ages," she faltered. "I didn't know he was still around."

"Bound to give you a bit of a shock. You OK now?"

TC nodded and went to hand back the water bottle ... "Thank you, I needed that."

"It's OK. Keep it."

When they'd gone, TC looked around again. She knew he'd gone, but she also now knew he was somewhere in that world and it changed everything.

The question was, where?

Green and Blue

Sunday, September 19th

In contrast to some, Peter Harker had slept well and was back at his temporary desk in Drumnadrochit police station by half-past eight. The modelling programme had been running overnight to produce a map like the boffin's, and it was almost done. It couldn't do it from Harker's data alone as he'd only scanned certain parts of the glen, so he'd reconfigured the software to merge the two sets of readings. The original data would again show up in green, and the latest would be in blue.

After a short while, a tone sounded and *Render complete* appeared on-screen. Harker hit *Print*. The station only had a standard office printer, so the detail wouldn't be great, but with any luck, it would show him what he needed. He'd, therefore, set the printer to maximum print quality, so it took its time, but slowly the sheet of paper emerged. When he came back from the drinks machine with what claimed to be tea but smelt suspiciously like oxtail soup, it had finished. Harker looked at the map, compared it against the architect's plans he'd been given, and went out to the front desk.

"Have you got a magnifying glass I could borrow by any chance?"

"I can do one better than that, Professor," smiled the duty sergeant.

With that, he left his desk and disappeared into a back room, only to re-emerge a minute later carrying a magnifying lamp with an articulated arm.

"Will this do?"

"Perfect!" replied Harker, gratefully taking the lamp and heading back to his office. A few minutes later he was back at the front desk, only this time he was visibly agitated about something.

"I've got to go back out there."

"To the glen, Professor?"

"Yes, I need to get back out there right away."

"OK, let me check with the inspector. I should be able to drive you."

Twenty-five minutes later, Harker and the sergeant drew to a halt at the far end of the gravel track. They quickly unpacked the crate again, and Harker set off towards the other side of the glen. He was almost running. Watching him from the Land Rover, the sergeant saw him pull the latest map from his pocket and begin work. As before, he put on the headphones and started walking a criss-cross pattern over a section of the landscape.

It was a smaller area than previously, and he walked slowly, yet deliberately as before. Even so, there was a palpable urgency to the way he moved, and when he was done, he sprinted back to the vehicle. After reloading the equipment, they set off.

For the next hour, he paced about the police station waiting for the tell-tale beep to say that the new map was ready. He was only reprocessing a small section of the map, so he knew it shouldn't take long. Even so, he almost leapt out of his skin when the beep finally sounded, This time, rather than hitting *Print*, he enlarged the image on the screen. What he'd spotted earlier was still there.

He excitedly took screen grabs of the image, one showing the whole station and another showing the enlarged section. Then rummaging in his pocket for the card the DG's advisor had given him, he typed in the email address, attached both jpegs and hit *Send*.

Life being what it is, there are often things that work out better for some than for others. In this case, Professor Harker was in the latter camp, whereas a certain gentleman behind an orange door in Lossiemouth was one of the former. Why? Well, let's just say Professor Harker should have turned the advisor's card over for instructions on how to send his findings by encrypted email.

He hadn't though, and given the algorithms Erica's source had set up to catch interesting data packets flying across the web, it wasn't long before a phone call was being placed.

"Hello, Erica McBride."

"All that we see," said a familiar voice.

"Oh ... Er ... All that we see or seem is but a dream within a dream."

"I'm sending you something. Print it and destroy the email."

The line went dead.

It being a Sunday, it only took Erica ten minutes to drive to the offices of the *Northern Echo* where she did as she'd been instructed. The first part anyway, and she was about to delete the email when the images slid out of the printer. She frowned. Working for a newspaper had its benefits though, and this was one such time ... She hit *Print* again, only this time she selected *Poster size*.

Once the printer had spewed out the massive sheets, Erica went across to a side meeting room and laid them out on the table. One was an original plan of Crianloch Station, another a map of Glen Crian as a whole, and the third, a close-up of one corner of the map. She looked at the first two and took a moment to get her bearings. The plan was clear enough, but why did the other two have today's date at the top? What was she looking at? Some sort of residual image? She re-read his email.

See the date at the top of the OS map, and the lines superimposed on it, then compare them to the architect's plan I've enclosed. Look especially at the southern corner and let me know what you find.

Southern corner? Erica flicked her eyes between the plan and the map of the overall valley, then traced the fuzzy green outline of the base with her finger. Suddenly something caught her eye. She pulled out the detailed map and there it was too. A second line on the southern edge of the map. Short and fuzzy like the rest, but blue this time. Could that be what he meant? A line that didn't match up with the original plan?

Erica dashed into the newsroom to where they kept Ordnance Survey maps of the local area. She ran her hand along the shelf until she came to number 431, then went back to the meeting room and spread it out next to the others. She pursed her lips as she followed the line with her finger again. Whatever the blue line was, Erica now saw where it led.

She rolled the maps into a tube for carrying, hit *Delete* on her source's email, and emptied the trash folder to be sure. Even as the *crunch* sounded from her MacBook, she was dialling Liz's number. When Erica spoke, she could hardly get the words out quickly enough.

Liz Benning had overslept, and when she eventually surfaced, the first thing she did was to check her phone for new messages. There was a single email from Steve Guthrie. It was short and to the point.

> *Hi prof. I've visited Effington to do some more tests on your sensor problem. No news yet but I've spoken with Seismic Dynamics and have another call with them tomorrow, so hopefully we'll have something for you by Monday. If you want to pop into my office, I'm free before 9:00 or after 10:30. Cheers, Steve*

Liz looked at the date on the email. It had been sent the day before, and he was having a call with the US the next day? *What warrants a call on a Sunday?* she wondered to herself. She deleted the email and was considering calling him back when her own phone rang.

"Liz, it's Erica."

"Oh, hi. How are ...?"

"Look, I've found something. You've got to come up."

"What?"

"Sorry, I rushed into that, but something big's come up."

Liz could hear the excitement in Erica's voice, and it was infectious.

"Hold on."

All thoughts of Steve now banished, Liz rushed downstairs where she found Jenny and Nigel having coffee in the lounge.

Erica could make out their muffled voices in the background as Liz mouthed *Good Morning* to each of them and gestured to her phone.

"Are you still there? I'm putting you on loudspeaker. I'm with the people I went to Scotland with. Erica, this is Jenny and Nigel."

"Hi, both."

"Would you go from the beginning, Erica? Start with what you told me yesterday?"

Erica went through the story she'd told Liz the night before, and although Jenny had already relayed as much as she could remember to Nigel, it was good hearing it from the horse's mouth.

"What do you think it is?" asked Nigel. "The blue line."

"Could be an error on either the plans or the map I suppose."

"Somethin' they built durin' construction but never updated the paperwork?"

"It could be nothing."

"But it might be something, and I haven't told you the best bit yet. The extra line goes directly to what on the OS map looks like a cave."

"Now that *is* interestin'."

"It's got to be worth a look."

The momentary silence that followed, consisted of Jenny, Liz, and Nigel exchanging glances. They nodded in unison.

"OK, we'll come up. We can be in the area tonight, and meet you somewhere nearby tomorrow?"

"Great. Let's go for Drumnadrochit. I'll text you somewhere for us to meet."

"OK. See you in the morning."

Erica hung up.

"She's very sure of herself," said Nigel.

"I wonder who this source of hers is."

"Well her editor obviously trusts him."

"A guy who wears a monocle though? An' has his own Faraday cage? It sounds like somethin' out of a conspiracy movie."

"He's either seriously deluded, or very much for real."

"I guess we'll find out."

So just like that, they were off to Scotland again ... for the second time in under a week. In Liz's car this time though, so she drove the first leg while Nigel googled somewhere for them to stay. He chose Fort William, which was going to be an eight-hour drive, but it would leave them only an hour and a quarter to go the following day.

As for Jenny, once they were on the M5, she drifted off into thoughts of her own. Thoughts of the past she'd never told Nigel about. Her childhood.

So Professor Harker's email had put one set of wheels in motion, and when the DG read it, he was both fascinated, and unusually for him, furious. The furious part of his brain was because of the email not having been encrypted. The fascinated part immediately called in his chief scientific advisor, and when they rang Harker a few minutes later, the DG was his usual, soothing self.

"What do you think, Professor?"

"Given what we're dealing with here, my best guess is that the coloured lines are a sort of heat signature left behind by the station. The one that doesn't match the plans is interesting though."

He went on to outline the same possibilities as Nigel, Jenny, Liz and Erica had.

"So what's your opinion?"

"I honestly don't know. It could be as simple as an error on the plans, or it could be something more significant."

"How can we be sure?"

"It's hard to say, but if I had access to a Quantum Detector, it might help[46]."

"Where would we get one of those from?"

"They have one at the University of Aberdeen, and they've got a team studying The Great Glen at the moment, so you might be lucky and find they're using some rooms at the University of the Highlands and Islands in Inverness. Otherwise, it would be Aberdeen itself."

"OK put DI Hendricks on, would you?"

Hendricks quickly agreed to track down a detector, and the DG ended the call. Next, he rang the Defence Secretary, who in turn, immediately got on the phone to the Prime Minister's office. A meeting was set for four o'clock that afternoon.

"Good afternoon gentlemen, what's so urgent that it couldn't wait until Monday?"

"It's Operation Carter, Prime Minister."

"I see. Something has gone awry?"

"You could say that."

The Defence Secretary explained the events of September 10th, and what they'd been doing in the days since.

"And you didn't think to alert me to this sooner?"

---

[46] Yes, such things really do exist.

"We didn't consider it appropriate, Prime Minister, as we didn't know about the radiation until Friday, and it was only this morning we had anything we felt we could act on."

"I see. So what's the prevailing theory?"

"As to what caused the base to vanish, we don't yet have one, but the Hawking radiation appears to be real. That's why we need to send in people to do a further assessment of the site."

"And I suppose you want my authority to mobilize troops?"

"Actually no, Prime Minister. We've established a collaboration between the local police and the people at RAF Lossiemouth, so we propose sending in a joint team. Keep it low key for now."

The PM considered this for a moment. "What's the danger to the public?"

"None as far as we're aware. The station is several miles from the nearest village, and if it becomes necessary, we'll equip our people with protective clothing. Purely as a precaution, you understand."

"Very well. Keep me informed, gentlemen."

Once the two men returned to the MoD building, it only took them a few minutes to reach DCI Croft and Group Captain Finch. The Defence Secretary opened the call as usual and immediately got down to the matter at hand. Half an hour later, DI Hendricks, Professor Harker and Finch's two officers were on their way back to Glen Crian. Being that much closer, the Drumnadrochit team had a ninety-minute head start on the others, and thanks to a Quantum Detector having been available in Inverness, Hendricks and Harker were able to take it with them when they set off.

The first time Hendricks had been there, it had been a

pleasant Autumn day. Now it was vile, with freezing, horizontal rain lashing the landscape, and a wind howling around the peaks like an agonised wolf. Given the mountainous terrain, the weather seemed almost appropriate, but that didn't help matters, and there was no sign of the constables on guard duty either. As always though, Hendricks had her all-weather jacket in the Land Rover, and this time she'd brought a spare for Harker as well. So, bowing their heads against the elements, they left the vehicle and set off across the glen.

They had a copy of Harker's map, and they'd both been there before, so they found their way easily enough. Even so, the weather made it hard going, and the undergrowth didn't help. After only one misstep into a boggy patch though, they eventually made it to the far side of the glen. Once there, it didn't take them long to work out where the rogue line led, and they were soon looking down at the formation Erica had tried to make sense of on the map. It was a hole about the size of a *Stop* sign, surrounded by a cluster of rocks.

After exchanging a glance with Hendricks, Harker knelt down and turned on the Quantum Detector. The needle instantly snapped to the right and sat there quivering against the end-stop as if it was trying to give a higher reading than the dial would allow.

Once they were back in the Land Rover, they waited for over an hour before the headlights of the blue SUV swept into sight behind them, and soon after, they were joined by the two RAF officers.

"You look like you've been for a swim Inspector," greeted the man as he climbed into the back seat.

DI Hendricks smiled.

"And judging by your expression, I'd say you've already found something."

"Well you can trust us on that, or you can check it out for yourselves."

The two officers exchanged a look.

"We'd better see for ourselves," said the woman.

By now there was barely an hour left before sunset, and with the weather as it was, the day had pretty much given up already. Hendricks and the others couldn't do that though, and when they reached the cluster of rocks, Harker again turned the detector on and bent down. The two officers followed suit, then the woman leant forward and peered into the opening.

"Looks like a cave entrance," she yelled over the sound of the wind.

"That's what we thought," yelled Hendricks in reply. "Unless you want to take a look inside, I suggest we call it a day. The mobile signal is rubbish in this weather, so let's go back to Drumnadrochit and set up a conference call with Inverness and Lossiemouth. Kill two birds with one stone."

DCI Croft and Group Captain Finch listened carefully to their officers, and when Drumnadrochit dropped off the call, the two men were left to agree on what to do next. After several minutes Croft left to make another call, leaving Finch to wait for a call back.

A little under thirty minutes later, Finch's video app beeped, and he pressed *Connect*. Three familiar faces appeared on the 4-way screen.

"Good afternoon Group Captain," said the Defence Secretary.

"Good afternoon, sirs."

"The Detective Chief Inspector tells me you've had a joint report from your people and are of one mind."

"That's right, Minister. The hole is apparently large enough to crawl into, so we felt we should consult with you before proceeding." The laziness in his voice had almost gone now, and if he'd turned his webcam round, the others wouldn't have seen a single golf magazine.

"And you, Chief Inspector. What do you expect to find? With no evidence of the base on the surface, why should there be anything underground?"

"Honestly, Director, I don't know. There may be nothing, but with the radiation traces and now the quantum readings, it's the best we've got."

"And your people are aware of the danger?"

"Naturally, sir."

"Very well. When can you get them back out there?"

"In the morning, sir," replied Croft. "It's almost sunset, and there's quite a storm in Glen Crian at the moment. Plus, I can arrange for hazmat suits from SOCO first thing, and high-intensity lights in case the weather hasn't cleared."

"Very well, keep us informed."

In Crianloch Station, Doug Smoke shifted in his chair. He didn't like the idea of them having jumped to a parallel world, even though proving their existence had always been part of the base's remit. As a result, it was with some reluctance that he'd finally had to accept the notion that something must have gone badly wrong.

"First question, Doug," began Marston. "Are we confident we're in a parallel world?"

"Yes, sir. The boffins see it as the only viable answer, and frankly, the evidence supports that."

"What have we got so far?"

"Nothing's changed, sir. The external comms still don't work, and to one degree or another, nowhere in the surrounding area is quite the same as we know it in our world."

"The conclusion being?"

"We're not in Kansas anymore."

"I appreciate the humour Doug, but that's it isn't it? This isn't our world."

The five people around the table could have debated the point, but they all knew it was true.

"OK, let's look at it another way. What's the same? Start with the air."

"Identical, sir ... 78% nitrogen, 21% oxygen and all the usual trace elements."

"Water?"

"H2O."

"Soil?"

"That varies, of course, sir, but right above us it's identical to what's in the construction records."

"Language?"

"Again, the same, sir, right down to the local dialects."

"Animals?"

"Going by what we've seen for ourselves, sir, they're all pretty much the same. We've also been able to do some research in a local library, and worldwide, the only big differences are that some species are extinct here that exist in our world, and vice versa."

"Such as?"

"Tigers aren't endangered here, sir, but moose are. Dodos

still exist, but there don't seem to be any flamingos."

"Interesting. What about food, habits, social structures, things like that?"

"Culturally everything seems much the same, albeit with a few differences, but no more than we expected."

"Than we expected?"

"If you remember, sir, research worked up a few hypotheses when the station was commissioned. Some of them assumed minor differences, some medium and some major."

"Remind me."

"Major meant Dinosaurs, medium meant humans, but not as the dominant species, and ..."

"And minor was pretty much anything we'd recognize as normal."

"Indeed."

"What about history? World events?"

"Many of the major events appear to have turned out the same, although some of the politics here are very different."

"Such as?"

"JFK was never assassinated and retired after two terms as president. The Spanish Civil War never happened. Japan still runs on a feudal system. Like I say, different."

"Countries?"

"Given how much change there's been in our own world in recent years, they're not that far apart."

"Which just leaves your favourite subject, Doug."

"Well, it's interesting, sir. There are computers, TV, satellites, mobiles and so on, but they're just ... well, different."

"Different how?"

"Think of it like Microsoft vs Apple, Android vs iOS, region 1 vs region 2 DVDs ..."

"Same experience, different means."

"That's right, sir."

Marston sat back in his chair, then stood up. He walked over to the kettle and reluctantly opened the jar of instant coffee.

"Anyone else?"

Three hands went up, and Marston went about his task. After several minutes, he re-joined the table to a small chorus of thank-yous, and thoughtfully stirred what passed for his coffee.

"So the good news is, we're in a world where we can survive indefinitely if we have to. On the other hand, protocol states our first priority in these circumstances is to try to return. I can't quite believe we have protocols for that, but we do, so we're back to the question of how we got here, and how we get back."

In reply, Doug Smoke stood up, went to the door, and beckoned in the seven experts he'd briefed in advance. It was a decisive moment.

"I take it we have an answer, Doug," said Marston, looking at all the new faces.

"We believe so, sir."

"Great, let's hear it."

"As you know, we were sure from the start that the problem lay with a Basement Project. So we've been looking at all of them, and we think we've found the culprit."

"Go on."

"We believe it's the TDE."

"Which is?"

"Sorry, sir, the Time Displacement Experiment. We started it up a few days before the incident."

"So what do we do about it now?"

"One school of thought says we turn it off, simple as that."

"OK."

"*But ...*"

"The other view is that we'd be better off winding it down gradually over a few hours."

"*But ...*"

"Which is it? Pros and cons?"

"*Sir ...*"

"The best option seems to be to wind it down gradually, sir, as even the advocates of a hard switch-off don't see any downsides to that."

"*Sir but ...*"

All through this conversation, the person who had been trying to interrupt was Jessica Williams, and finally, Doug turned her way. He was polite, but none too happy.

"You had something to add Jessica?"

"It won't work. What I mean is it won't make any difference."

"We've been through this, Jessica, and everyone agrees the TDE is the most likely cause."

"And they're wrong. This isn't a time problem."

"We're not saying it is, just that the experiment has had unforeseen consequences."

"But that's like saying an unforeseen consequence of making an omelette is having a helicopter land on your house!"

As usual, it was a bizarre analogy, but she kept going.

"What I mean is we've experienced a reality shift, not a time shift. They're simply not the same thing."

"We know your views Jessica, but it's not your experiment, so I'm inclined to go with the views of the people who know."

It was a polite but firm put-down, and Jessica knew she was beaten. She was therefore surprised when Marston spoke.

"Jessica, is it? A question. Do you foresee any dangers in shutting down the TDE?"

She hesitated before answering. "I don't know it well enough to say."

"So I take it you'd have no objections to us trying it?"

"It won't help though."

"But if it won't hurt, we try it. Yes?"

She nodded reluctantly, and Doug took this as his cue to set the wheels in motion.

 So where was he? The thought of it filled TCs mind so completely, she didn't notice the three-week deadline pass ... and that was all it took. Much like the day she'd ventured out of her flat for the first time, the world was new again. This time she felt new with it too, and as she sat contemplating some sponge cake one morning, an idea came to her. She'd get a job.

"Big deal" you might say, but it was, for without putting it into words, she'd decided to stay. In reality, it was all about *him*, of course, and with that one, simple decision, the universe had no further hold over her. Cake or no cake, this was now her home.

A year later, she was driving into a beer festival when some floppy-haired idiot walked out in front of her camper van, and she hit him.

She slammed on the brakes and let out a small scream as his body bounced neatly off the front grill. When she got to him, he was rolling on the ground, moaning and clutching his stomach. A crowd had gathered already, and expecting broken bones or even blood, she knelt down beside him.

"My beer," he moaned, "you smashed my beer."

He rolled over to reveal that in the collision, she'd smashed a large jug of beer he'd been carrying. In a funny sort of way, it had acted as a beery kind of airbag. The crowd laughed, muttered and started to disperse, leaving TC free to stare.

"Nigel!"

"You broke my beer!" he insisted.

"I'm so sorry. I'll buy you another."

There he lay in worn trainers, faded jeans and a beer-soaked *Doctor Who* t-shirt, but it was all she could do not to throw her arms around him. It was him! The man she'd seen die on that street corner eight and half years before and yet here he was ... Nigel. Her Nigel.

"What?"

"I said I'll buy you another beer?"

"Bloody right. What did you say before that?"

"Come on, let's get you up, and we can sort out that beer."

She'd replied on instinct, but it seemed to work. Evidently, as much of the beer was already inside him as was on the t-shirt, and he wasn't about to pass up the chance of more.

At half-past ten that night, TC meandered back to her van with a smile on her face. They'd talked beer, politics, music, literature, and she was pretty sure she hadn't dropped herself in it. Part of her wasn't surprised they got on so well. Then again, she'd met enough people over the years who weren't the same as the ones she remembered for her to be wary. She didn't need to be though, and they even swapped phone numbers. Admittedly he'd passed out somewhere between his sixth pint, and a bowl of French onion soup, but it didn't matter.

She was over the moon.

Parallel running

Monday, September 20th

Everyone had slept badly. Nigel had been his usual sleepless self, Liz was too anxious and excited about what they might find, and Jenny ... well, her nerves were building with every passing minute. The morning was no better either, by when Jenny needed something to concentrate on, so she took the first turn at driving. With that taken care of, Liz grabbed the opportunity to phone Steve Guthrie.

"Morning, Steve."

"Oh morning Prof'. You're up early."

"You've got some news for me?"

"Absolutely."

With that, he explained the spontaneous hard resets and took her through the power surge theory.

"So that's why you had me call the farmer."

"Have you heard back from him yet?"

"Not yet, no."

"Well never mind, it's why I went back out to site myself."

"And?"

"I didn't find anything new at Effington, although Seismic Dynamics has discovered something intriguing. Another set of sensors went wrong on the same day as ours."

"A bad batch?"

"Unlikely, as ours run bespoke software, but I'll be speaking with the other user later on, so I'll let you know. Are you coming into the University today?"

"No, not today Steve. By the way, where were these other sensors?"

"Northern Scotland somewhere, hold on." There was a sound of rustling papers as he looked for the one he's scribbled notes on the day before ... "Got it," he said at last. "Crianloch. A place called Crianloch."

Erica, meanwhile, had also had trouble sleeping and was already waiting in the *Apple of my eye* café as Jenny and the others approached Drumnadrochit. As the last half mile sped by, Liz was chatting with Nigel about her moles, leaving Jenny to concentrate on the road. You'd think so anyway, but she didn't need to as it was a route she'd travelled hundreds of times before. The road curved sharply to the left to go over the river, and ignoring the right turn to Crianloch, Jenny drove across the old, stone bridge. As she did, the skies opened. The previous day's storm wasn't finished, and was still throwing everything it had at locals and visitors alike.

Erica spotted the others as soon as they walked into the café, and after ordering teas and coffees all round, they moved to the table where she'd already spread out the various maps and plans.

"I see what you mean about the lines," said Nigel.

"They look like a sort of ghost image or something."

"I thought that too."

"Which makes the blue line all the more interestin'."

"I know. Take a look at this."

Erica unfolded the 1:25,000 Ordnance Survey map she'd borrowed from work, and pointed to where she'd carefully pencilled in the route of the blue line. At the end of it was a small ring of black dots and dashes. It wasn't clear what it was, but there was clearly something there.

"It looks like a gravel pit or a cutting of some sort," said Nigel, peering at the key at the bottom of the map.

"Rock outcrop?"

"Possibly."

"I think it's a tunnel," put in Nigel.

"A tunnel?"

"Think about it. We're talking about an underground base, aren't we? Which presumably had lifts in and out. So isn't it likely they'd build a backdoor as well?"

"It's a bit small."

"Well, whatever it is, if it's got something to do with David, I want to know."

It was Liz who'd interrupted, and the words had come out before she realised what she was saying.

"David?" asked Erica.

Liz looked embarrassed and glanced from Jenny to Nigel.

"Ah ... well ... you remember the other day when you asked me about Group Captain David Marston?" she said slowly.

Erica nodded.

"Same David. He's my fiancé."

Erica raised both eyebrows. "I take it he's not been in touch or something?"

Liz nodded.

"Anything else you haven't told me?"

"There was my brick," interjected Nigel excitedly, and was about to tell the story for Erica's benefit, when Jenny interrupted.

"There *is* something else," said Jenny softly, "I think they're all connected."

The others turned to look at her, and she paused to push the hair from her eyes before continuing.

"The moles, the brick, the base, David. I think they're all connected. In fact, I'm sure of it, and I reckon I know what's at the root of it all too."

"Go on, Jen," said Nigel quietly.

"I don't think the base is in our world anymore."

This shut them all up. She'd said it in such a matter of fact tone.

"You'll have to explain that one," said Nigel at last.

"It was something someone told me once ... about parallel worlds."

"Parallel ... Oh, you're havin' us on."

"No, seriously. I mean, an entire underground base can't just vanish, so why shouldn't it have gone somewhere else?"

"What are you on?"

"It's as likely as anything else!" Her voice had risen now, and she looked pleadingly at Nigel. He knew she was relying on him to back her up, and he hesitated before answering.

"Short answer, Jen, no. It's about as likely as ... I don't know ... somethin' very unlikely indeed."

He'd run out of inspiration halfway through that sentence, and there was another long silence before Erica spoke up.

"So why haven't we got theirs, Jenny?"

"I think we have."

"But we haven't. I've been to Glen Crian remember, and trust me, there's nothing there."

"No wait a minute," interrupted Nigel with a sudden glimmer of understanding in his eyes. "What you mean Jen, is that in this parallel world, there isn't a base there, an' Glen Crian's still just a valley. So, like that, we have got theirs."

Jenny smiled and nodded.

"But what's the connection?" asked Erica.

"David's *your* fiancé and *your* cousin," replied Jenny, looking from Liz to Nigel. "Plus, the moles and the brick did their thing on the same day as David vanished ..."

"... and I found out on my earlier call that some other sensors like mine went haywire on the same day ... and in Crianloch too."

These last few words fell not so much like a stone into a pond, as like a rhino into a swimming pool.

"So the parallel worlds piece ..."

"...ties it all together. The base shifts from our world to another, and it creates some sort of ... I don't know ... some sort of butterfly effect."

"With us as what?" asked Liz. "Iron filings to its magnet?"

Jenny didn't answer that, as her eyes were locked with Nigel's. He knew her moods, her jokes, her expressions, and the pleading look on her face told him everything he needed to know.

"I believe you," he said at last. "I do. I actually believe you."

"Me too," said Erica. "I've written about weirder things in my column, so why not?"

Liz looked at the three of them. She wanted to believe, but David had told her he was based in Lossiemouth, and they'd never kept secrets from each other before. Suddenly she was angry. He'd lied to her! She'd almost worried herself sick over him, and he'd lied to her. And to Gran as well!

Twenty-five minutes later Liz turned left at the T-junction in the centre of Crianloch. As she did, Nigel stared out the car window at the weather, while Jenny distractedly brushed a strand of hair from her face. It could just as easily have been a cobweb of memory, as everywhere from Drumnadrochit onwards had tugged at her heart. It was too late to turn back now though, and as Liz's Kia ground to a halt a few hundred yards up the gravel drive, they all gazed out at the pouring rain. It was the same spot where Erica and AGB had stopped three days before, only now, the landscape looked very different.

"Nice weather for ducks," said Nigel with a grin.

Luckily, they'd remembered to bring coats with them, and Liz got out first, pulling her seat forward so Jenny and Nigel could get out as well. As she did, the wind caught her, and she'd have lost her footing if Nigel hadn't grabbed her arm.

Once they were all out, Erica beckoned to the others, then led them up the rise to their left as her guide had done before. The four of them scanned the landscape. Unsurprisingly in the conditions, the police constables hadn't yet returned to their post, and without hesitating, Erica set off down into the glen.

After her went Nigel and Liz, with Jenny bringing up the rear.

The morning after TC ran Nigel over, she woke up to find a note under one of her windscreen wipers.

Thanks for the beers and sorry if my head dented your van. See you around. Nigel.

She beamed with pleasure, and a few days later took the leap of sending him a text.

Hi there. Dented any vans recently?

His reply was almost instantaneous ...

My limit's one a month so you should be honoured. Buy you a beer sometime? It must be my round.

Hers was as quick ...

The White Hart you mentioned? Friday at 8?

And his ...

See you there.

It was as simple as that. They met, they chatted, they talked about the same things as before, and Nigel bought crisps. It was easy and comfortable as friendships should be, and it wasn't long before they were meeting regularly. There was never any question of them dating, but they became friends, really good friends. After a few months, she moved to Penmound, and not long after that, she joined him as a regular in the pub. The following Summer, they started playing skittles[47] in the

---

[47] Skittles is a traditional game that's still played in pubs across England and Ireland. It's a bit like ten-pin bowling, only with smaller wooden balls, no technology to reset the pins, a lot more shouting, and quite a lot of beer.

local league together.

In many ways, he was very different from the Nigel she'd known before, although at the same time he was exactly the same. He looked just like him anyway. Sometimes TC forgot herself and said things he could never hope to understand, but generally, she managed to brush them off. He loaned her books, put up with her musical tastes and marvelled at her ignorance of old movies. They laughed about it though, and overall, Nigel relished having such a great friend in the village. Jenny, on the other hand, fell in love with him all over again.

The downside, of course, was that Jenny could never tell him about her life as TC, and yet here they were, battling a ferocious mountain storm as they walked across a highland glen together.

For once though *Fate* was on their side, and the wind dropped slightly as they reached the cluster of rocks. They all exchanged glances, then without hesitating, Liz knelt down and crawled into the hole. Moments later, she poked her head back out.

"It opens up once you get inside. I'm going to take a look."

They all looked at each other and without a word, followed her in. Whatever was down there, it had to be better than the weather outside. They were quickly away from it too, as the tunnel sloped sharply downhill for a hundred yards or so before levelling out. It changed, as well. One moment they were squelching through muddy darkness, and the next there was a well-lit concrete corridor up ahead. That wasn't all, because where the one became the other, there was an eerie green glow. It wasn't bright, but it danced. Like those Christmas tree lights that blink at you when you least expect it. Not only that, but the lights were making a low, crackling noise, rather like a log fire.

Liz reached out a hand and instantly snatched it back as a thrill of electricity shot down her spine. Ignoring her yelp of surprise, Jenny suddenly walked past them all, straight through the lights and into the corridor beyond. Immediately, klaxons went off, and a red strobe light started flashing 20 yards down the passage.

"What the hell?" demanded David Marston.

"That's the intruder alert, sir."

David flashed a look at his security advisor.

"The system shows where any incursions take place, so my people will already be on their way."

"Let's get up there too. It could be an animal, but if it's a person we've got a problem."

Walking as fast as they could without running, the two men left the room, went up two levels and along a series of corridors to where the alert had started. Up ahead were four heavily armed airmen surrounding a group of soaking wet civilians. *So, not an animal*, thought David.

Suddenly there was a shout, and one of the civilians broke away from the rest.

"Halt!" shouted one of the gunners. "Stop, or I'll shoot."

"David!"

Liz's voice cut through the air to a startled Marston.

"Stand down!" he bellowed.

"David!"

She ran full tilt at him, and they didn't embrace so much as collide.

She pulled away, took a step backwards and looked as if she was about to say something. Then she slapped him. Hard.

"Why aren't you in Lossiemouth?" she demanded in the same voice she'd used on the SUV driver.

"You're soaking wet," he said incredulously.

"Is that all you can say?" she challenged.

"What on earth are you doing here?"

"We came to find you!"

"To find ... so everyone knows about the base?"

"Well, no," she said, subsiding slightly. "We got lucky."

By now the airmen had escorted the others down the corridor and were waiting with them a few yards away ... sidearms at the ready. David scanned the three faces, and his eyes widened in surprise ... "Nigel?"

"Well, Gran was worried," he replied in an *I do this sort of thing every day* kind of voice. "Anyway, how often do I get the chance to help my perfect cousin out of a spot?"

"Ye gods, does the whole family know?"

"Just us," said Nigel with a grin. "Oh, this is Jenny by the way."

"At last. Hardly the ideal circumstances, but it's good to finally meet you."

They shook hands, and last but not least, Liz introduced Erica. "She's how we found you."

"Well, we definitely need to catch up," said David. "I want to know everything you know."

They started walking and had only gone a few yards when a massive explosion rocked the base, knocking them all off their feet. As the lights went out, David instinctively threw an arm around Liz. When the emergency lights flickered on moments later, a great cloud of dust was rolling towards them along the corridor. David quickly closed his eyes against it and pulled Liz to him. Moments later, the floor shook as a second explosion thundered in the distance, and this time, it was Jenny's turn to fling out a hand. She caught hold of Nigel's elbow as the concussion hit, and they were plunged into darkness again. There was a crash as one of the light fittings fell from the ceiling, and another as a fire extinguisher jumped out of its wall bracket and rolled across the floor. When the lights came back a second time, grit and paint flakes were raining down on them all. The air was thick with them and had turned a dirty, milky grey.

What the hell was that? wondered David as he helped Liz to her feet. He looked around to see Nigel and Jenny huddled together against one wall. A short distance away, two of his men were kneeling alongside Erica who'd fallen heavily in all the commotion.

"Is everyone OK?" he demanded.

There was a chorus of uncertain yeses as everyone staggered to their feet.

"Let's get going. And you men bring up the rear."

Halfway to the stairs, Doug Smoke appeared around a corner.

"What the hell happened Doug?"

"It was the TDE, sir. Turns out there was a risk to taking it down gradually after all."

"It exploded?" asked David incredulously.

"It shorted out a couple of circuits which caused a system cascade, and one of the generators blew."

"I didn't think that was possible."

"It wasn't supposed to be, sir, so things must be more different here than we thought."

He stopped in mid-sentence as he spotted Liz and the others. "Sir?"

"Yes, it seems we have visitors Doug ... This is my fiancée Liz, my cousin Nigel and two of their friends."

Even as David said it he knew how bizarre it sounded, but Smoke had been trained to cope with any eventuality, so he simply reached out and shook hands with each of them.

Once they were all back in the Senior Officers' Mess, David had one of the canteen staff make coffee while Liz and the others started into their story. He listened with rising incredulity.

"So you're telling me it's not been in the news at all?"

"Not a word."

"How on earth has it been kept a secret?"

"Well, someone's been looking into it."

"The map you mean," asked David. "How did you get that anyway?"

"Best not to ask," grinned Erica. "A journalist has to protect her sources. But I can tell you there's been a group of scientists in Glen Crian for the last few days. Taking all sorts of readings by all accounts."

"They can't have worked it out yet though."

"To be fair, neither did we," replied Liz. "Erica found what turned out to be the back door, and here we are."

"But do you realize what you've done?"

"Of course," chimed in Jenny calmly. "We've passed into a parallel world. Same as you."

She said it in the same tone of voice you'd use to ask someone if they fancied a cup of tea. Perfectly reasonable, without a hint of it being anything out of the ordinary. Nigel, Erica and Liz smiled. David raised an eyebrow.

"Why do you think that?" he asked guardedly.

"It's the only explanation, surely? And what with the moles not having left a trace either ..."

"Yes, why was that?" interrupted Nigel.

"What do you mean?"

"Well here, the whole base shifted to another world, but they just moved a few counties."

"Wait a minute. What moles? Don't tell me ..."

Liz nodded.

Just then there was a knock on the door, and Doug Smoke came in. The explosions had sealed off the tunnel everyone had come through, virtually destroyed one of the generator rooms, and one of the scientists' tropical fish had died of shock. Otherwise though, the base was fine ... albeit with a few hairline cracks here and there.

"Well, it could have been worse. What next Doug?"

He smiled a wry smile ... "I'm not sure the other scientists will like it, sir, but I'd like to call Jessica Williams back in."

"To hell with the others. If she's got a theory of her own, I want to hear it."

Five minutes later, Jessica Williams knocked on the door and entered. She was obviously unused to being summoned like this and didn't know what to expect. The unknown faces around the table confused her too, but David was smiling, and Doug Smoke even pulled a chair out for her, so ...

"No ill effects from earlier I hope," began Marston.

"No that's fine, I'm only junior, so I'm used to not being taken too seriously."

"Actually, I meant the explosions."

"Oh no, I'm fine, thanks."

"Let's go back to what you were saying before."

"About it being a reality shift?"

"Yes."

"Well, that's it really. Everyone agrees we're in a parallel world, and the only thing we have running in that line is the Pudding."

"Pudding?"

She smiled. "Sorry, it's a kind of science joke. Parallel

Universe Detection Device In Neutral Gravity ... PUDDING."

David smiled back ... "Neutral Gravity?"

"Technically weightlessness, but that wouldn't have made a good acronym," she grinned.

"And what's weightlessness got with this?"

"Nothing really. Theory suggests some particles might be able to float between parallel universes, and that made someone think of weightlessness, so ... Mostly though we just wanted a really neat acronym."

"So this PUDDING was designed to detect parallel universes."

"Exactly."

"And how long's it been running."

"Right from the beginning, which is where my theory comes in. When we lost comms, I started going through all the data we'd accumulated, and I noticed something. It was only small in itself, but as I went back further into the records, I started to see a pattern."

"Meaning?"

"Well, it turns out there's been a gradual build-up of particles since we turned it on."

"What sort of particles?" asked Smoke.

"They don't even have a name in scientific circles, but it's been proven there are both atomic and subatomic particles which can appear to be in two places at once[48]. You know, like with Schrödinger's cat[49]."

---

[48] According to Bill Poirier in 2010, particles from other worlds can seep into ours, and some can exist in more than one place at a time or communicate with each other over great distances. What Einstein called "Spooky action at a distance."

[49] *Schrödinger's cat* is a thought experiment, put forward by Erwin Schrödinger in 1935, in which there's a box holding a cat that is considered to be

"You've got the data for this I take it," said David, ignoring her last reference.

"Of course."

"So what's your hypothesis?"

"That the build-up reached a critical point, and rather than detecting the presence of a parallel world, it shifted us into one."

"What do your colleagues say about this?"

"Well the particles were never meant to build up, so they think I'm dreaming."

"But surely the data ..."

She looked a little sheepish. "My section leader refused to look at it. Said I was crazy."

"Well, I think we need to get him to reconsider. Doug?"

"Of course. With me, Jess."

And they left.

An hour later, showered and refreshed, Liz and the others were relaxing in David's quarters when there was a knock on the door. It was Doug Smoke again.

"Well, Jess's section leader has reviewed the data, and he grudgingly accepts she might be onto something."

"Great. What next?"

"They're doing some new data modelling, and we should have something later this afternoon."

"OK, thanks, Doug."

Doug Smoke went to leave, but Marston called him back ... "Have you got those papers I asked you for?"

Smoke nodded, handed David a thin brown folder and left.

---

simultaneously dead and alive. If we open the box, two worlds split apart with the cat being alive in one but dead in another. At this point, the worlds may stay linked irrespective of distance. This is *Entanglement*.

"So what now?" asked Liz.

"Well, seeing as you've broken into a top-secret military facility, I should really lock you all up," replied David.

There were protesting gasps all around.

"But as my Ops Manager has just handed me four copies of the Official Secrets Act, if I can get your signatures on them, I'll take you on a tour of the base. I take it, Miss McBride, that I can trust you to turn off your journalistic instincts for a while?"

Erica nodded reluctantly, and the others simply exchanged glances. David was no fool though, and although he took them to the civilian mess, a couple of laboratories and walked them the length of one of the station's 25 main corridors, they never left the floor they were on. As a result, they didn't see the server room, the underground aircraft hangers, the basement labs or any of the other really juicy bits.

They were thrilled by it all just the same, and when they got back to David's quarters, they were ready to sit down. Like everyone else in the station, he had a bedroom, a bathroom and a good-sized living area. In fact, the only difference was he also had an office which was the first room you went into from the corridor. It was also where he'd been supposed to hold most of his meetings, although as it didn't have a coffee machine, that was never going to happen. That was where they waited just the same, and where, later in the afternoon, there was another knock on the door.

"We've got a way forwards, sir," began Smoke without preamble. "The senior scientists are a bit embarrassed as Jess's data is definitely right, and what's more, the particle build-up is still going on. In fact, it's heading towards double what it was when we jumped from our world. So the fear now is that if we don't do something soon, we might jump again."

"Back home?"

"Or somewhere else. No-one's willing to commit themselves either way."

"What's Jessica's recommendation?"

"Turn it off, sir. Turn it off right away, and with any luck, the particle count will revert to normal."

"With no explosions this time I hope?"

"It's the best we've got, sir."

"OK, do it."

A while before, just as Liz was crawling into the hole, the official team had arrived back in Glen Crian. No Harker this time though, only Hendricks, her sergeant and the two RAF officers. The weather had quietened down a bit, and although dark clouds still clung to the peaks above, the rain had stopped. The first thing they spotted was Liz's car, which prompted a brief discussion about what hikers were doing out on a day like this.

Then they unloaded their Level A hazmat suits and set off across the glen towards the location of the cave entrance. *If that's what it is*, thought Hendricks. That wasn't the only question of course and the one which had occupied them on route from Drumnadrochit, was when to put the protective suits on. Prudence suggested they do it on leaving the Land Rover, but with the suits' full-face masks and breathing apparatus, they were unwieldy, to say the least. It wasn't their first visit to the glen either, of course, so given the number of gorse bushes per square yard, and the distance they had to walk, they compromised on about halfway. So that was where they stopped and transformed themselves from ordinary-looking figures into baggy, yellow spacemen.

When they finally reached the hole, Hendricks knelt down to poke her head inside. She'd just done so when she jerked it out and fell backwards onto the ground.

"Did you feel that?"

"What the hell was it?"

"It felt like an underground explosion."

Suddenly the glen was shaken by a second blast, and an immense plume of soil and smoke blasted out of the hole, knocking them backwards and covering them all in a layer of dirt. The TDE had done its work.

They clustered around the debris of the hole. It was well and truly blocked.

"Requisition a digger?" suggested Hendricks after she'd picked herself up off the ground.

"Better still, we've got some heavy equipment at Lossiemouth," offered one of the airmen. "Keep it in the family, so to speak."

Hendricks nodded. They couldn't very well bring in civilian contractors with the danger of radiation.

As Hendricks was getting on the radio to Lossiemouth, yet another knock sounded on the door to David's quarters.

"Come in."

Doug Smoke and Jessica Williams entered.

"I take it you have news."

"Exciting news, sir. Over to you, Jess. It's your baby."

"Well, first things first. The particle count is dropping."

"How fast?"

"Fast enough. It'll take about a day to get below the level it was at when we shifted here, but it's definitely dropping. So at least we're not going anywhere else."

"Fantastic. So we just need to make sure no-one is off-base after when? This time tomorrow?"

"That should be fine."

"Great. I wish I'd listened to you the first time, Jessica."

She was pleased to hear this, but it had the sound of a dismissal, so she spoke again.

"That's not all though."

David raised an eyebrow.

"Well, you do realize what this all means?"

"That we can get home."

"Well, yes, but apart from that."

"I don't follow you."

"We shifted here when the particles got above a certain level, and when they drop below that, we should shift back."

"Yes I see that, but ..."

"So we could do it again."

"I beg your pardon."

"According to my figures, this is a replicable experiment. We could come back here in future if we wanted. It'd make a fascinating study of an alternate planetary evolution."

She paused to let that sink in before continuing ... "In scientific terms, it would be huge."

"One question," piped up Jenny before anyone could answer. "As you've already got people off-base, could we explore a bit too?"

"Where would you go?" asked David, momentarily distracted away from Jessica.

Jenny didn't hesitate, and after a short discussion, David agreed, on the condition that she and Nigel take a driver with them. Something about Jenny's eagerness unnerved him, and everyone in the family knew how vague Nigel could be. Either way, he didn't want to risk them getting caught up and not making it back in time.

And so it was that a short while later, Jenny, Nigel and the others stepped out of the vehicle lift into a strange, yet utterly familiar world. It was late afternoon by now, and after David briefed the driver, the three set off.

As they drove into Drumnadrochit, Nigel gazed intently at the scenery, soaking up every minute of the adventure. In contrast, Jenny's eyes were darting back and forth across the landscape, and as the car reached the outskirts of the town, she uttered a little gasp. Neither Nigel nor the driver noticed though, and a few minutes later they found themselves sitting in an alcove at the appropriately named *A Stranger Calls* public house. The beer tasted much the same as they were used to, and as Jenny started sipping her second pint, she fixed Nigel with her most serious expression.

"What?" he asked at last.

"What do you mean, What?"

"You're starin' at me."

"Well ... yes ... I need to tell you something, and I'm not sure how you're going to take it."

"I'll take it with beer, please," replied Nigel with a smile.

"Seriously Nige. The thing is, even after everything that's happened, I'm afraid you might think I'm crazy."

"Course you are; you hang out with me, don't you?"

"No, really."

She gave him what he called her Paddington hard stare[50], and

---

[50] According to Paddington Bear's creator, Michael Bond, that famous young troublemaker has a very persistent stare that he uses on people who've annoyed

he immediately fell silent.

"The thing is ..." She braced herself before continuing. "The thing is, I'm from a parallel world."

"Well, so am I"

"Oh, you know what I mean."

"I shouldn't worry about it. I feel like that after four or five pints myself."

"No, I am." she insisted, now getting annoyed.

"Go on then, I'll buy it. You're from another world."

"Yes."

"Is it nice there?"

"It's just like home," said Jenny cautiously. "Only different."

"Only different."

"They all differ slightly."

"What all?"

"The different worlds," she replied.

"So, there's more than one."

"Well ... yes. Quite a lot actually."

Nigel looked from her to his beer and back again.

"So that's how you know about parallel worlds."

She nodded.

"Not somethin' someone told you."

The moment had arrived.

"Actually that's true. The thing is ... I've spent all of my adult life jumping between parallel worlds."

"You've ..."

"I didn't know that to start with of course. In fact, I thought I'd gone mad, but when someone explained everything about parallel worlds to me, it answered so many questions."

---

him. It's very handy too because anyone on the receiving end of it immediately feels too embarrassed to keep talking.

"An' you just believed them!"

"Yes. Well no, not as such. Not straight away."

There was a long pause as Nigel absorbed this. Then with a *whatever* kind of shrug ... "Go on then. Tell me all about it."

She'd been dreading this for years, and her fear had grown the longer she'd been in his world. Only now, she no longer thought of it as *his* world. It had become hers too, and the idea of telling him the truth bordered on terrifying. Still, ever a believer in pulling plasters off in one go, she took a deep breath and launched straight in.

She told him what she remembered about her own world, and the others she'd visited over the years. She told him about the similarities, the differences, the oddities, and everything else she could think of. How in one world, Microsoft had invented the iPhone. In another, Antarctica was a French colony. And in another, chicken pies were illegal in Finland. She told him the trivial, the interesting, the major and the personal. Once she got started, it all came pouring out.

When she was done, she sat back in her chair, exhausted. Now it was all out, she realised how much she'd wanted to tell him. She sighed and waited. For a moment Nigel just sat there, then he stood up, and without a word, walked out of the pub.

Jenny couldn't believe it. After everything she'd gone through, he'd walked out on her.

She jumped up and looked out the window. Nigel was standing in the middle of the car park, and as far as she could tell, he was going through his extensive range of confused faces. After several minutes, he turned and headed back in.

He sat down and in a surprisingly calm voice, said ... "So, when did we first meet?"

"The Merry May Beer Festival."

"What were you drivin'?"

"My camper van. Don't you remember?"

"Of course, I remember. You knocked me over with it!"

Jenny nodded as Nigel took a long drink. Then another.

"You know what," he said at last. "It actually makes a lot of sense."

Jenny gaped at him.

"No, really. Remember that time when you didn't get the joke about England not havin' won the World cup since '66? Or when you got all flustered over children havin' teddy bears instead of toy squirrels? An' the classic was when you insisted Clint Eastwood had been president of the US? I thought you were havin' a senior moment."

She punched him on the shoulder.

"Ow! ... So it's true?"

"Uh-huh."

Jenny was nonplussed, but as she watched, Nigel's face slowly split into a broad grin.

"You're OK with it?" she stammered.

"What's to be OK with? You're the same person I've always known, aren't you?"

"Well, yes."

"There you are then."

"There's one other thing though," she said quietly.

Nigel cocked his head to one side.

"I think this might even be *my* world. Where we are now, I mean. I spotted something as we drove into town and ... well ... I think this might be the world where I was born. If so, my parents might still be alive ... probably wondering what happened to me all those years ago."

"Oh, you have to go find them!" said Nigel excitedly. He was

back in puppy-mode, and Jenny beamed. This was precisely what
she'd hoped he'd say.

"I want to, but I need to tell you something first."

"You already said that."

"This is the last thing; promise."

"Go on then."

Jenny took another deep breath. "When I went away to
college, I knew someone else called Nigel, and he looked just like
you."

"That explains a lot too."

"Yes. I mean, no. What? Look it was years ago, and I admit
it's weird you looking like him, but I love you for who you are."
And there it was, the word was out. Jenny hadn't meant to say it
and didn't even realize she had. Nigel had heard it though, but
he neither reacted nor said anything. Instead, he went over to
their driver who was sitting at the bar, and told him a surprisingly
plausible story about why they needed to head off for a while.

Nigel figured there was no point in telling him the truth, and
whether the driver believed him or not, he was happy enough to
let them go. The way he saw it, the beer was tasty, and the food
smelled good, so what did he have to lose?

So off they set; down the High Street, past *McDonald's*,
through the traffic lights and round a maze of side roads until
they came to Woodman Terrace.

"Let me go in first. You wait here."

"Good job I brought a coat."

"Wimp."

She flashed him a smile and walked off. Past the first few
houses, until she reached the third on the left where she
hesitated. Her heart was in her mouth as she walked up the path,
and almost leaping out of it as she rang the bell. She heard voices

inside. Then the door opened.

Her father stood there.

His face went through every emotion from shock to elation and back again. He went white, pink, red, and finally, with tears streaming down his face, he gathered her into his arms.

"Who is it?" came her mother's voice from the kitchen.

When she got no reply, she went to look for herself only to see her husband hugging a young woman on the doorstep. She was about to say something when the auburn head looked up from his shoulder, and she almost fainted.

"Jenny!"

The door closed amid the sound of a million tear-filled questions.

Some while later, the door opened again, and Jenny called out Nigel's name.

"Pleased to see you?"

"You've no idea."

"I bet."

"Look, they want to meet you, but there's one more thing I haven't told you."

"I thought we'd done all that."

"Yes ... well ... the thing is ... the other Nigel I mentioned ... Well, he died. So this is going to be quite a shock for my folks."

She didn't give him time to process that information before pulling him into the house. Her parents were sitting in the lounge, waiting for her to bring in her friend. When she did, her mother almost fainted again.

She wasn't the only one either, for when Nigel saw Jenny's parents, a tremor of familiarity leapt up his spine. When he shook her dad's hand, he felt a jolt go through him. It was like a stab of static electricity mixed with the sort of shudder people sometimes get in graveyards. It wasn't unlike the feeling TC had experienced on her first few jumps between worlds.

There was a bottle of wine open on the table, and leaving Jenny to talk with her parents, Nigel went through to the kitchen to get an extra glass. He knew the way, and opening the right cupboard without thinking, the jolt hit him again. He'd been here before. Maybe not *him* exactly, but that part of himself we bump into when we get déjà vu.

He stared at the wine glass, and as he did, he became aware of the voices in the other room. He didn't know why he listened, but he did, and like when he'd pressed *Play* to listen to his grandmother's message all those days before, what he heard changed his life.

"You've got to tell him, dear," Jenny's mum was saying.

"But I can't. I've told him I knew another Nigel who died, so that's enough, isn't it?"

"Your mother's right love. He needs to know you used to be together."

"But that wasn't him!"

"He looks just like him."

"I know, but *that* Nigel died. Don't you remember!" Jenny's voice rose as desperation and fear took over. "How can I tell him he was my boyfriend, and I watched him die?"

So it was a day for revelations all round, and when Nigel re-entered the living room a few minutes later, he was a quieter, more subdued version of himself. Several hours later, still struggling to process what he'd overheard he, therefore, leapt at the chance of getting away for a while and slipped back into town to let the driver know they were staying over. The airman had already figured as much and had found somewhere for the night, so they agreed to meet back at the pub at four o'clock the following day.

All's well that ends well

Tuesday, September 21ˢᵗ

So, the family was reunited, Jenny was able to tell her parents everything about the intervening years, and although it was only for a short time, her mum and dad had their daughter back. If *An idyllic, perfect day* ever needs redefining, this was it, and as they neared the appointed time, Jenny's mum took her on one side.

"We were so worried love. All those years of not knowing. I can't pretend to understand half of what you've told us, but I can see you're happy, and I'm glad for that at least." She paused ... "But do you really have to go?"

It was the question Jenny had been asking herself all day, and it was tearing her apart. She desperately wanted to stay, but she couldn't lose Nigel again, even if they were destined simply to be friends. If only they had more time or could come back. She thought about what Jessica Williams had said, and she wondered.

Just then she felt her father's arm around her

shoulders and she turned to look at him. They'd always been close, and this was one of those moments when words were unnecessary; they both just knew. He'd lost his little girl and found a young woman in her place, only now he was losing her as well. His biggest concern though, was whether she was happy. He asked her about her life, about her friends, her job, her cats ... and about Nigel. He saw the way her smile brightened whenever his name came up.

"And him. Does he love you too, sweetheart?"

"We're really, really good friends Dad and what with everything I've been through, that's enough for me."

He frowned. He'd always rather fancied being a grandfather, but he supposed if she was happy ...

The driver was waiting when they got back to the pub. It was 3:45, so barely enough time for goodbyes.

Jenny's mum hugged her so tightly she thought she might never breathe again. Her dad did the same. Then he took Nigel by the shoulder and pulled him to one side. As Jenny watched, her father spoke, Nigel nodded, and her father smiled. Then they shook hands and rejoined the others.

"I'm sorry, but we need to go," said the driver, reluctantly interrupting the four of them. After one last round of hugs, the car drove away.

Twenty-five minutes later, it arrived back at the base where Liz and David were waiting anxiously by the guardhouse. They were the last of the groups off-base to get back, and knowing what Nigel could be like, David had been starting to question his decision to let them go. But they were back now. He watched as the driver drove the car into one of the vehicle lifts and stood aside as everyone followed it in. Then taking one last look around, he joined them. The doors closed on the other world, and they headed down to the mess.

When they got there, Doug and Jessica were waiting for them.

"How long Jessica?"

"An hour at the most."

The particle count ticked down on Jess's laptop until it was just a few away from the magic figure.

"Whatever happens next, it's been an amazing trip," said David. "Thank you, Doug and you, Jessica. And as for the rest of you ..." he continued, taking Liz's hand "... Well, thank you for coming to find us."

As the *s* of his final word died away, there was a sudden flash of green. Impossibly bright and short, the blinding pulse of light filled every corner of the room for half a second, then nothing.

As it did, Glen Crian glowed with the same green light, and a sound rolled down the valley like a hundred bubble-wrapped elephants falling onto a field of prawn crackers. With it came a massive shock wave that flew across the landscape, spraying the stream beyond its banks, and ripping rocks from the surrounding peaks as it went. As if in response to all this, the sun suddenly broke through the clouds, glazing the still-wet valley like honey.

People in the village felt the vibration, the next day's newspapers called it an earthquake and in the same instant, the moles transported back to Effington.

Hendricks and the others had just arrived back on site when the shock wave hit, and for the second time, they were blasted off their feet. This time though, as the dust cleared, and Hendricks shook her head, she found herself inches from a wire perimeter fence. One second it wasn't there, and in the blink of an eye, it was.

The brick? Yes, that vanished too, returning to its real home, which was near the top right-hand corner of the guardhouse at Crianloch Station. No one had realised it was missing mind you, so it contented itself with having had something of an adventure.

Crianloch Station was back.

Late September to Christmas Eve

Over the following weeks, all sorts of things happened.

Hendricks reported back to Inverness, Harker to London, and Finch's two officers to Lossiemouth. Then Croft and Finch briefed the Defence Secretary and the DG, who in turn, filed their report with the Prime Minister. After a week, the status of the case in the official records was changed from *Investigation* to *Analysis*. That was far from the end of things though, as dozens of questions remained unanswered.

While all that was happening, David Marston, Doug Smoke and Jessica Williams were taken in for debriefing. But apart from recording their stories, what could be done? The base was back, and other than the tropical fish, everyone was OK. Plus, the scientific community had exabytes of new data to go through, and Jess's discovery had seemingly rewritten the laws of physics. So for the time being, that was that.

Erica, on the other hand, had quite a time of it. She spent the whole of her first day back writing up the story, only to have it returned by her Editor. With it was a curt note saying they didn't publish science fiction, so she should start again. She was annoyed at first, but as the day passed, she concluded that on balance, maybe some secrets were better left untold. That didn't stop her from reporting everything to her source in Lossiemouth of course, and he thanked her with a smile that held no hint of disbelief whatsoever. Her front page therefore never happened, and Erica's oddities that week featured an artistic anteater and a psychic weasel. Nigel would have been so pleased.

In Crianloch, some of the locals were disgruntled not to have been able to sell their story to the tabloids, while others were just happy none of their sheep had been injured. Mostly though, people went back to their everyday lives. As for the milkman and the paperboy, they simply resumed deliveries as before, and the latter even got a pay rise on account of all the copies of *Physics Monthly* and *Science Fiction, Science Fact* he now had to deliver.

Steve Guthrie meanwhile had been back to Effington several times. In fact, slightly to his own surprise, he was now an established member of the darts team. It no longer felt that far to the university either, and he was even thinking of moving there.

Liz and David, on the other hand, had talked non-stop during their final day in the other world, and now wanted to look forward rather than back. They'd spoken about their careers, about Scotland, and most of all about their future together. Liz hadn't fully forgiven him for lying about where he was based, but in the end, they made one decision ... never to be apart again. National security or not, David also knew he couldn't keep secrets from her either, and their time apart had shown them just how much they both needed each other. As a result, David called his commanding officer the following week to arrange a meeting to discuss career options.

The moles too were returning to normal and had started re-acclimatising to their original home. They didn't like it at first because they'd preferred the sandier soil on Lundy, and now had to get used to something heavier again. Still, as before, they merely grumbled a bit in a moley kind of way and started digging. The shrews missed them though.

But why?

Not *Why did the shrews miss the moles?* After all, moles are cute and furry, so what's not to like? But why had they relocated in the first place? Why did the brick end up in Penmound? And why for that matter had Crianloch been hit with so many failures, even before it did its vanishing trick?

As it happens, that last one was easy to explain, as in the weeks following the base's return, Doug Smoke had his team conduct extensive studies around the base, as part of which, they made an interesting, albeit embarrassing discovery. Remember his triple redundancy play? Well, turns out it wasn't immune to animal intervention, and thanks to a handful of rabbits, a small herd of deer and one over-curious sheep, several of the cables coming into the base had been nibbled through[51].

And the other anomalies? Well, for one thing, the government's scientists were noticeably uncomfortable hypothesizing about misbehaving bricks and vanishing moles.

---

[51] Cris Thomas (no relation), a Cyber Security Researcher, tracked power cuts caused by animals between 2013 and 2017, at the end of which time he told a security conference that in those four years, squirrels and other creatures had caused over 1,700 power cuts, affecting five million people in the US alone.

But why only those things anyway? And why, had the entire base moved to another world when the moles had just taken a short holiday by the seaside? For that matter, what about the connections with Nigel and David's family?

Whatever the answers to those questions, the scientists were either baffled or couldn't come up with a version of events they liked. In the end, the best they could offer was that the base's reappearance had created a sort of ripple in reality, which had caused everything else to happen. Erica wasn't satisfied with this though. It was too non-specific. The only thing was, when she queried the findings of the final government report (which her source had kindly acquired for her), she was told politely but firmly that no such events had ever occurred.

As for Jenny and Nigel, they'd experienced something the others hadn't, and it was going to take them a while to adjust.

Jenny was struggling to cope with having seen her parents, only to lose them all over again. It brought back so many memories, and she didn't know how to deal with it. She could have turned to Nigel as she had so many times before, but there was a change in him, and it held her back. In the end, like so many of us, she threw herself into her work.

Nigel, on the other hand, was fine with her being from another world, but he'd been unnerved by the mention of the other *him*. More than that, there was what he'd overheard about *them* being a couple, and he wasn't sure how he felt about that. OK so it had been ten years before, and at least she'd had the good taste to fall for someone who'd apparently looked like him, but something about the whole business niggled at him. As ever, he decided to cope with this by pushing it to the back of his mind in the knowledge that an answer would eventually find its way out. In the meantime, he buried himself in his writing and without meaning to, he also retreated from the world.

All in all, they both had some adjustments to make. Oh, they met, they drank beer, and they shared crisps, but something had changed between them.

In the middle of October, they each received an invitation to Liz and David's wedding. It was to be on December 15th, and would be held at the tiny parish church in Wensbridge. Erica and her wife received an invitation too, so the evening before the ceremony, they all met up. It was good to catch up, but oddly tense too, and it was only when her wife went off to the bar that Erica opened the conversation for real.

"What's it like to be back above ground David?"

That broke the ice, and soon the conversation was flowing like they'd known each other all their lives. They talked about the road trips, the brick, the base, the green light, the moles, everything. The only thing they didn't talk about was Nigel and Jenny's trip to Drumnadrochit, as although Liz knew a little about that, she figured it was up to them to mention it ... or not.

The wedding itself went without a hitch, and the service finished with David and Liz leaving church under the crossed swords of an RAF honour guard. It was unlike anything most of the guests had seen before, and was followed by a reception with the usual mix of food, champagne, and embarrassing speeches. When the evening came, everyone threw themselves into the ceilidh until long after the happy couple had left.

Jenny and Nigel were staying with his grandmother, and while Nigel was loading the van the following morning, the old lady took Jenny to one side.

"Are you two alright dear?"

Jenny sighed. "I honestly don't know Gran; the whole thing was quite an experience for both of us. Me seeing my parents, and him finding out about the other Nigel."

"The other Nigel?"

Like Nigel, Gran had often wondered why Jenny never spoke of her parents, and she waited as Jenny marshalled her thoughts. Silence reigned for what seemed like minutes, but once Jenny started, it all came flowing out again. Jenny stared fixedly at the floor as she told Gran the whole story, and only when she was done did she look up once more.

"He's so different now, Gran. He's so distant, I can barely get two words out of him some days."

"I know dear, but …"

"I think I'm losing him," sobbed Jenny

Their eyes met, and the old woman pulled Jenny to her. After a while, with the shoulder of Gran's dress now wet with tears, she let Jenny go.

"I'm sure it'll work out, dear. You two have always been so close."

Which they had, but that all seemed to be in the past now, and as the days rolled towards Christmas, Jenny's usual smile started to slip.

Then on Christmas Eve, her phone rang.

"Hello?" she replied noncommittally.

"Hello madam, this is *Claridge's Tea Room* here."

"Oh yeah, very funny Nige."

"Well the thing is madam, we're triallin' a special outreach programme at present. If you'd like to join our representative in

The White Hart public house, he'll be pleased to see you."

"Tea in the pub."

"Well no, but hopefully you can make do with beer an' crisps."

"Yeah, OK."

She wasn't enthusiastic. It had been a stressful day in work and what with everything else, she was feeling very fragile. She looked at her watch, picked up her keys from the little bowl by the front door, and set off.

When she got to the pub, Nigel was waiting in their usual chairs by the fireplace. It was almost like old times. Luckily, he hadn't seen her come in, and feeling as she did, she made a quick detour to the toilets to wipe away some tears. She walked back into the pub, all smiles.

"I've often wondered," began Nigel, "why you call your cats Tommy and Tuppence."

"That's easy, Poirot and Miss Marple are big here, but where I grew up, it was all about Tommy and Tuppence Beresford[52]. Christie's other characters were just also-rans."

"I thought it might be somethin' like that."

"Why do you ask?"

"I'm curious, I guess. About all the other places you've seen. How many other versions of me were there?"

"Only the one I told you about."

"An' you knew him at college."

"Uh-huh."

"So how much like him am I?"

Jenny paused. This was a line of conversation she hadn't prepared herself for.

---

[52] There are 33 Poirot, 12 Miss Marple, and 4 Tommy and Tuppence novels in our world, but the tables were turned where Jenny came from.

"Well ... apart from your looks, you're very different."

"Hmm."

"I found that with a lot of the people I met in different worlds. Some were the same, some weren't, some didn't know me at all."

"So, he an' I are unique."

"You certainly are."

"And you love me."

"I what?" she replied quickly.

"You said it before we went in to meet your folks."

"I did not!"

"Fraid so."

She was quiet now, and it fell to him to resume the conversation.

"An' now?"

The silence between them was broken only by the sound of logs crackling in the fire. It was as if every world was waiting for her reply. She dropped her eyes and stared into the flames.

"Yes, I love you," she said at last. "To begin with, I had to keep reminding myself you weren't my Nigel, but as I got to know you, I started to forget him, and you became my Nigel ... even though you're not."

As she spoke, she broke down, and tears streamed down her cheeks. To her surprise, she suddenly felt Nigel take her hand, and when she opened her eyes, he was kneeling in front of her.

"What the hell are you doing down there?"

"Will you marry me?"

"What?"

"Will you marry me?"

"But you ... I mean, I ... no, we ..."

"I've been in love with you since the day you ran me over.

You always seemed so .... I don't know .... Too .... I just never liked to say."

"You didn't like to say! You bloody idiot! You ..."

She didn't finish the sentence though, because he leant forward and kissed her.

After two and a half years, it was about time.

What came after

The following Spring

Given the unpredictability of the English weather, holding an outdoor wedding on the first Tuesday in May might sound like madness. That didn't matter to Nigel and Jenny though, because the date marked three years to the day since she'd run him over with her camper van. What's more, the venue they'd chosen for the wedding was the field where that had happened.

And so it was, that on a beautiful May 3rd afternoon, friends and family gathered in the grounds of Weston Manor, near Penmound, to witness one anniversary become the start of another.

No moles were present, and sadly, of course, neither were Jenny's parents, but even so, with Liz and Erica as bridesmaids, and David as Nigel's best man, it was a wonderful day just the same. Relaxed, devoid of formality and full of the sense of fun that typified the happy couple, even *Fate* smiled down on them in the warm

Spring sunshine.

As for the reception, it seemed only fitting they hold it at *The White Hart*. And with Nigel and Jenny both being people the landlord knew well, he excelled himself decorating the function room. Garlands of tulips, daffodils and white ribbon hung from the ancient rafters, all the windows were edged with roses, and on the walls were wreaths made up of peonies and daisies. To complete the effect, every table had a rough-cut slice of tree trunk in its centre. And on top of each one, sat a small vase of wildflowers and an assortment of unmatched glass jars, all with candles in.

Even in daylight, the combination gave the room an intimate, rustic feel, and the day as a whole was quite simply, joyous. Liz and David made speeches, Gran smiled constantly, and Jess Williams danced with Doug Smoke. Nigel's parents threw themselves into the disco, Dot and Steve were there together, and Erica was excited about her wife's impending promotion … even though it meant them moving to Edinburgh. Evidently, everyone was starting new lives, so it was the perfect way for all of them to close one door and open another.

As darkness fell, candles were lit on the tables, and hanging from the ceiling shone large, warm bulbs in pierced metal shades which sent shadows flitting around the room. Nigel and Jenny's first dance together? You can probably guess, as it just had to be *Crazy little thing called love*.

The only thing is, it turns out I lied. Not about there being three constants to remember about parallel worlds because there are. There's a fourth though, and Jenny and Nigel proved it, because even the universe likes a happy ending.

So, do you believe that Jenny kept jumping between worlds because of her fondness for cakes? Or was it because she and Nigel were so entangled, the universe had to find a way of reuniting them? Perhaps it was both, who knows.

In any event, it had all worked out. They were happy together, the cats enjoyed playing hide-and-seek between Nigel's piles of books, and the only thing that ever played on Jenny's mind was her parents.

Then, a few months after her and Nigel's wedding, Jenny was sitting outside with a coffee, staring at a home pregnancy kit. She'd been there so long, the drink had gone cold, and she was about to go in to make a fresh one when she made a decision.

Picking up her phone, she dialled a number, and after four rings, it was answered.

"Hello, Jessica Williams."

"Hi, Jess. It's Jenny Bellroy here, Jenny Stevens as was. Look, what can you tell me about replicating the experiment and going back to that other world?"

THE END
Until we meet the characters again in *Transference*

Some words of thanks

Thank you for reading my first, published novel. I hope you enjoyed reading it as much as I enjoyed writing it. As you might guess, it's been a big part of my life for quite a while, and also, it turns out, a journey of discovery. Both about myself, and also regarding the process of writing, editing and self-publishing.

Before *Entanglement* I'd written on and off all my life but never tried to publish. Then in March 2018, I'd hit a block on another project, so I picked up my old copy of *The Hitchhiker's Guide to the Galaxy* to clear my head. I'd always loved it, and a page or two in, I had another reason to thank Douglas Adams. Something in it had sparked an idea, and two hours later, I'd written a few thousand words of what became *Entanglement*. Much of that is still in the book too, and unlike writers who have their stories fully mapped out from the start, mine evolved as I wrote it. At times it even seemed like I was reading it as I went along, rather than writing it, which was an amazing feeling.

In October, I sent the first version to family and friends, and after making numerous subsequent changes, I sent the next version to professional editors in February 2019. It was a huge moment, sending it to strangers, although even sending it to friends had felt big at the time. They were all constructive in their feedback too, although when the professionals' comments came in, and I realised the scale of the suggested rewrites, everything changed. Yes, the plot remained, but the book morphed from 24 chapters to 17-ish, I deleted one character, and virtually every paragraph was modified in some way. Sections moved around to increase the pace, duplication was removed, character voices were strengthened, and to my surprise, I discovered how open to feedback I'd become. In any event, the process was consistently both fun and rewarding, irrespective of whether I spent a day writing several thousand words, or took hours agonising over a single paragraph.

On a personal level, though, it was a difficult time for me, as in July 2018, my mother suffered the second of two major strokes. Her first was in 2009 and had started her decline into dementia, but with her second, she worsened considerably. As she did, I felt my perspective on life shift. I didn't feel it as deeply as with my own heart attack a few years before, but with mum's gradual deterioration, I now had a new urgency to complete the book. I just had to give her a copy while there was still time.

On top of that, in June 2019, my cat Watson died. I'd had him and his brother, Holmes, since they were 8 weeks old in 2003 so as you can imagine, Wattie's death hit me hard. Where did I go from there? Well, like every book on writing advises, I kept going and stuck to my daily routine, either finalising the novel or working through the myriad challenges of self-publishing. Then one day, with *Entanglement* finished and searching for the central themes of its two sequels, a friend gave me an idea which necessitated a rewrite of the last chapter here. And with that, I was done. Most importantly, I was able to give Mum her copy.

So, hopefully, this has given you a small insight into me and my journey, so let me close with a fresh word of thanks, first to my marvellous dad and my various readers, but also to the other contributors and many more who either encouraged me or just didn't laugh when they heard what as doing! Thank you all. ☺

If you'd like to know more, have ideas for where the stories and characters might go next, or would simply like to keep in touch, I'd love to hear from you.

ANDREW J THOMAS was born in Bristol, England, and after writing on and off during a successful career in IT, he turned professional with this novel. He's inspired by the likes of Douglas Adams, PG Wodehouse, Neil Gaiman and Agatha Christie.

His work is quirkily funny, with characters you'd enjoy a drink with, events that are just strange enough to be believable and footnotes that'll have you rushing out to buy the ingredients to bake your own cakes.

He lives in a 17th century thatched cottage with his cat and a large DVD collection.

Web	www.andrewjthomas.net
Instagram	@andrewj.thomas
Facebook	@andrewthomasnovelist
Twitter	@andrewthomas109

Lightning Source UK Ltd.
Milton Keynes UK
UKHW011001120919
349645UK00001B/44/P